Sweet, Sweet Poison

Books by Kate Wilhelm

Sweet, Sweet Poison

KATE WILHELM

St. Martin's Press
New York

Design by Judy Dannecker

Library of Congress Cataloging-in-Publication Data

Wilhelm, Kate.
    Sweet, sweet poison / Kate Wilhelm.
       p.   cm.
    ISBN 0-312-04433-X
    I. Title.
    PS3573.I434S88 1990
    813'.54—dc20   89-77847
                                      CIP

First Edition

10 9 8 7 6 5 4 3 2 1

For Geoffrey Simmons, with gratitude.
There are debts that cannot be repaid,
but only acknowledged.

Sweet, Sweet Poison

CHAPTER 1

Al Zukal drove into the driveway of the new house with caution. You never knew out here in the country, he thought; things happen, dead animals, trees down, sinkholes. . . .

"They ain't got here yet," Sylvie muttered. And, in fact, no one else was in sight.

There was the gravel drive close pressed by evergreen trees at the county road and dense undergrowth that neither recognized, with grass that already needed cutting and probably would need it on a weekly basis. The driveway curved a few times, and at those places neither the county road nor the house was visible; it was like being in a wilderness, they both thought uneasily. The yard had not been maintained for many years. Untrimmed roses sprawled with dead lower branches; lilacs grew as high as trees and made a thicket with too many spindly new sprouts. Spent blossoms hung in brown clusters. Sumac had crept in and threatened to claim the entire acreage but was contested by many young trees—maples, pines, a few oaks—all too crowded and weak-looking. There were fourteen acres altogether, reverting back to a natural state where nature would do the thinning.

But no moving van was in sight. Al pulled in behind the house, where he stopped and turned off the motor. There was a two-car garage, unusable until tons of junk were cleaned out. He looked at Sylvie.

She had been a red-haired girl when they married, thirty years ago, and she would die red-haired at the end, no matter how long-delayed it was. He was used to her red hair and liked it. He liked her pear-shape, too, and would have admitted readily that they made a good couple, each pear-shaped, with her rounder end down, and his up. It made for better sleeping that way, he liked to think.

"What if they don't make it today?" she demanded, not yet moving to open her door and get out.

"They'll make it. They want to get paid, they get here. Simple arithmetic. Come on, gives us time to make sure where we want the bed."

Actually the only thing they were moving of any consequence from their Bronx apartment was the bed. "That was my mother's bed!" Sylvie had said early on, as if that settled that. And it had. Just about everything else in the van that had not yet arrived was new. The new station wagon had boxes of bedding, two feather beds, also inherited from her mother, God bless her soul, and a mishmash of dishes, no four alike. But Sylvie knew when and how they had acquired each and every one of them, and when the missing pieces had vanished, or had been broken. "I want them all," she had said through tight lips, and there they were in the wagon waiting to be lugged inside. There were also boxes of new clothes; at least she hadn't insisted on keeping every rag they ever owned.

He said, "Well, why don't you get on out and let's get at it?"

Actually he said, "why doncha," and when she responded she said, "Well, aincha the impatient one!" But they didn't hear it like that and presently they were both standing before their new home. It was a two-story building, the lower half finished with river stone, the upper section white clapboard. It had an attic that would sleep many grandchildren, and a basement that would probably hold more junk than they could accumulate in the years remaining to them—they were both in their fifties. The house was large, five bedrooms, a den and breakfast room besides the kitchen, a big dining room, and even bigger living room. The biggest apartment they had ever lived in had had three bedrooms, and one of them was really a dining room or a parlor or something. But with four girls growing up in the house they had needed bed space more than eating space or sitting space. Now they looked at their new home with silent awe.

Looming over the many trees behind the house the mill rose, and that was theirs also. The mill had been built in 1848 and operated until World War I, or thereabouts, and used as a school at one time, and a bootlegger's production site at another, but for the past twenty years it had not been used for anything.

Sylvie cleared her throat and said, "Listen." It came out as a whisper.

"I don't hear nothing."

"That's what I mean."

Before, when they had come out to their house, they had been with the real estate man, and then with their daughter Flora and her husband Bobby and their two kids, and there had been noise. But now there was a breeze shaking the trees a little, and off beyond the mill the rustle of water, and a faint sound of the falls, not much, not enough.

"I don't know, Al," Sylvie said softly.

"Jaysus Crackers! Now you don't know! Come on, grab that first box and let's get at it. Wait and see. When Flora and Bobby are here, and the kids yelling, the radio and stereo blasting, it'll be just like home."

They began to carry the boxes inside and stack them on counters in the kitchen, and soon the movers came, and the sight of the four-poster with the pineapple knobs comforted

3

Sylvie. She began to relax. She fussed at Al for getting in the way, and he cursed the movers for bumping the bed against the stair rails, and everything was normal again.

The movers also brought in a new sofa, new chairs and tables, dining table, kitchen table . . . a new stove, a Jenn Aire that had a grill and six burners, and a refrigerator with two doors. Al had stared at it in the store. "Jaysus Crackers! You know what I grew up with? A little box this big, with a chunk of ice delivered every Monday, and by God it had to last until the next Monday."

After the movers had finished, Al nudged Sylvie with his elbow. "Well, watcha think?"

She nodded. "We need more furniture than I thought we would. It's a big house, Al."

"You don't have to fill it, you know."

She was surveying the living room with narrowed eyes and did not answer. The spanking-new and factory-clean furniture looked barren somehow, and that was because there was no clutter, no piles of newspapers and magazines, no sneakers in corners, no beer cans on the tables, no pretzel bags, nothing to make it look like home. It even smelled strange, Al realized, not liking the untouched, unlived-in look and smell. Sylvie would fill it, he knew, and after the kids got here, they would help, and for now, well, there was work to do.

A while later she was stashing things in cabinets in the kitchen when he decided to do the shopping they had agreed on ahead of time. "You coming?"

She shook her head. "Too dirty. I thought they just had this many cabinets in them fancy magazines with houses that no one really ever lives in."

She'd fill the cabinets, too, he thought gloomily and left her there. Spender's Ferry was less than three miles away, one hour and twenty minutes out of New York City, with a commuter train station and everything. Goddamn suburbanites, he thought in surprise. That's what they had suddenly become. Al's father had come over from Czechoslovakia to strike gold and had set himself up in a butcher shop, which Al inherited in due time. Then the Bronx caught on fire. That was how he thought of it. The shop vanished, and Al got a job butchering for a supermarket. At least, he often thought when things got tough, they always had meat on their table. Stolen meat, meat carried home in pockets, in his lunch box, meat sometimes slipped to Sylvie when she came in to shop. When things got really bad Sylvie worked too, cleaning offices in the middle of the night. Somehow they had made out okay. Not great, but okay. Then, almost a year ago, Al Zukal had spent five dollars on the lottery and had won big. Just like his father always said, he thought: work hard all your life and you'll make it. Guaranteed income of two hundred twenty-five thou a year, he thought, as he had very, very often over the intervening months. Goddamn suburbanites!

Jill Ferris was leading the way across a swinging bridge below the mill at that moment. "Dad's always maintained the bridge, just because he likes it," she said over her shoulder to a tall man behind her. Jill was thirty, a bit underweight, with long pale hair, no longer really blond, although she had been very blond as a child. Now it was the color of darkening golden oak; it gleamed with red highlights when she moved into sunlight. The man following her was Sebastian Pitkin, a few years older than Jill; he had a solemn expression, lank hair darker than hers, and large blue eyes that bulged a little. The bridge swayed and he clutched the handrail involuntarily; she seemed not to notice.

Jill stopped near the end of the bridge and pointed. "Pretty, isn't it?" Below them was Spender's Lake, seven acres in all, with a short strip of beach at the upper-right end. That was on the side of her father's land, several hundred acres, mostly woods, with an orchard that was invisible from here. On the other side of the lake was the university experimental farm. The narrow bridge, twenty feet across, swung a few inches above the dam; the water-fall had a drop of eight feet. The stream that wound away through a gorge was only two feet wide below the dam, although farther on it widened again to become Spender's Creek. The setting was incredibly beautiful, untouched-looking. The trees were massive in the forest, the lake shockingly blue, grasses edged the water in places, and even the picturesque swinging bridge was like an illustration in a book from the turn of the century.

"See, that's state forest land," Jill said, pointing again. "Dad's land borders it on this end and the creek and mill property make up the boundary here. The experimental farm is on the other side of the mill property. No one will ever be able to encroach in any way. Perfect, isn't it?"

Sebastian was nodding thoughtfully, eyeing the mill that towered over them. The waterwheel looked intact, al-though some of the buckets probably would need replacing. Hard to tell, though; there was too much moss on the lower portion. . . . No water flowed through the diversion trough, but of course it wouldn't, not with the mill shut down. "You say the mill's in good shape?"

"Absolutely. They built it out of cypress, cedar, and oak, and they built it to last forever. The upper floors would be great for dormitories and the entire lower part could be classrooms, mess hall, kitchens, meeting rooms. Wait until you see." She started to walk again; the bridge began to swing again. He caught the handrail and followed cau-tiously.

There were mammoth double doors that had admitted horse-drawn wagons loaded with grain at one time, but no longer opened. Weeds grew thick at the base of the doors, all around the mill. White Queen Anne's lace, blue forget-me-nots, pink and yellow sweetpeas trailing everywhere. Almost too pretty, too planned. Jill led the way around to a normal-sized door that opened at her touch. The interior was dim; makeshift partitions had been added at one time or another, obviously temporary additions that never had been torn down again.

"See," Jill said, in the center of one of the small rooms, "a private meditation room, or a sleeping cell, or even a meeting place for a group of four or five." The room was about eight by ten, stifling, bake-oven hot. The single window appeared to be painted shut.

They left the room and were in the central, open space where the mechanism for the grinding of the corn and wheat was all there, gears and wheels and chains and pulleys, but the stone grinding wheels had been removed. This section was pleasantly cool. They went up very sturdy stairs and looked around, came down a different staircase, and roamed the back part of the lower floor.

They were emerging from around one of the partitions when Jill gasped at the sight of a figure in the open doorway.

"Who are you? This is private property," Jill said, louder than she intended, startled.

"I could say the same," the woman snapped back at her. "It's private property, all right, my private property, me and my husband's. What are you doing in here?"

Jill could only stare at this awful woman, with her awful, thick Bronx accent and voice that sounded like a demented duck quacking. She was dressed in awful dirty, baggy pants, with a dirty shirt, and she had awful red-dyed frizzy hair poking out from under a grass-green kerchief.

"I'm sorry," Sebastian said. "We certainly didn't mean to invade your privacy. I thought the property was for sale. Mrs. Ferris was showing it to me. Please forgive us." He smiled gently. "This is Mrs. Ferris, and I'm Sebastian."

For a moment, with his light blue eyes fixed, his gaze on her so directly, she felt confusion. A kind man, she thought, understanding, but then the girl made a noise and Sylvie looked at her, the moment broken, gone, leaving a bewildering set of contradictions in its place. Sylvie crossed

7

her arms over her chest and nodded. "Right. Well, the mill and the house ain't for sale, not no more. Me and Al bought it all last week and we're moving in right now."

"Come along," Sebastian said to Jill then. "It's a mistake, after all. No harm done."

Sylvie watched them narrowly as they left the mill and stepped onto the bridge. She waited until they had vanished among the trees on the other side before she went back to the house, muttering to herself. A politician, or a preacher, she thought. She shook her head. Preacher. Not just because no politician would ever own up to a name like Sebastian, but the way he looked at her. Making up to her, she thought with surprise. The kind who got on Sunday television and looked at you like that, like he'd be all over you in a flash if he could, like if he could just lay on a hand, you'd say yes no matter what he asked. Making up to her, at her age, she muttered angrily. Sylvie didn't trust religion that relied on sorrowful blue eyes and the laying on of hands, and the intimate little smiles that suggested he knew your secrets. Religion should be cooler than that, she thought, more dignified. And that skinny girl. Putty in the hands of a man like that. Her lips tightened at the thought of the girl. *Who are you?* Like she owned the world. Well, she showed them, Mr. Sebastian-let-me-save-your-soul, and Mrs. I-own-the-world Ferris.

She was still grumbling under her breath when David Levy turned up at the kitchen door of the house. He was a stick of a boy, way over six feet, with a great big pumpkin grin, and wanting a haircut, like always. Ever since she knew him, he had needed a haircut. Must get it done sometime, she thought, but it never showed. Great mop of black hair. Rosa, their youngest daughter, had told David they were looking for a place in the country, and David had told them about this, and now here he was to lend a hand. A good boy. And Rosa didn't know good when she saw it, off in California on a scholarship, studying to be some kind of ocean scientist, and some other girl would see David Levy and not be so blind. . . .

"What can I do?" David asked. "I wanted to come earlier but we've been pretty busy at the farm. Anyway, here I am." He had a backpack slung over his shoulder. He put it on the table and she began directing him exactly the same way she directed Al and the girls and their husbands and children.

Pretty soon Al came back with the station wagon loaded with groceries, and they got to work carrying them inside. "I told my boss about you," David said, putting a box down on the table. "I hope it's okay if she comes by to meet you."

"Grand Central," Sylvie muttered. "Fine, David, fine. Al, put that on the table until I have a chance to see what all you've got. Did you buy some hot dogs like I told you?"

"Sure, sure. And buns, what you didn't tell me. And catsup. And beer. And I'm for a beer right now. David?"

He shook his head. Al opened two cans and handed one to Sylvie. David rummaged in his backpack and brought out a thermos. "Lemonade," he said, and drank.

He put the thermos down and went to the door then. "Here she comes," he said. In just a moment a woman appeared and he opened the door for her.

"Dr. Wharton, these are my friends, Mr. and Mrs. Zukal."

She was dressed in jeans and a T-shirt and sneakers. She had the kind of sturdy little body that would let her wear clothes like that for many more years. Her hair was short and straight, dark with streaks of gray at the temples. When she smiled, a dimple appeared in her cheek and her eyes smiled along with her mouth.

Sylvie nodded. "You want a beer?" she asked. And then, "You're a doctor?"

"Just a professor. And call me Lois," she said. "I'd love a beer." She was looking around at the furniture, at the

9

boxes, and cartons with undisguised interest. "This has been a hell of a day."

Al Zukal popped another can and handed it over to her and she drank thirstily. "For us, too," he said. "Moving's a bitch."

"I was really surprised when David said you had bought the place," Lois said. "Not you, but anyone. This property has been on the market for years."

"Two looks," Al said. "All it took. Two trips and me and Sylvie, we seen it was exactly what we're after. Believe you me, we looked at a lot of dumps, real dumps, and a lot of mansions, too."

Sylvie began to talk about some of the other places they had inspected, and Al was still talking, now about the realtors who would sell a doghouse and call it a palace. Lois finished her beer and caught the look of affection and amusement on David's face. She grinned again and although both Al and Sylvie were talking, she did, too.

"Anyway, welcome, and thanks for the beer. I have to go and scrub. I'm all over muck. Why don't you join us for a cookout? David, you know the way up the trail, don't you? You can be guide. Seven or thereabouts."

Sylvie and Al exchanged glances; hers said sure, why not, and he nodded.

"Good. No one should have to cook on moving day, and restaurants are just too much trouble if you've been working hard. Don't dress up or anything. It's a real cookout, first of the season, and with the weather cooling off the way it does as soon as the sun goes down, it's not likely to be a late-night affair." She reached out to put down her empty can, and somehow her arm brushed David's thermos and it teetered, then fell with the unmistakable sound of breaking glass.

"Goddamn it," Lois said with a sigh. "David, I'm sorry. As I said, it's been that kind of day. I'll replace it, of course." She bent over to pick it up, but he was there first.

10

"It's all right," he said hurriedly. "Really. Don't worry about it."

But she would get him a new one, Sylvie thought. Lois left then, and Sylvie turned to the bags and boxes on the table. "Now, let's see what you got and try to figure out where it should go."

Al was looking thoughtfully out the door. "David, she said up the trail, walk to her place. Where? There ain't no place out there that I know about."

David squirmed uncomfortably. "I didn't know she'd invite us all over," he said, not looking happy. "I mean, she's my boss, a professor, Dr. Wharton, and all, but she's also Mrs. Wollander. She lives in the big house at the other side of the lake."

As Lois walked away she continued to hear Sylvie's raucous voice, and Al's equally raucous voice in some kind of weird harmony. She was still grinning.

"What's so funny?"

She looked up, startled, but not really surprised to see her husband Warren approaching with both hands outstretched.

"Hi! Didn't see you there. Sun in my eyes maybe."

He drew her close and kissed her. Warren Wollander was six feet tall and large through the shoulders and chest, strong-looking at sixty-two. "I didn't intend you should see me," he said, softly. "That's just about where I was standing the first time I saw you. Remember? I like watching you when you don't know I'm there."

"Who could forget?" she said, and put her arm about his waist. His arm was across her shoulders as they started up the trail.

He had taken the walk that day even though there was still snow in every shadowed cranny, thick on the north slopes, piled up behind stone walls. And across the lake he had seen a person who, he thought, was spiking the experi-

11

mental trees. A short, shapeless figure in a down jacket, heavy pants, boots, with a red stocking cap that had a long tail that swung back and forth as she applied a drill to a tree, braced for purchase, and started to drill.

"I thought you were a yeti," she said gravely, and they both laughed. Actually, she had been drilling out core samples to measure for growth. He tightened his arm around her shoulders. "I was smiling at our new neighbors," she said. "Mr. and Mrs. Zukal. I invited them to the cookout. And David, too. It's time you met David, I think."

The pressure of his hand on her shoulder tightened, just for a moment, and perhaps not in response to what she had said, she thought. She did not look up at him, but watched the trail. It was well-groomed, with dense mayapple colonies on both sides.

"Well, well, the place finally got sold? That will surprise Jill, I suspect."

"I guess so," she agreed, and suddenly felt tired, and unhappy about the invitation that she had issued without thought. "Do you mind that I asked them over?"

This time she knew his hand tightened, but it was a reassuring pressure, and reassurance was in his voice when he replied. "Lois, this is your house, not Jill's. Remember? You're the lady of the house. You want company, invite them. Tell me about our new neighbors."

She began to talk and presently he was chuckling, and then laughed louder. "God, it will certainly surprise Jill."

She laughed, too, but she was bothered about his daughter Jill. What if Jill came on in one of her bitchy moods? She could do that. And this man, this guru, whatever he was, what if he was impossible? She knew that Jill's husband Stanley would be all right, and Warren would treat the Zukals exactly the same way he treated everyone. With a politeness that would be excessive if he didn't like them, and with warmth and humor if he did. She sighed and wished she could take back the spontaneous invitation. And even with the thought, she found herself denying it.

No, by God, she thought firmly; this *was* her house, she *was* the lady of the house, and Jill had to be reminded now and then. Jill had arrived for a visit three weeks ago and Lois was beginning to think of her as the Woman Who Came to Dinner. Yesterday Jill had announced plans for a cookout, even though the late April weather could be as fickle as any poet ever suggested. She had invited a stranger, Sebastian, and had taken it for granted that it would be fine with everyone else. Well, it was, only the party had suddenly increased by three.

Sometimes she wondered if Warren was fully aware of the cautious maneuvers she and Jill used with each other, and usually she knew the answer was that he was fully aware. She suspected that he knew exactly why she had invited their new neighbors, and she suddenly felt ashamed of herself, and immensely grateful for his support. His position was not enviable either, she knew. He was deeply in love with her, no doubt about that, and he loved his daughter without reservation, even though she could be . . . difficult was the kindest word Lois could think of. She gave his waist a little squeeze when they had to separate to walk single file. She appreciated these short periods together more than he could realize; she knew he was the wisest man she had ever met, and if he thought it would all work out, that made her think so too. Most of the time anyway.

CHAPTER 2

This was one of the worst evenings of his life, David Levy thought as he and the Zukals approached the big house. They had come up the trail, as Dr. Wharton had suggested, and Mrs. Zukal had been watching for animals or snakes or bugs the entire way. Now they emerged onto a meticulously maintained lawn that stretched out forever. Already, some people on the patio behind the house had turned to watch them. David felt like a pinned butterfly. He swallowed hard and deliberately looked past the group of people to study the house.

The original structure had been tall and narrow, three stories up with a peaked roof, but wings had been added, and now it sprawled and the central part looked almost like a ship's mast to which the lower sections were tethered. The patio was flagstone; a long trellis covered with the first extravagant flush of red and white roses screened what lay beyond.

Although he intended to keep focusing on the house, his gaze was drawn to Lois as she came to meet them. She was dressed in chino pants and a gray silk shirt that made Sylvie's blue polyester pantsuit look tawdry. She got between Sylvie and Al to take their arms and steer them to her husband. Her greeting was warm and cheerful; she made it seem natural for the three newcomers to be part of the group, and to David's surprise no one else seemed to think it strange either. He mumbled something to Mr. Wollander, and then to his daughter Jill who looked like a movie star in skintight jeans and a scoop-neck sweater that accentuated her sharp collarbones. He nodded to the other man whose name was simply Sebastian.

"You've certainly come to a beautiful setting," Sebastian said to Al as they shook hands. "We were just marveling over the lake."

It was about twenty feet lower than the lawn where they were standing, and in the evening sunlight it gleamed like a sapphire without a ripple to mar it.

"Yeah, it's pretty, all right," Al said, and Sylvie said something at the same time; behind them David suppressed a groan. But Sylvie shut up and the moment passed.

"I have pictures of the mill that go back sixty years or more," Warren said then. "I bet you'd like to see them."

Before they could respond, Jill said to Sylvie, "This afternoon I acted like an idiot. You gave me such a start. We used to play in the mill, you know how children will get into a place like that. We told ghost stories and there you were suddenly, just like out of one of the stories. I'm sorry."

"You started me, too," Sylvie said. "I thought you was squatters or something. No harm done."

"She was absolutely forbidden to go there, just as I was," Warren said, laughing. "We did the same thing when I was a boy. Come on, let's look at those pictures."

As he led them inside, Lois began to relax and she wondered why she had been tense at all. Jill had behaved like a perfect lady, and had taken the news of the addition to her party with such good grace that Lois had felt ashamed. She went to one of the long tables where drinks had been prepared.

"David, Sebastian? What would you like?"

They both took juice and she had gin and tonic. Jill helped herself to white wine. Sebastian was still regarding the lake.

"I had no idea this was back here in the hills," he said after a moment. "I'm surprised that people aren't swarming to it. Isolation and peace are priceless commodities these days."

"Too small and too out of the way," Lois said. "And hiking's better on the other side of the village, up into the mountains. But when hunting season opens, they swarm." She stood at his side and also gazed at the unlikely blue of the water. "You realize that color comes from the fact that the lake is dead?"

Sebastian looked at her with disapproval, she thought, surprised at his expression. "Acid rains did it in," she explained. "Unfit for fish or plant life. It's doing the same to the experimental farm," she added, and heard the bitterness in her voice.

"Perhaps," Sebastian said in his gentle voice, "we are seeing a warning sign that must be acknowledged. A lake here, a farm there. The earth is speaking to us. But who is listening? Perhaps there has been too much experimenting already."

Lois felt a surge of anger that caused a trembling in her fingers. "Not just a lake here and a farm there," she snapped. "Whole forests are dying. In Bavaria, the whole damn Fichtelgebirge forest is at risk. More than fifty percent of the mature trees are dead. And it's happening in Vermont, on the West Coast. Not just a little patch here and there, I'm afraid."

"I understand the peril," he said gravely, "and what I suggest is that if we can restore the harmony of humans and nature, of living with nature instead of pitting ourselves

16

against it over and over, perhaps even this peril can be overcome."

He believed it, she realized, when she turned to study his face, to see if he was mocking. He looked as if he wanted to touch her, to soothe her, calm her; he looked as if he ached because of her pain and anger. Suddenly she remembered a high school teacher, more than twenty years ago, who had looked at her pityingly and said, "Do you really believe we can pollute all the oceans of the world?" Then, as a girl, she had been comforted by such knowledge, such serene wisdom, such absolute faith. This man, Sebastian, with his understanding, his sympathy, his empathy, his firm convictions could be just as soothing, just as comforting. He would dispense faith, trust, harmony with a word, a gentle smile. And meanwhile the trees were dying from causes so complex that few people even attempted to define them, and those who studied them walked in fear. Looking at him, she had the wild impression that he was following her thoughts, that he was telling her she did not have to live in fear, that she could recapture the same kind of tranquillity that softened his face. The tranquillity of ignorance, she said to herself sharply, and lifted her glass and forced herself to look away from him.

She drank, and then remembered that she had not yet asked David about his weekend plans. She turned toward him. "Are you free this weekend? I thought we might start the lime before another rain comes."

Too late she realized that Jill had been talking in a low voice with David; she bit her lip in exasperation. "Sorry. I can't leave my work behind, it seems." But David had left Jill with an embarrassing swiftness and was already at her side.

"I wasn't going anywhere. The lime shipment came this afternoon. And a couple of the hands will be around."

She shook her head, and waved him away. "No. No more work today, no more talk about lime or trees or acid

17

rain." Then, as if to prove her point about no more work talk, she returned to the table with the decanters, and asked over her shoulder, "Sebastian, can you leave your work when the day is over?"

"I'm going to the village to pick up Stanley," Jill said, and walked stiffly off the patio to vanish into the house.

Lois sighed and refilled her glass.

"But how does one say a day ends?" Sebastian asked as if bemused. "One day flows into another, and then another endlessly. And my work . . . That, too, is endless. I am never not working, if that is even the right word."

Lois glanced toward the house, wishing Warren would come back and bring Al and Sylvie with him, let them do the talking. She said to David, "Sebastian is a . . . what, counselor, preacher, teacher? What do you call yourself?"

For a moment, when he had come to her side to talk about lime, David had looked almost at ease, now he looked wretched again. But Sebastian paid no attention to him, he kept his gaze fixed on Lois.

He smiled. "None of the above, I think. A guide at times, when I have found a piece of the path myself. But most of the time I think I am a student, a searcher, and the few stretches of path that have opened to me have revealed that the path is as endless as the day, as my work. . . ." He stopped speaking and regarded her for a moment. "You have a headache?"

After a brief hesitation she said yes. "Tension, I know. Stiff neck, stiff shoulders. Working too hard, racing the clock most of the time. It will pass."

"Let me demonstrate one of the techniques I found along the way," he said. "It will help very fast, or not at all. But first you have to sit down."

It was a challenge, she thought, one she did not have to accept. But his expression was guileless and kindly, and with reluctance she seated herself at the table. At the other side of the table David swirled his ice cubes around and around in his glass.

18

A few minutes later when Warren returned, laughing with Al and Sylvie, she was still seated at the table. "Warren, let Sebastian show you how to get rid of a headache. It works like magic!"

Sebastian demonstrated on them all. Sylvie was stiff all over as he approached her, confirming her worst suspicions, that he was a laying-on-of-hands minister, and Al was wishing they could go back inside and look at more pictures. What a house, he thought. Made theirs look like kid's stuff. David was wishing he had never been born. He had known this would be the worst evening of his life, but he had not known just how bad it would get. Seeing Dr. Wharton—Lois—with her husband, and then with Sebastian's hands on her neck and shoulders. . . . He had thought he was braced, but that was before he had realized just how bad it could get. Women were fussing with another long table and that gave him hope that they would eat soon, and the evening would end.

"See," Sebastian was saying to Sylvie. "You are stiff with apprehension, and that causes the muscles to contract, and that is the source of pain."

"I ain't even got a headache," she said.

"But you are not relaxed, either." His voice was soothing and kind, and when he felt her neck, his fingers were gentle at first; they became probing, and hurting. He pressed at the base of her skull, and then at the top of her shoulders, and it seemed to her that she did loosen up a little. But there wasn't no miracle cure, she added. He went on to Al who steeled himself as if getting ready for hand-to-hand combat. Sebastian laughed.

Soon after that Jill returned with Stanley. His arm was around her waist, her hand over his on her hip, as if to keep it anchored there, not let it roam. His face was round and smooth, his eyes pale blue. Like a little doll, Sylvie thought. A bright and smiling little doll. She guessed that Jill had told him about the company for supper; he acted like a proper little gentleman with Sebastian, didn't look

19

him up and down or anything, just shook hands, and then turned to her and Al. At first, she expected him to cold-shoulder them; he looked like one of the magazine ads for the type who made a million before thirty and had no use, thank you, for anyone who didn't. But instead, he was like a school kid with her and Al.

"Wow! You guys won the big one! Hey, that's great! Do you have a financial advisor yet?"

Warren burst out laughing. "He can turn carrot juice into oil fields, folks. If he gives out advice, listen."

Al surveyed Stanley thoughtfully. "Financial advisor? What's he do?"

"You don't, do you? Oh, God! Let's take a little walk." When Al started to move toward the side of the patio where the trellises were heavy with roses, Stanley took his arm and drew him instead out onto the lawn. "No flowers. Allergic. Mostly to bees, but it's been my experience that if you avoid flowers, you're more likely to avoid the little bastards. Now look, you need someone who makes it a career thinking about money, someone who really likes to see it grow, see. . . ."

It wasn't that he had snubbed Sebastian, Lois thought, but he had shown no enthusiasm either. She listened absently as Jill explained to Sebastian that with Stanley money was a vocation, and a hobby, which made him a happy man since there was so much of it to work and play with. And Sebastian murmured something to the effect that Stanley might be very good for Al and Sylvie. With a start Lois understood that Jill had been apologizing for her husband and that Sebastian had accepted the apology. Lois wondered if Jill had planned this whole cookout simply to bring Sebastian and Stanley together in a friendly manner, and she decided she simply did not care.

David didn't know exactly how it happened, but Warren Wollander asked him a simple question or two, and the next thing he knew he was talking about the need to introduce new foods that would grow in marginal lands, the need to supply complete proteins in crops that could be maintained by peasants everywhere. The need to develop fast-growing trees that would supply fuel and food and fodder and hold the soil, restore the balance of atmospheric gases. . . .

"You can't do it," Jill said flatly when he paused for a breath. "You can't keep up with human fertility through food. You have to educate people, reduce fertility first, and then maybe you will accomplish something."

"But you can't just let them starve if they're already here," Sylvie said.

Al and Stanley returned, apparently having reached an agreement of some sort. Al looked at Sylvie fondly and said, "First thing, we get that check, and first thing, ten percent right off the top, to charity. Her idea."

Stanley groaned.

"And where do you stand in this perennial problem of distributing the world's largess, Sebastian?" Warren asked. Lois felt herself become very still at the tone of his voice, too polite.

"When enough people find the path, realize the human potential, experience the wholeness that is available to all, then there will be no problem," Sebastian said softly. "It doesn't take everyone, just enough to lead the way. We all find different ways to help bring this about, some through the green revolutions that arise, some through other means."

"Well, the means I intend to apply this minute are at hand at the grill," Warren said. "Steaks in five minutes."

It turned out that neither David nor Sebastian would eat meat; Lois felt, with a twinge of irritation, that she should have known, and she went inside to advise Mrs. Carlysle, the housekeeper, that they would also need a lot of cheese. Her headache had come back.

The steaks were superb. Al asked for the name of the butcher, the grocery, wherever they got them. The supermarket he had worked in never had meat like that. Mrs.

Carlysle had found smoked salmon that David accepted although Sebastian did not. "To hell with it," Lois said distinctly under her breath. Sebastian was not her problem. Let Jill see to his diet. Warren talked to Sylvie about growing up here, how he and his brother, who was killed in Iwo Jima, had played up and down the hills, in the mill. Stanley talked to Al about money matters and to Jill about the hideous mess the painters were making in their New York City condo that was being redecorated. Jill shrugged. "I told you to move into a hotel until they're finished. You keep telling me how awful it is, but you don't do anything about it. You knew it would be a mess." She was quiet for most of the meal, her smile forced and mechanical. Sylvie caught her glancing from David back to Lois, and saw the little glint in her eyes as she reached some kind of conclusion. "You swim every morning, don't you?" Jill asked David, who blushed and nodded. Jill shivered. "I couldn't stand the idea of leaving a warm bed and plunging into that cold water before breakfast even." It was innocent, Lois told herself. It was. David looked agonized and averted his gaze to his plate. Sebastian and Stanley launched into a tortured philosophical discussion about the ethics of feeding the poor. Sebastian's voice was melodious, his accent softened by a touch of the south. Now that Lois had disengaged herself from trying to entertain him, she listened to the rhythms of his voice instead of the actual words. It was almost as if his first language had been French perhaps, or Spanish, and he had learned English from a southerner who had lived many years in the north. Lois smiled to herself over her own tortured path in trying to identify his origins, and she wondered what Warren had seen in the man to cause his distrust. Aside from the fact that he was some kind of guru, she added.

"But don't you think it would be cruel to give them vitamins and adequate food for a limited time, knowing that tomorrow they will be starving again?" Sebastian asked. His voice had become sorrowful.

"You have to work with it one day at a time," David said, sounding nearly desperate but unable not to join the discussion, his words too fast and sharp. His New York sound, Lois thought.

Sylvie had grown increasingly restless, certain that none of them was talking about real people, just ideas. "What you're saying is just like don't go to the doctor today because maybe you'll get sick again or get hit by a truck tomorrow. Well, maybe if your belly's full and you're healthy tomorrow you can face whatever's around the corner better." Her voice rose in indignation. "It's crazy to just give up. Might as well not be born in the first place. Or have a bat ready to bash every baby's head the minute it shows up. Is that what you mean?"

"Of course not," Sebastian said. "But I think people should accept what happens. Endless, futile struggling destroys whatever peace is available, and peace of the soul is more important than a full stomach."

"Yeah, but peace is easier with a full stomach than an empty one," Sylvie muttered. "You don't know that, you ain't talked to the right people."

Warren laughed. "She's got you, I'm afraid."

It was the signal that that conversation had drifted too far into unpleasant matters to continue at the dinner table, Lois knew. Apparently Stanley understood the message also.

"Speaking of vitamins and such," Stanley said, "I read that if you take bee pollen in increasing doses, you can build up a tolerance to stings."

Jill toyed with her food and looked terminally bored.

David began to talk about the health food and vitamin catalog that he ordered his vitamins from and Sebastian promised to send him a price list from the company he used, less expensive, he said, than David's supplier. Stanley asked if they carried bee pollen, and Sebastian said coolly that anyone with the right thoughts, the right attitude, reverence for all living creatures never got stung to begin with.

"Right," Al Zukal said with a satisfied grunt. He pushed his plate back, finished. "And them people can whistle snakes up out of baskets and climb ropes that ain't hooked on nothing, and their shit smells sweet. Yeah."

There was a long silence, broken when Warren rose from his chair. "I'll see if coffee's about ready," he said, his voice strained.

Belatedly Lois realized that he was nearly choking to keep from laughing. "I'll help," she said and followed him inside where they collapsed holding each other in the hallway to the kitchen, laughing out of control.

That night in bed, Al said, "Well, watcha think?" And Sylvie said, "Doncher get ideas."

"What's that supposed to mean?"

"We're not their kind and they know it and so do we."

"Stanley's all right."

Stanley had insisted on driving them home, to Sylvie's great relief. She had been terrified of the dark trail, and the probable dangers it held.

"Sure he is. They all are. But don't get ideas. Listen. What's that?" They both listened, and she said, "Wolves."

"You crazy or something. There's no wolves anymore. Except on TV. Dogs."

They lay in rigid silence listening to howling that sounded more like wolves than dogs.

"Stanley gave me some good advice already," Al said after a moment. "And he's coming over Sunday to talk before he goes back to town."

"What advice?"

"He said . . . Well, not all that much, I guess."

"Spit it out," Sylvie said. "You won't go to sleep and neither will I until you do."

"Yeah. Well, he said I should first thing, next check next month, take out insurance, a big policy."

She was silent for a long time, then said, "You already got insurance."

"I mean big. Really big. You know that lottery ticket was mine, and if I kick, that's all she wrote."

Sylvie drew closer to him. Out here in the country it was cold at night, not like back home, she thought. "Well, don't kick," she said finally. "Why should you? You're as healthy as a horse. Listen. What's that?"

After a moment he said, "Frogs or something. Crickets maybe."

After another minute or two, she got up and stood at the window looking out. The blackness seemed to start right at the end of her nose. "I can't see a thing, not a light, nothing. Black as a coal bin out there. I want a dog."

She groped her way to the bathroom where she switched on the light, and then returned to bed, leaving the door open a few inches. Now the dimly lighted bedroom seemed more natural, like the bedroom in their old apartment where streetlights had filtered in no matter what she did.

"Dog's a good idea," Al said, as they adjusted themselves to fit each other again. Her feet were like ice. "Yeah, real good idea. Tomorrow, you and Flora should do that, go out and get a watch dog."

They both began to think about the visit of their daughter Flora and her husband Bobby and their two children, and the noise they would bring with them, and they thought that somehow light would come with them, too. Finally they could drift off to sleep.

The dog was a golden retriever, two years old, female. They named her Sadie. Al regarded her with great distrust. They had never owned a dog before—who wants to clean up dog shit on the streets? Or take it out for a walk in the rain? But out here it seemed the dog took care of herself. And she slept on the porch so no one had to take her out. But his distrust was focused on the fact that she acted like a kid, just like Flora's two kids, running, romping, having a good time. Not like a watchdog should act, he decided. Mikey held her while Janie went off to hide, and Sadie tore out after her when he let go and found her in two shakes. They tossed a stick and she brought that back. She played Frisbee like a pro. So, Al brooded, good-time Sadie, what good was a dog like that, one that loved everybody? And she did, it seemed, love everybody. She laughed at the kids and smiled at Flora and Bobby, and treated Sylvie like she was a Marine sergeant and Sadie a recruit in love with being a Marine.

On Monday morning when Lois appeared on the swinging bridge Sadie stiffened and growled, although she couldn't see that far, or hear either, Al was sure. He and Sylvie went with the dog to the edge of the property where Lois was just about to step onto their land, and Sadie was shivering, growling. She began to bark and Lois stopped in her tracks. It was the first time Al had heard the dog bark, he realized with approval. Not that she should bark at Lois, but it was a good sign.

Sylvie had to introduce Sadie to Lois, real polite and formal like; the dog sniffed Lois all over, and then wagged her rear end in approval. It was embarrassing to Al the way Sadie stuck her nose in Lois's crotch, but she seemed to have to do that; she had done it to everyone she was introduced to so far.

"She's beautiful!" Lois said when the inspection ended, and she had been accepted. "Has she been in swimming yet? Retrievers usually love the water."

Al hadn't even thought of letting the dog in the lake. But that afternoon he and Sylvie went down and he tossed in a stick, and Sadie tore out after it as if she were half fish. By then he was sold on her, anyway, but it was another good sign. If one of the kids ever fell in, or anything like that happened . . . he thought vaguely, not quite ready to admit aloud that he sort of liked the silly animal for herself. She had set up a hell of a ruckus when the carpenters came to work on the mill, and after they left she went over every inch of the ground they had walked on, everything they had touched. She repeated this the next morning, and the next;

they had not introduced her to the carpenters whom she continued to treat as trespassers. But she met Lois at the bridge and smiled, waving her plumy tail, and escorted her to the break in the fence that separated this property from the experimental farmlands. She did not step through with Lois and she refused to go on the swinging bridge unless under direct order by Sylvie.

Now, when Al and Sylvie went to bed, they didn't lie in rigid silence, holding their breath, listening. Sadie was on the job.

On Saturday Flora, Bobby, and the kids came back, and the kids wore themselves and Sadie out again, as they had done before. When the kids had gone on to bed, Al shook his head at the dog, lying in exhaustion on the porch. "That's how it's gonna be," he said. She raised her head and smiled at him. She thumped her tail on the porch once, sighed, and made no further attempt to be polite.

Al was the first one up the next morning. He went to the kitchen to start coffee, and glanced out for Sadie. She would take food from him now, and he liked to feed her, but she wasn't on the porch. He walked out and whistled, expecting her to come bounding in from the fringe of woods, or up from the mill, overjoyed to see one of her people, the way she was every morning. He had disturbed the early birds, silenced them; gradually their twitterings resumed, and there was a slight breeze in the treetops, but no other sound. He walked a few feet from the house and whistled once more, a little louder; when she did not appear, he started to walk toward the mill and the water, vaguely concerned that she might have fallen in, even though he had seen her swimming like a fish before.

A lot of trees had grown up between the house and mill, not as thick as the real woods, but enough so that he could not see the mill until he stepped out from the thicket, and then he came to a full stop.

"Sadie? Sadie!" He ran to the dog, lying on her side in high grasses. "Jaysus!" he whispered hoarsely and knelt on the ground near her, not close enough to touch her. "Oh, Jaysus," he said again, and it sounded like a whimper.

CHAPTER 3

The problem was that when she was gone the house changed, Charlie Meiklejohn brooded, sitting at the kitchen table, scowling at the rain that continued without letup. It had rained yesterday, too. Too damn much. It was a comfortable house, if a bit untidy at the moment because he believed in carrying out papers and stuff only when they began to get in the way, and that point hadn't been reached yet. This was Wednesday, and Sunday's paper was still there; soon it would be time. But this little bit of clutter wasn't the real difference, he knew, even though when she was home, clutter seemed to disappear without anyone's doing anything about it. When she was around, he would see something and think vaguely that next time through he would pick it up, but next time through, more often than not, it was gone.

For one thing, he thought then, pursuing the cause of the difference in the house, it felt too big and too empty, and when she was home it never occurred to him that the house might be too big. Three rooms upstairs, one of them her office with her computer now nicely covered, everything in

29

place, awaiting her return. Their bedroom, and their grown daughter's bedroom that was now their official guest room. His office on the first floor was a jumble of miscellaneous stuff. He kept the door closed, he said to keep the cats out. There was the living room where they spent most of their evenings, a dining room, and a tiny room that they never could figure out what to call. They had put the television in there. Earlier that day he had made a tour of the house wondering that he never had noticed before that there was too much room. And that was when the mystery had started. When she was home the house was exactly the right size, and with her gone, it was ten times too big.

There were dishes in the sink from last night, and from that morning, and eventually he would rouse himself and cram them all into the dishwasher, but not yet. There was this mystery to solve: What was it that vanished with her gone? How could her presence fill an entire house no matter where she was physically within it? The house was the same. The yard beyond the sliding glass door, with flowers in bloom, the patio awash at the moment, but not changed, everything tangible exactly the same as usual, but everything different anyway.

Even the cats were different. Brutus was not speaking to him at all, disdainful of any attempt at friendliness, accepting food grudgingly, without appreciation, and spending far too much time simply staring at Charlie through slitted eyes that could turn into devil's eyes altogether too easily. That cat was too damn smart for his own good, Charlie brooded. He had come to them in New York, nearly full grown, and street smart; he had looked them over, looked over their apartment, examined the two other cats and found them acceptable, and moved in. But he had never fully forgiven them for retiring out to the country, not yet, probably never would. And he blamed Charlie; that was obvious in the way he stared at him through devil eyes. Ashcan, the cowardly gray-suited one, kept prowling about, as if Constance might be found under the sofa, or behind the

30

drapes. And Candy, the big-mouth, had gone into her invalid act. She did it very well, dragged herself from room to room, lay without motion for hours at a time, and looked at him with her butterscotch eyes in a way that suggested death was near, and it was his fault.

It wasn't perfume, he knew, returning to the mystery; she seldom wore any. But she had a fragrance that came from her shampoo, her own physical body, whatever. That was part of it. Not enough. Her soft steps throughout the house, the sound of the sliding door opening and closing, her low murmurs to the cats. Another part of it. Not enough yet. A few days ago Mrs. Grayson had come to do her weekly cleaning and she had talked to the cats, and had even elicited a response from them, and that hadn't been enough to fill the void. So it wasn't just another person, another voice that was lacking.

He missed her in bed, of course, the warmth of her body next to his, the rhythm of her breathing, a sigh now and then, and that wasn't enough either. After all, he didn't spend all day every day in bed with her. Not any more anyway. A grin softened his face, smoothed out deep lines, as he thought of the various times they had tried to do just that. Stop, he told himself. That made it worse.

Charlie had been a New York City fireman, an inspector, a city detective, altogether more than twenty-five years, and he had seen enough, had done enough to put those lines on his face. It was as if, when Constance was home, a curtain was drawn somewhere in him that screened out all those lines, those many years, and with her gone, the curtain was removed, his past was written clearly on the landscape of his face. Although he had taken an early retirement, it became evident when he was alone that it had not been too early. He was not generally introspective, and never gazed on his own face except during the act of shaving; he had no way of realizing the change he was fretting about was internal, and he continued to try to find a

31

cause for the palpable difference in the surroundings of the house.

When the phone finally rang he scooped it up before the first peal ended. "Do you believe in auras?" he asked.

"Sometimes. Charlie, are you drunk?"

"Nope. How is she? How's your dad? How are you?"

"She's coming along fine. We get to spring her on Friday. Dad's going crazy. And I'm lonely. How are you?"

"Swinging from the chandelier. The Mitchums are so concerned they've taken to sending the boys over to keep an eye on me."

She chuckled. Now that the crisis with her mother was over—gall bladder surgery that had gone sour—she could laugh again, but for several days the strain in her voice had made him feel as if he were choking. Another mystery. They chatted; he read her a letter from an associate of hers who wanted permission to reprint one of her papers in psychology; she reported on her father's eccentricities in restaurants—nothing with sauce because you never knew what they were trying to hide—and they both laughed. When he hung up, the house felt emptier than ever.

Candy was regarding him with tragic eyes. "All right," he snarled at her. "She didn't ask to speak to you. So there."

He started to load the dishwasher then and was still at it when Pete Mitchum tapped on the back door. With him was another boy. Young man, Charlie corrected himself, as he crossed the kitchen to admit them. Pete was about twenty and his friend looked a year or so older. Dressed in dripping ponchos with hoods, rubber boots, they looked like Christopher Robin twice.

"Hi, Mr. Meiklejohn. This is David Levy, the guy I told you about."

Charlie motioned toward a chair under the wide overhang out of the rain, and they deposited their wet gear and then came on inside.

David Levy was very tall and angular, with a lot of thick

black hair, and blue eyes. "Thanks for seeing me, sir," he said as they shook hands. His grip was surprisingly strong.

Sir, Charlie thought with a feeling of resignation. He asked if they wanted a beer, a Coke, coffee, which he was at that very moment going to make, and motioned them toward the table. They both refused his hospitality, and he abandoned the coffee project and joined them.

"Before I ask you anything," David said awkwardly, "I should find out your consultation fees, I guess."

Pete looked mortified and Charlie said seriously, "Advice is cheap, so cheap that it's held to have no value, and no one takes it anyway. For advice, no fees."

Pete had already told him a long story about how he had met David, through a network of mutual college friends that seemed to stretch out over the country. His friend, he had said, needed some professional advice, would it be okay to bring him over? Since at the time Charlie had been at the Mitchums' dining room table eating chicken and dumplings it would have been churlish to refuse. Now he regarded the young man patiently and waited.

"What I need to know is how do you go about proving that someone poisoned a dog. I mean, if it's something you really know happened, then what?"

"Your dog?"

"No sir. You see, I work at the university experimental farm over at Spender's Ferry, about forty-five minutes from here, I guess. And my friend Rosa's parents won the lottery last year and they were looking for a place in the country and I told them about the old mill over there . . ." He took a deep breath.

"Take it easy," Charlie said. "There's no rush. Rosa's folks won the lottery. She's your girlfriend?"

David blushed. "That's what my dad asked. It's not like that, sir. I mean, she's female and she's my friend. I think men and women are friends more than they used to be maybe. Anyway, her parents won the lottery. And they decided to move out of the city. They've always lived in the

33

Bronx, I guess. And because I'm doing graduate work at the farm, I knew about the mill. They were looking for a big place. Anyway, they liked it and bought it, and Mrs. Zukal bought this dog, a beautiful golden retriever, because she was afraid out in the country. And someone poisoned the dog. We all know it was poisoned. But now what?"

"Did they send you? Mrs. Zukal and her husband? Why didn't they come themselves?"

David shook his head. "No one sent me. They don't even know I came here. I guess I feel sort of responsible because I found the place and suggested they look at it, and all."

Charlie grunted and stood up. "I'm going to make that coffee. You guys sure you don't want something? Cold drinks are in the fridge. Help yourselves."

Pete helped himself. "He just drinks juice or herb teas," he said, opening a can of Coke.

"Sorry," Charlie said. When *she* was home there was always freshly squeezed juice, but he never thought of it. He busied himself with coffee and then returned to the table. "Okay," he said. "There is a problem with proof. Dogs get into things. You said a mill. Maybe rat poison, something like that. Maybe a neighbor put out something that he ate and died from. Did a vet look at him?"

David shook his head. "Her," he said. "Her name was Sadie. They found her the next morning, I guess. She was good and dead. No point in the vet. Mr. Zukal buried her."

"Then you don't really know what she died from."

David shook his head even harder, a stubborn look settling in on his face. "One day she was playing, chasing a ball, in great shape, the next morning she's dead. We know. And the mill hasn't been used in half a century maybe. There aren't any rats there. Sadie was trained in a special school to be a watchdog. She wouldn't go chasing around the neighborhood. She had to be poisoned on her own property by someone. I just don't know what to do about it. How to go about finding out anything."

"Okay," Charlie said briskly. "You haven't ruled out accident, you know. She could have caught a diseased animal, or a poisoned animal. A squirrel or a rabbit, even a rat. They're everywhere even if you don't see them. And no doubt dogs are susceptible to a host of things you also don't know anything about. So the first thing you'd have to do is find out what killed her. That means exhumation. You would take her remains to a veterinary pathologist and have tests run. Then you have something to start with. Right now all you have is suspicion. Is there any one person you suspect?"

David had turned very pale at the word exhumation. Charlie pretended not to notice.

"I can't think of anyone, or a reason," David said faintly.

"Right. So, after you learn the actual cause of death, if it was poison, you would call the county animal control office and ask if other poisonings have been reported. If there have been, they might take over at that point. If not, you're still on your own. But the first step, in any event, is to find out the cause of death."

"If I find out that she was really poisoned, will the sheriff investigate? Or the animal control office? Will anyone?"

Charlie felt a stab of pity for this earnest young man burdened with his load of guilt and responsibility. "Maybe," he said slowly. "But, David, I won't kid you, unless there have been other cases, and unless livestock gets involved, probably not much. Someone might ask the Zukals a few questions. But it's almost impossible to prove something like this unless you actually catch the person in the act, and even then, chances are good they'll get off with a slap on the wrist. And the animal pathologist will charge, you know. It will be expensive, and you'll run up against indifference. Just the way it goes."

"That's really shitty!" Pete protested.

"Yep."

David stood up then and held out his hand. "Thanks, Mr. Meiklejohn. I appreciate your talking to me about this."

Charlie wanted to pat him on the head, but he knew that would not be welcome, and besides, he would have had to get on a chair. Instead, he shook hands with David, and then stood in the doorway watching the boys walk across the backyard in the rain. So young they probably would splash in every puddle they came to, getting a sampling of how truly shitty the world could be. They would climb the fence, walk through the pasture that separated the Mitchum house from his house, and that would be that, he thought, almost wishing he had told Pete no, not to bring his young friend around. The advice he had given had left a bad taste in his mouth.

Saturday morning Lois was surveying the greenhouse that held her cloned trees. Some of them were outgrowing the bench already and would have to be moved onto a lower one, and that was going to be a mess, she knew. It would take several hours to do them all, and meanwhile she had the metabolism studies to work on, and the measurements . . . She glanced at her watch again. At ten-thirty she walked outside and started for David's apartment, but then she saw Tom Hopewell emerging from his corn rows, and she slowed down.

He waved at her and she waved back, glanced toward the apartments, and waved again.

"Are you busy right now?" she called.

"Sure. But I can stop. Why?"

Sometimes she felt a bit of confusion with Tom, but she had no idea of what caused it. He was a year or two younger than she was, and he dressed like a ragged child, and like a child he could grin so disarmingly that people often forgot that he was a truly fine botanist with a Ph.D. There was something unfathomable about him, about the way he looked at her, the way he could stop what he was doing just like that. He looked and acted like a child playing at being a scientist, his hair too long, knees out of his jeans, dirty hands.

"It's probably nothing," she said, as he drew near. "David's so late, and I need him. I was going to go wake him up, but it might embarrass him if I walk in. Would you mind?"

"Oh, it might embarrass him indeed," he said gravely, but his eyes were dancing with amusement, and she didn't know what he found funny.

They walked on to the apartments together, and she knocked on the door. There was no response from inside. Tom entered and continued on through to the bedroom; Lois stood in the doorway uncomfortably, keeping her gaze averted.

"Oh my God!" Tom said in a voice that was low but carried to where she was standing. "Lois, there's been an accident or something."

She ran into the apartment, into the bedroom where he was standing ashen-faced, staring at the bed, at the figure that had covers drawn up to his chin. She reached past Tom and touched David's cheek, then jerked her hand back. She heard a moaning sound and did not realize she was making it until she found herself standing at the sink, hanging onto it as if to keep from falling, and behind her she could hear Tom on the telephone.

The day before, Friday, Charlie had gone to the city to give a deposition in an arson case he had worked on, and he got talked into a poker game that lasted too long, but made him feel filthy rich afterward. And because on Monday Constance was due, he stayed in town to meet her at Kennedy, and then they celebrated by staying the rest of the week and seeing two Broadway shows. By the time they returned home, the weather had changed dramatically, into summertime, and the house was filled with her presence and once more was exactly the right size.

He had forgotten David Levy and his problem and never would have thought of him again, except in a passing moment, if Constance had not come looking for him in the basement a few days later.

"Charlie, there's a man to see you. A Mr. Levy. He's pretty upset."

"David?" Charlie put down the spinning reel he was trying to fix. It kept snarling the line, and for the life of him, he thought moodily, he couldn't see why. He wiped his hands and followed Constance back upstairs. It was a pleasure to watch her move. She was long and lithe and moved like a dancer. When they emerged from the dimness of the stairs into the sunlight in the kitchen, he got another jolt of pleasure in seeing her hair gleam when she moved through the brilliant light. Only God knew how much of that color was the original color, how much was because the original color had started to turn into spun platinum. His own black crinkly hair was unmistakably turning gray, but she was keeping her secrets.

She preceded him into the living room where a tall, gangly man stood. "This is Mr. Levy," Constance said.

Charlie felt bewilderment. Not David. He started to extend his hand, but the other man stepped backward, swaying. He looked very ill, cadaverous almost, with sunken eyes and a pallor that suggested confinement, hospital, sickbed. Deathbed.

"My boy came to you for help," Levy said heavily. "He did what you told him and they killed him. I just wanted to look at you. See you. What kind of a man are you to turn him away like that? Send a boy off to get killed."

CHAPTER 4

Charlie watched in icy shock while Constance took Mr. Levy by the arm and maneuvered him to the kitchen table with a cup of coffee before him. She said little as she managed him, and what she said made no difference; Levy allowed himself to be led and now he picked up the cup and sipped from it.

"Tell us what happened," Constance said gently, when he put the cup down again.

In his mind's eye Charlie was seeing the lanky boy unfold himself from that same chair; he remembered his own impulse to pat him on the head, remembered watching the two boys trudge out into the rain toward the Mitchum house.

"They called me," Levy said. "They said there's been an accident. They said they had to do an autopsy. They released him to me and I took him home and buried him. Today they said the investigation is over, accidental death. They said he used drugs and overdosed."

He looked into Charlie's face across the table from him

39

and shook his head. "My boy didn't do drugs," he said with finality.

"No, he didn't," Charlie said. "Mr. Levy, do you know why he came to see me? Did he tell you?"

Constance would have taken it slower, he knew; she would have gentled Levy some more, got him to relax some more, but Constance hadn't met that string bean of a boy. Maybe she didn't realize that Levy was a dying man. Constance didn't have the icy rage that filled Charlie at that moment.

"He told me in a letter," Levy said after a hesitation. He pushed his cup back.

"Hold it a minute, Mr. Levy," Charlie said, his voice suddenly harsh. "Just hold it a minute. He came here for advice and I gave it to him. Did he tell you if he followed up on it, what he learned?"

Levy faced Constance, directed his words at her. "He couldn't get anyone to help him, the sheriff, the animal agency, no one. Your husband. I told the sheriff about the dog, what Davy was doing, and he said Mr. Meiklejohn was high-priced and wouldn't get involved with a dead dog, that no one in his right mind would get involved with it. He said Davy took the drugs himself and that's that. He didn't even read the letters. Pretended to, that's all. He already had his mind fixed on what he thought he knew."

Constance was totally bewildered by all this information. Charlie had not told her about David Levy or a dead dog. And this poor man, she thought, had not fully accepted the death of his son, no matter if there had been a funeral; he still had hope behind the desperation in his eyes. And he was so very ill. The skin was drawn tight over the bones of his face; his eyes were bloodshot, sunken, the rims red. There was a tremor in his hands.

"Mr. Levy," she said, "did your son find out who killed the dog? Did he tell you?"

He sighed deeply and shook his head. "I think he knew,

but he didn't say who it was in the letter. I'd better be going. It's a long drive."

His pain was so wrenching that Constance wanted to hold him and soothe him, and she knew that would be absolutely wrong. Not now. "Mr. Levy," she said, and Charlie heard her professional voice, the crisp manner and tone of a trained psychologist, "you made an accusation about Charlie that we have to air. When did your son die?"

"Saturday, the twentieth, in the morning. Today they said the investigation was over. I came to get the stuff they were holding and to show them his letters. No use."

Charlie's eyes were narrowed in thought. He shook his head. "He couldn't have followed my advice already. Listen, let me tell you what we talked about the day he was here. That was on Wednesday, late afternoon. He said the Zukals' dog had been poisoned and I said he would need to exhume it and have tissue examination tests to find the cause of death. There's no way on earth he could have done that and got the results in two or three days, by Saturday."

"Just like the sheriff," Levy said with weary bitterness. "You're all alike." He started to get up.

"Just sit still, will you?" Charlie snapped at him. "Maybe there's a connection and maybe not. I sure as hell don't know at this point and apparently neither do you. But, Mr. Levy, neither do I believe your son took drugs of any kind. Now let's talk about it."

"Why?" Levy asked. "I can't afford to pay you anything."

"For crying out loud! Do you have a buck? Just haul it out and put it on the table."

Levy looked from him to Constance, and then withdrew a shabby wallet and fished out a dollar bill.

"You're paid in full. Now, just answer a few questions, will you? Honey, is there more coffee?"

*　　*　　*

Two hours later they walked to his car with him, a twelve-year-old Ford. Home for him was a veterans' hospital in New Jersey, a long drive.

At the car he hesitated briefly, then held out his hand to Charlie. "Let me know what you find out," he said, and got in and started the engine; he looked almost surprised when it turned over. "All he wanted to do was help feed the world," he said softly, looking straight ahead, his cavernous face twisted. He shook himself and engaged the gears and left without speaking to either of them again.

"We'd better find out something pretty damn fast or he won't be around to hear it," Charlie said, as the old car backed out to the road. "Let's go read those letters."

In the kitchen once more, Constance gazed at the dollar bill that had been pushed aside to make room for the letters that Levy had produced. He was dying, he had said candidly; he and his son had pretended that death could be put off until David was through with school. And now he could go ahead and die, Constance thought, but she knew that he would try to hold on until he knew the truth.

She began to arrange the letters chronologically. David had been a faithful correspondent, had written at least once a week; there were a lot of letters to go through. Levy had also left a box of personal effects that the sheriff had released to him—snapshots, a few magazines, a calendar, catalogs, a grocery list, bills, a checkbook, and several bank statements. It was a pitiful assortment.

"Look at this," Charlie said a few minutes later in a grumpy voice. "Three pages about the party at Wollander's place, a blow-by-blow account of a cookout! And half a page with one line about the goddamn dog, the last letter he wrote."

Constance nodded.

Charlie read it in disgust: *Remember Sadie, the dog that got killed, I think I'm onto something about that. More next time.*

42

He tossed the letter down on top of the others and stood up. "Want to go for a ride in the country?"

"Where to?" she asked. "Spender's Ferry?"

He grinned at her. "Why ask anything ever? Just say the answers. Works just the same."

"Charlie." She began to gather up the letters. Watching her hands, she said, "If a boy came through that door right now and asked what to do about a possible dog murder, you'd tell him just about what you told David Levy, and you know it."

"Yeah," he said. "I know that. Somehow it doesn't seem to help much. And, like the sheriff said, maybe there's no connection."

"The sheriff must be Greg Dolman," Constance said a few minutes later in the Volvo, drawing up a memory of the sheriff. Middle-aged, paunchy, amiable, good politician, and he did not want trouble. That was how he put it, he didn't want trouble, kept a clean county. At one time, it was said, he also had run a speed trap that had netted someone a lot of money that never seemed to show up on the books. The next election his vote had been bigger than ever; his constituents understood the value of free enterprise and approved. But someone had put a stop to that, without publicity, without scandal; it just stopped.

Having sorted him out in her mind, Constance began to regard the passing scenery with great pleasure. God must have been having a very fine day when he invented June, she thought. Today the sun was warm, without the cruel heat that could come later in the season; the leaves were at their brightest, most tender stage, flowers abounded, and even the traffic seemed manageable, civilized and polite.

They drove through Spender's Ferry slowly. Like most New York villages, it had been discovered by tourists, and it played up its picturesque appearance. A grocery store with a boardwalk in front, and a mammoth parking lot behind it; three antique shops, one with a sign that said: CUSTOM-MADE ANTIQUES. A gift shop. A church with a

43

white steeple and a golden bell. Red-brick elementary school, a restaurant that probably was very good, housed in a beautifully maintained Victorian three-story house—it had a sign that said only HAZELTINE'S.

"Hokey," Charlie said.

"But nice."

"You betcha. Pays to look nice."

She sighed as the fleeting romanticism disappeared. Beyond the village, working farms stretched out on the right, fields and fields of satiny corn six inches high, and on the left the experimental university farm began. It looked very little different from all the other farms they had passed. Then Charlie turned into the driveway of the Zukals' house.

"Now, this is nice," Charlie murmured when he drew up to the house and stopped. He opened his door and got out as Constance got out on her side, and they both stood very still.

A woman's raucous voice was screeching; a man's equally raucous voice was yelling at the same time. Just then Sylvie and Al appeared from the trees behind the house. She had a green kerchief tied on her head; wisps of red hair had escaped and clung to her sweaty brow. She was dressed in baggy pants and a man's shirt. He was in jeans that rode too low on his ample belly, and sneakers with shoelaces flying. He had a fringe of pale hair and a bright red scalp.

"You want they should nail you to the floor? Why doncher just leave them to their work?"

"You hear anyone saying I'm in the way? You hear that? I don't hear nothing like—"

They broke it off when they saw Charlie and Constance, and now the sound of hammering could be heard, and a loud radio.

"You another lousy inspector? Go inspect already! Watcha waiting for? Go inspect until your eyes fall out!"

"Mr. Zukal? Mrs. Zukal?"

"Yeah, who you think, Queen of Sheba or something? It's over there!" Sylvie began to stamp toward the house, muttering over her shoulder to Al. "And stay out of their way! They don't need help!"

My God, Charlie realized suddenly, with amazement, he had missed this! He had known people like this all his life and he had missed them. Constance had come to his side; he took her hand and walked forward.

"Hold it, Mrs. Zukal. I want to talk to you about your dog."

Well, he thought, satisfied, as they both froze, he had their attention. The stillness was short-lived, and one of them was demanding to know what for, and the other who did he think he was, and either or both, what did he know about their dog, and other things that got lost in the tumult. He held his hand up, shaking his head.

"Let's sit down and talk," he said firmly. "I'm Charlie Meiklejohn, and this is my wife Constance, and we are not inspectors of any sort. We are private investigators. Can we talk?"

Sylvie looked them both up and down, and then nodded toward the house. "But don't you go to the living room," she snapped at Al. "All that sawdust!"

They went inside the house and stopped at the kitchen. "This is fine," Charlie said; he pulled out a chair for Constance, another for himself, and sat down at the kitchen table.

The Zukals sat down after hesitating briefly, and Al demanded, "Now, you. Who sent you and what you want here? And what do you know about our dog?"

"Not enough by half," Charlie said, and went on to describe David's visit again. "Today his father hired us to look into David's death," he finished. "His father doesn't think he ever took drugs in his life."

"See!" Sylvie cried. "See! I told you! That David, he wouldn't even drink beer!"

But Al was scowling fiercely at Charlie. "You sure as hell didn't do David no good."

"I know that," Charlie said quietly. "That's why I'm here now. Will you answer a few questions?"

Sylvie yanked the kerchief from her head and ran her fingers through her red hair until it looked like the hair of the bride of Frankenstein. "You axe, then we see," she said.

"Yeah, just axe. No promises," Al said.

"Right. First. Did David actually dig up the dog?"

"Nope. Didn't even know he was thinking about it. Never said a word."

Sylvie contradicted him instantly. "He nearly cried when I told him. He would go stand by the grave and just look. You knew what he was thinking, all right. It hurt him. He was such a good boy. Rosa should have seen it, that he was such a good boy."

Charlie asked where the dog had come from, and was rewarded with an avalanche of information. He let them both talk without interruption.

"Brenda Ryan's kennels over by Albany. Me and Flora, she's our girl, me and Flora and the kids took the wagon and went over. I thought it might need lots of room in the car, you know, chains and stuff like that, but she was like a puppy, after Brenda introduced us, I mean. Introduced us like she was a person. Sadie, this is Sylvie, and this is Flora, and this is Mike and this is Janie. Just like that, and the dog smelled us, and then began to wag her whole rear end."

"And when they got her home, we had to take her all around the place and let her pee now and then, and smell the trees," Al chimed in. "She had to do that, you know, to find out where she lived. And if we wanted her to be nice to people we had to do like Brenda done and go Sadie this is David, or Sadie this is Lois. Don't do no good to put it any other way. I mean, you can't just go meet the gang or nothing."

46

"Brenda Ryan weighs three hundred and forty pounds," Sylvie said suddenly, in awe.

"Jaysus Crackers! What difference does that make? You told me that a hundred times already. Who cares?"

Sylvie turned to Constance. "I just axed her right out. That's the way. People don't care if you just go ahead and axe instead of beating the bush like. She said lady dogs are even better than boy dogs to guard things. They take their responsibility seriouser or something. I thought it would be one of those great big ugly black dogs like on television all the time, you know, all big teeth and hair like painted on. But Sadie was real pretty, and she liked to play—"

"Sylvie, who cares if she was pretty! Let the man axe his questions, will you?"

Constance glanced at Charlie who looked absolutely at ease and relaxed, as well he might, she thought. This was going to take the rest of the day.

Slowly he drew the story out of them. Sylvie had brought the dog home and for the next few days they had felt secure, well guarded, and then the dog died. They had it one week.

"But dogs don't just die any more than people do," Charlie murmured at that point. "They die of something."

Al and Sylvie exchanged uneasy glances.

"Who did you introduce the dog to during those days?"

"David, of course. He was in and out all the time, just like he was at home like. And Lois. Mrs. Wollander. She cuts through the property walking to work and home."

"So on Sunday morning you found the dog dead?"

"Yeah. Stiff already. Puked a lot first, then kicked."

"Were you here Saturday night?"

"Sure. And Bobby and Flora and the kids. They come on weekends, but as soon as school's out, they're moving in with us. Anyways, they was here. Kids played with Sadie right up to bedtime. Crazy about her. Real smart, she was. They'd hide things and she'd go find them. Real smart."

"Where did Sadie sleep?"

"On the porch most nights. But she'd be up prowling around all hours. Investigating noises, I guess."

"And did she eat outside, too?"

"Yeah. On the porch . . ." Al's voice faded out and Sylvie said, "But we found her dish way over by the mill. Remember, Al?"

"Yeah, just thinking about that. But the kids was hiding it on her. They must have left it there." The certainty that had been in his voice was gone, however.

Charlie was feeling more and more unhappy as they talked, and when Al asked if he wanted a beer he nodded gratefully. Al brought one for Constance, too, and, bless her, Charlie thought with appreciation, she pretended she wanted it.

"We'll have to exhume the dog's remains," Charlie said a few minutes later. "Can you tell me anything about David? He didn't tell you he was coming to see me, I know. I asked. But something made him decide to poke around himself. Any idea what it was?"

Al began to pick at the beer can as if the painted-on label might be peeled off, and Sylvie began to pat her hair down, suddenly aware that it was unkempt.

Charlie waited. If there was anything people like the Zukals could not stand, he knew very well, it was silence.

"It was the insurance," Sylvie muttered. "Set him right off."

"I'll be damned if it was. It was them letters. You had to go show him, didn't you?"

From then on Charlie listened. The Zukals had met David when he and their daughter had attended a special science-oriented high school in the Bronx. The kids had become good friends and David had spent a lot of time at their apartment. His father was ill even then, in and out of the hospital, and David was lonely. They had treated him like a son, and maybe that was the problem with him and Rosa, Sylvie added thoughtfully. Anyway, they didn't try to

48

hide things from him. When they were broke he knew it, and when they struck gold, he knew that, and when the letters came, it had seemed natural for Sylvie to show him. Gently Charlie drew her back to the letters.

"Yeah," Sylvie said heavily. "They don't want our kind here, you know. Don't much blame them, but here we are. And here we stay, like it or not. Anyways, Monday, after Sadie died a letter came, nasty like. *Go back where you belong.* That's all. Looked like a kid must have wrote it. And the next Monday another one came. *What does it take? A bullet? Would that penetrate your thick skulls?* David seen that one and I told him about the first one."

"And two days later he came to see me," Charlie said. "Did you keep the letters?" They both shook their heads. "Have there been any more?" They shook their heads again. "Okay. What about insurance?"

"Nothing to it," Al said. "Sylvie got spooked, is all. See, Stanley, Wollander's son-in-law, he tells me I should get more insurance just as soon as the next check comes, seventh of July. He's talking a big policy, something no load, or front load, or something like that. I can borrow on it even, and Sylvie tells David, and he goes maybe it's not so safe out here for us. But, hell, wouldn't do nobody around here no good if I kicked."

"Someone might think Sylvie wouldn't hang around out here if you were gone," Charlie mused.

"Well, someone's got another think coming," Sylvie screeched.

And now Al told in great detail how his two sons-in-law were geniuses. "See, we get the big check and first thing Sylvie tops it right off, ten percent by Jaysus, to a school for girls."

"Well, there's boys' camps everywhere, homes for troubling boys, special schools, and girls get the short stick every time. Sure I did, and next time another ten percent."

"Yeah, yeah. We been all over that. Okay by me. See, we got these four girls—"

"And whose fault is that, Mister? You got the special doohickey that makes a boy baby, not me. Rosa told me all about that," she explained to Constance. "She's a scientist. Or will be some day. Real smart, Rosa."

"Jaysus! Will you let me finish! Anyways, we was going to spread the dough around, you know, let the girls and their husbands have some, and they all got together and talked it over, and they go, not the way to do it. If we really want to help, we'd help Bobby and Harmon start a business, this year and next, and then help Les and Nola get a bait shop they been wanting, and like that. Seeds, they call it. So Bobby and Harmon—Bobby can make things out of wood, really good stuff, chairs and tables, stuff like that, and Harmon can do business, sell stuff. They make a good pair. They're going to have the mill for a shop. Handmade furniture. Won't make a fortune right off, but it'll grow. Bobby comes out and looks it over and he goes, you know, Pop, that mill can make electricity, all we'll ever need, and more, and the electric company has to buy all the leftovers. We'll break even right off the bat, and that means profits faster than anyone thought at first." Al looked puzzled, then shrugged. "You can have leftover electricity? I don't know about that. But . . ."

Now Sylvie chimed in and her voice overrode his. "That's what we mean, you get it? We bought this place, and they can send inspectors and zoners and whatnot, but we're here. And we're here for good."

Charlie asked a few more questions and got more answer than he wanted each time. They had not seen David after his visit to Charlie's house. What with the kids all over the place Saturday and Lois working David's butt off over at the farm, Al said, it hadn't struck them as unusual not to see him. And she's working her butt off, too, remember, Sylvie put in, and they went on from there.

They hadn't even known anything was wrong until Lois had come to tell them. When David didn't show up on time, even though it was Saturday, she had gone to his

50

place looking for him, and she had found him dead. She was real shook up by it, Al said soberly. It hurt her real bad.

"So she came to tell you?"

"Yeah. She thought it wasn't right for us to find out in the village, or something like that."

"Did you believe he overdosed himself?"

Al and Sylvie looked at each other, and she said in a low voice, so low it was hard to catch her words. "You know, we're from the Bronx. We wanted out, want to get our kids and our grandkids out of there. Sure, we know it's not everyone shooting up, snorting, messing themselves up, but who's to say who is and who ain't anymore? I didn't believe it about David but I don't know. We seen too much. Been fooled too many times. You know what I mean?"

Charlie nodded. He knew.

He asked Al to show him where they had found the food dish, and where the dog was buried, and for permission to dig it up for tests. And when Al asked him with incredulity if he was going to dig it up himself, Charlie shuddered. He said he would send someone. They all went out to walk over the grounds, down to the bridge, around the mill, to the mound that was Sadie's grave, to the spot where Al had found her dead. Al and Sylvie talked over the noise of the carpenters in the mill with their radio turned on at maximum volume. Lois was going to help choose which trees had to come out. Al was going to put in a little beach at this end of the lake. Here was the place in the fence that Lois used every day to go to work. They planned to put in a real gate and fence off the bridge, because of the kids. . . .

Charlie paused at the break in the fence and looked back at the mill, several hundred yards away; the loud music was dimmed by distance but still too clearly audible. A path led from this point, skirted the lake side of the mill and continued to the swinging bridge. No comparable path led to the house through the tangle that many years of neglect had produced. Beyond the break in the fence the path was even more sharply defined, three stone steps down, then a hard-packed trail.

He glanced at Constance and nodded toward the path. "Let's see a bit more of it."

"It's like a sidewalk," Al said behind them as they started down.

And it was, almost. It led them through a few feet of brambles and low sumac and suddenly they were in a grove. The ground still sloped, but more gently here, hardly noticeable as they walked slowly. On the left the trees were all about twenty-five feet tall, straight up to a canopy, but on the right the trees had been allowed to keep their lower branches and they made a thicket that would be all but impenetrable. They had been planted precisely, meticulously, and looked totally artificial in almost military ranks. Every tree was tagged.

Constance looked at the experimental trees with a sense of unease. No grasses, no vines, nothing grew under them, but more, the trees themselves looked alien, foreign to her. Not like oaks or maples or conifers, these had smooth, pale tan trunks, leaves too shiny and thick, and many small round nuts no bigger yet than peas, and they also looked alien. Orchards were always arranged carefully, she reminded herself; she had planted their apple trees according to the book, so many feet from one to another, but every one was different from the next, gnarly, unique, with the differences more apparent year by year. And these were all the same.

They came to a different section, smaller trees, obviously younger, identical. . . . Abruptly Charlie stopped, shaking his head. The path continued but it wound here and there and the end was not in sight. Neither was the lake. Stippled sunlight, rows and rows of identical trees, and finally silence; they had gone far enough to lose the rock music.

"How far to the farm?" he asked Al over his shoulder.

"Three, four hundred more feet of trees and the buildings start. It's all like this, all the way. Up at the fence you coulda turned toward the lake, and that's different, right down to the water, but let me tell you, I sure don't like this way."

"Yeah. See your point," Charlie said, and turned back. "Is this the way David came, through the trees?"

Al nodded. "Closest this way. Lois uses the path every day. Lots of people seem to, why it's all packed down."

They returned to the mill property and the noise of hammering and music. They walked to the bridge and surveyed it and the dam.

"That dog, Sadie? She wouldn't set foot on the bridge," Al said. "Can't blame her none. Bridges ain't supposed to move when you do, way I see it."

Silently Charlie agreed. Finally, he and Constance got in their car to leave and he felt that he had missed whatever it was he had been looking for.

"You think the dog was poisoned, don't you? Deliberately," Constance said as he backed and turned around, headed out to the road. "But, Charlie, a dog trained the way that one apparently was wouldn't take food from a stranger, would it? And how could anyone have gone in that far? The dish was at least three hundred yards from the edge of the property."

He grunted. "On my list," he said. "Both items. Tomorrow we ask Brenda Ryan a thing or two. And not how much she weighs."

After a moment, Constance murmured, "Lois Wharton Wollander is the only one outside the family who was introduced to the dog, apparently. And David, of course. And David worked for her."

"It'll be a busy day tomorrow," Charlie said, slowing down at Spender's Ferry. "Brenda Ryan, Lois W. W., Sheriff Greg Dolman. A busy day. Let's check out Hazeltine's." He drew up before the Victorian mansion that housed the restaurant and turned off the engine. "You know who Wollander is?"

"Vaguely familiar name. Tell me."

"What Al would call a crowner. A kingmaker. A man who knows which closets hold skeletons, and how to unlock the doors to get at them, and where every body is buried."

"Oh, dear," Constance said. "Al said all those inspectors, zoning people."

"Yep. Someone must have sicced them onto him."

CHAPTER 5

That night after dinner in the Wollander house, Warren Wollander said, "Jill, would you mind if we all go to the study for a little talk?"

Lois felt her muscles tighten at his tone of voice. Carefully she placed her napkin on the table and just as carefully she did not look across the table at Jill.

"Let's talk here," Jill said. "What now? I feel like I'm twelve years old again."

"You're not a child," Warren said evenly, "and that's part of the problem. People are talking in the village about your . . . involvement with Sebastian and his group."

"What I do is my own business," Jill said coldly. "I don't give a damn what they're saying in the village. And you never used to."

"Now I do. Mrs. Carlysle tells me you've ordered a special diet for yourself and tonight you barely touched your dinner. Is that at Sebastian's suggestion?"

Jill flung down her napkin and started to jump up, then decided not to, looking intently at her father. She took a deep breath. "Yes. He understands nutrition thoroughly. I am to eat meat sparingly, drink a lot of milk and juice, no alcohol in any form, make sure I have plenty of fresh vegetables and fruits, many of them raw. I am to watch my weight and not gain more than sixteen pounds, and get plenty of exercise."

"My God," Lois said softly. "Jill! That's wonderful!"

Warren looked confused for a moment, then a wide smile spread over his face and he blinked rapidly. He jumped to his feet and took Jill's hands, drew her from her chair, and wrapped his arms around her, held her hard against him. After a moment he pulled back and examined her face; his eyes were bright. "Are you sure? I thought you couldn't . . . Your mother said—"

"She was wrong," Jill said. "That's what the meditation has been all about, why I've practiced and practiced. And it worked. I had to learn to relax, to center myself, become receptive. It worked! That's what Sebastian was trying to explain out here: If you can master yourself, you can do anything."

"Let them talk," her father said then, and laughed and hugged her fiercely again. "Let the bastards talk all they want. When? How are you? Have you seen a doctor yet? Will you stay here until it's time, afterward if you want?" He looked at her closely again. "Stanley doesn't know yet, does he?"

Jill turned helplessly to Lois and shrugged. "I wasn't going to tell anyone for a couple more weeks. It's too soon. But *I* know. Next weekend, when Stanley comes up, I'll tell him, now that it's out anyway. But let me be the one. Promise. Not a word yet."

Lois nodded, smiling. And Warren said, "We should have a toast in champagne. A tiny preliminary celebration."

Jill shook her head. "No alcohol, remember? Don't tempt me. You two go ahead. I want to walk a little bit and then read, and then sleep. I should get as much sleep as I can, too."

She kissed Warren's cheek, nodded to Lois, and started to leave the dining room. At the door she paused, her hand on the knob, her head bowed. She looked like a too-thin adolescent in her long pale skirt and tank top. Her arms were nearly fleshless, her hands sharply boned. She turned to look at them and said softly, "Dad, I'm really sorry. The things I said when Mother died. I'm sorry. I was a little bit crazy. And, Lois, I'm sorry. You've been wonderful to me, and I've been a bitch. I know. I know. I'm sorry. Can we all start over, now, tonight?"

Warren started to move toward her; she waved him back again and smiled slightly. "No emotional upsets, either. Let's just pretend this is day one and go on from here. Okay?" She gazed at him steadily, then at Lois, and nodded. "Thanks." Then she opened the door and left.

Lois tried to convince herself that the glint in Jill's eyes had been happiness, not triumph.

"Well, let's take a walk, too," Warren said then to Lois. He was beaming, his eyes glistening.

They walked slowly down to the lake, and then along the tiny beach to where there was an immense log. All around them the night sounds were like music not quite in harmony, stopping and starting, speeding and slowing. Cicadas, crickets, tree frogs, the whir of wings—a night hawk or an owl. Overhead, the sky was clear, midnight dark with myriad pinpricks of stars. The air was warm, but cooling fast. It rarely stayed warm throughout the night, not until late July, or even August.

They sat on the log, his arm around her, her cheek on his shoulder. "I'm so happy for her," Lois said. "And for you."

He squeezed her slightly. "She surprised the hell out of me. The last thing I expected her to say. She made me forget altogether the other matter I wanted to bring up with both of you."

Lois started to pull away a bit, but he held her firmly. "I've been in the spotlight for more years than you've lived," he said after a moment. "I've made enemies. And some damn good friends. But there are enemies. And some of them are nothing but slime."

Lois shivered, whether at the falling temperature or the harshness of his voice she could not have said. The chill entered her and stayed.

"I want you to promise me something," he went on.

"You know I will."

"Maybe you will and maybe you won't. We'll see. Promise me that if you get any poison-pen letters, you'll bring them to me. Will you promise that?"

She jerked away from him with a suddenness he could not counter. She leaped up and backed away from him. "You've had letters like that? About me? Someone's found out, hasn't he? I told you it would happen!"

He stood up and caught her hands and held them tightly. "Not about that. That's what I'm afraid of, that someone will send such a letter to you. I've had filth like this before in the past. Slime can't face a man directly, they act like this, underhanded, mean, nasty, hurting. Today I got a letter about Jill and Sebastian. Last week one about you. Both lies. Meant to destroy, to kill something fine and wonderful."

"About me? What about me?" Her mouth had gone dry, and she was shivering uncontrollably.

"It doesn't matter what it said. Believe me, I know how this kind strikes out. They don't want to hurt you, just me. And they know the way to do it is through the two people on earth that I love. They always know how. If he doesn't see a reaction from these first two, I'm afraid he might send you a letter. If he does, will you just hand it to me?" He pulled her to him and held her, and she stared, unresponsive, dry-eyed at the lake. Starlight reflected from its surface in an unquiet shimmer that appeared and vanished with the motion of a breeze. Dead lake, she thought, and felt as dead as she knew the waters were.

"It must be Coughlin," she said finally. "He must have found out what you're doing."

"*Shh.* No jumping to conclusions. It could be a number of people for a number of reasons. Let's leave it at that for now."

She might not have heard. "If it's Coughlin, he won't stop. He'll dig and dig until our grandparents' private lives are on the line."

Warren sighed. "Darling, this has no payoff. You can speculate all night, all week, for nothing. You'll just lose sleep. Either this slime will keep it up or he won't. Either he'll make demands or he won't. Either he'll send you a letter or he won't. I just wanted to prepare you, in case. Now we leave it alone." He released her and stretched. "Speaking about grandparents, how about Jill? My God, I'll be a grandfather! And you a grandmother!"

They began to stroll and he talked about his strategy for keeping his daughter here, at home, during the pregnancy. "Can't pressure her," he admitted, thinking out loud. "Through Stanley. He'll see that it's for her own good, fresh air, rest, no stress of the city, no muggers. That's the ticket. A little chat with Stanley. No pressure."

She said the appropriate things at the appropriate times, but her thoughts were on Bill Coughlin, who had told Warren to keep out of his way because he had every intention of becoming governor first, and then president when the time was ripe. Over my dead body, Warren had murmured, and Coughlin had nodded. If it takes that, he had said. Two weeks later Warren had started writing his memoirs. But no one could have learned what he was doing, she told herself firmly. No one knew yet except her, and his secretary, and, no doubt, Jill. His secretary, Carla Mercer, had been with Warren for over twenty years; she knew more of his secrets than he could remember, he sometimes said. When Warren began to chuckle, she realized she had heard nothing for a long time, and she realized that her thoughts

59

and worries were spinning in all directions and had become too chaotic to track.

Later that night, unable to sleep for thinking about his grandchild, grandson, he corrected firmly, Warren stood at his darkened window gazing at the land his grandfather had bought so many years ago. A moon sliver shed enough light to see the oak tree that he had built a treehouse in, and had fallen out of. But even without the moon, he knew every inch, where every shrub lay, every rise and fall of his land. And now another generation to maintain it, preserve it, love it.

He always had known that Jill would come home, he thought then. She had spent her first eight years right here, and after those good years, at least half her time had been spent here, absorbing the countryside even if she had not realized it then. She knew this piece of land as well as he did, it had reached out to claim her exactly the way it had claimed him, and her son would know and love it, too.

Suddenly he stiffened. A figure was hurrying up the driveway toward the county road, a woman dressed in a long black coat with a hood, a raincoat from the downstairs closet, he knew. She was out of sight almost instantly, behind the clump of birch trees.

He felt leaden as he turned from the window. His room was too dark to see anything, but he crossed to the door, out into the hallway where dim lights were always on. Moving like a stone man he walked through the hall to the wide stairs. Halfway down he realized that he had no slippers on, but he kept going, to the first floor, to the den which was dark. Without turning on a light he went to the bar and poured a drink from a decanter there; he knew it contained scotch. He added no water. He took the glass across the room and sat in his favorite chair, his father's favorite chair before him, and he drank deeply.

At first he had thought to await her return, confront her, accuse her? Even that, he admitted to himself. Accuse her.

Drive her away? Possibly, he admitted, and got up for another drink. The first half hour passed, then a second half hour. He was certain he had not dozed, certain he would hear the door open, would hear steps eventually, but the deep silence persisted. Another half hour. Then he cursed himself under his breath. She could have entered through the back door, or the side door. He wasn't even sure which door she had left by. He went to the front hall and looked inside the closet. The black coat was there, as usual. Heavily he returned to his room where he stood for a long time regarding the border of light outlining the connecting door to Lois's bedroom. He did not touch it.

Behind the door Lois lay with her face pressed into her pillow. Trapped, she kept thinking. This was what it meant to be trapped. She couldn't stay, and neither could she leave. She was not weeping although her eyes felt afire with unshed tears. And the word, trapped, repeated like a drumbeat in her temples. She had told Warren in the beginning that it wouldn't work, and he had assumed she meant the difference in their ages. *No, no, no!* she had cried and had told him about her first husband. They had been in Hazeltine's, a corner table, she remembered distinctly. The vase had two irises in it, a velvety deep blue one, and one that was only faintly touched with blue.

"He got in trouble at school," she had said that night, speaking of her first marriage. "He was my advisor, and then we married, and my name was on the paper along with his. We both were in trouble. He . . . he fudged some results and it was discovered. He was ruined, and I dropped out and went to California to start the degree process all over, using my maiden name, Wharton. When I applied here, in New York, I had to tell the committee, of course, but no one else knows. Not my colleagues at the farm, no one. The name on the paper was L. Malik, his name; L. Malik is dead and buried, and she has to stay dead and buried. She could ruin both of us if anyone ever makes the connection."

Warren had looked blank. "History," he said. "What does it have to do with us now?"

"You don't understand how serious something like that can be. If anyone brought it out, smeared me with it, I would have to go away. But you could be hurt, too."

He reached across the table and put his finger on her lips. "One question," he said softly. "Did you do anything wrong?"

His finger pressed against her lips. She shook her head.

"I thought not. Will you marry me?"

Lois turned over in the bed and stared at the ceiling. She should have known, she thought wearily. She had known. Secrets always surface again. Nothing stays buried. But now that Jill was pregnant, Warren would have his grandchild, his heir . . . She bit her lip. Six months ago she had brought home a new prescription for birth-control pills, had filled her little silver box, and then had stood holding it tightly for a long time, and finally had put it away without taking a pill. She had prayed, if only she could give him the heir he so desperately wanted. She had not told him, afraid that if nothing happened he would be too disappointed, and now she was relieved that she hadn't mentioned it, hadn't talked about it. And she realized that she had better start them again.

She did not move yet, but continued to stare straight up at the ceiling. And the pulse in her temple beat *trapped, trapped* over and over. When she finally rose to take a birth-control pill, she could not find the container, the little silver one-a-day dispenser that she had bought the day after Warren's proposal and her acceptance. She was so tired she could not remember where she had put it, when she had last seen it even. It was three in the morning and she was too tired to think anything. She dragged herself back to bed.

Then, in that state of not yet sleep, but not awake either, she realized that Warren must have taken the pills. In her mind's eye his face shaped itself, smiling at her, coming closer and closer, and she smiled back and held out both hands to him, and they laughed together and made love.

"What they needed was a good watchdog, and a good dog for kids, and good around water. Sadie all the way," Brenda Ryan told Charlie and Constance the next morning. She was probably more than three hundred forty pounds and she was enraged. Her face was red-splotched, her jowls shook as she talked. She wore a tentlike garment with great pink blossoms of some improbable flower, and the garment shivered and rustled and shook also, as if her rage had communicated itself to her clothing. Only her hair, a mass of tight golden curls, did not move. They were in her office outside Albany.

Very mildly Charlie said, "You're sure the dog wouldn't have taken food from a stranger?"

Brenda snorted and everything about her shook harder. "Look, I train those dogs myself. You don't want a dog that'll take poisoned meat from a burglar, now do you? I see to it they don't. We see those caper movies just like the burglars do, and we take care of that. Mr. and Mrs. Zukal, they could feed her, that's it. And I'm not too sure about him. Her, I know. I trained her, too. Mrs. Zukal, I mean. If she doesn't handle the dish, handle the food, Sadie doesn't eat. It's like that. I tell her, Mrs. Zukal, I mean, it's good to have a backup or two. I mean, she gets sick or something, dog doesn't eat from strangers, dog dies. I never saw it happen, but it could, that's how they're trained."

"You never even met Mr. Zukal, did you?"

"No. I told her how to teach Sadie to take from him, too. They both handle it for a few days, and then he can do it alone. Not until two, three days. One of them kids could have dropped a steak under her nose and she'd leave it there. That's how they're trained. Poisoned? God, I don't see how."

She talked on about the dog, wanted to show them the

kennels, demonstrate how she trained them, but Charlie and Constance declined, and left in morose silence.

He slouched in the passenger seat and she drove. "Maybe Sadie wasn't poisoned," she said.

"Maybe. Maybe Sylvie did it herself."

"Hah!"

"Right."

Miles later she said, "Maybe Al did it."

This time he said, "Hah!"

It was midmorning when she pulled to a stop in front of the administration building of the experimental farm. If there hadn't been a sign on the door they might have mistaken it for a farmhouse. There was a wide porch and a nice lawn out front with well-trimmed hedges and specimen shrubs but nothing to suggest that it was a university facility.

Charlie had the feeling that if he rang the bell a plump little housewife in a starched apron would appear and the fragrance of apple pie would fill the air. He ignored the bell and tried the doorknob instead. The door opened onto a long hall. On one side there was a narrow table with metal in-and-out baskets, some of them nearly overflowing with mail, others empty. Above each basket was a hand-lettered nameplate. He looked them over and spotted one that said Dr. Wharton; the basket below it was empty. There were several closed doors on both sides of the hall and a staircase. No carpeting, no other furniture, no other person.

Somewhere a typewriter was going and there was the sound of an air conditioner that apparently was in serious trouble. A door closed somewhere out of sight. Charlie shrugged at Constance and they moved on down the hall looking for a person, anyone. A door opened and a young woman in jeans and a faded Pink Floyd T-shirt stepped out carrying papers. She regarded them uncertainly.

"Are you looking for someone?" she asked.

Charlie turned to Constance. "See? I told you we

weren't the last man and woman on earth." To the be-wildered young woman he said, "Dr. Wharton."

"Oh." Her relief was evident, she even smiled. "Out back. You can go through here."

She indicated the hallway, possibly to a second door to the outside.

"And after we are in the open air again, then where?" Charlie asked gravely. They all looked at the stairs as a man began to descend, speaking to someone still out of sight on the second floor.

"Just tell them if they can't be in and out again within two weeks we'll have to get someone else." He saw Charlie and Constance then. "Hi. Can I help you?"

"We're looking for Dr. Wharton."

"I'm going that way. Come along. I'm Tom Hopewell."

Charlie regarded him with interest. One of the hand-let-tered nameplates had been Dr. Hopewell, but this man looked more like a rag picker than a doctor of anything. His worn shirt was a faded, red-tinged mud color, and both elbows were out. His jeans were shabby, one knee out, never hemmed, and now ragged at the bottoms. He had what looked like a two-day-old stubble. Thirty-five at the most, slender with narrow shoulders, and very dirty hands.

"Lois is back in the tree section," Tom Hopewell said, setting a brisk pace through the hall, out to the back of the building. The appearance of a family farm stopped abruptly here. Rows of tomato plants came to the door almost, and they seemed to be all tagged. Beyond them were rows of immature corn that looked bedraggled and stunted. Some of the plants had plastic tents over them. Some had plastic bags over portions of them only. Small boxes spotted the ground here and there. Tom Hopewell ignored it all and maintained his fast pace. Suddenly he stopped and pointed. "There she is. I've got to go." Although his words indi-cated a need to hurry, his body seemed of two minds about it. The lower part started to turn, the feet started to move in the other direction but his head did not move immediately as he gazed another moment at the woman he had pointed out. Then, abruptly, he turned all the way and trotted off.

The woman had just emerged from a greenhouse near the start of the tree plantings; she stood in the doorway talking over her shoulder to someone still inside. She nodded and walked toward a quonset hut. Another farmhand, Charlie thought, another worker dressed in jeans, T-shirt, and sneakers. Doctors were not what they used to be, he added to himself, as he and Constance went forward to meet Lois Wharton Wollander.

They caught up with her outside the quonset hut. "Dr. Wharton," Charlie said, "can we have a few minutes?" At first she had appeared to be as young as the woman in the building—thirty maybe, with very attractive gray streaks in her dark hair that were dramatic enough to have been added at a salon—but close up it was obvious that she was a bit older than that. She wore no makeup and was very good-looking in a careless sort of way, as if she hadn't thought about other ways to fix her hair, or how beautiful her wide eyes actually were.

She glanced from him to Constance and back. "Why?"

He introduced himself and Constance. "We've been hired to investigate the death of your student, David Levy."

One moment her expression had suggested preoccupation, a bit of impatience, and not a lot of interest in them, but now she simply looked startled and puzzled. "But why? I thought . . . The sheriff said he overdosed."

"Yes. But his father isn't convinced, and, frankly, Dr. Wharton, neither am I. Can we talk?"

She hesitated, then nodded. "I have an office in the admin building. I guess we could go there."

"Where did David live?" Constance asked suddenly. "One of the units over there?" Off behind the greenhouse, only partially visible, was a long, low building that looked like a motel of the fifties.

Lois looked at her more sharply and nodded again.

"I stayed in a place just like that years ago, a summer at Indiana State," Constance said. "I bet they used the same plans. Can we talk in there?"

Reluctantly Lois said the units were open and they started to walk. "Is the whole operation here organic?" Constance asked, and this time Charlie looked at her sharply. "The bees," she said. "All those little boxes. Hired bees. You can't bring in bees if you're using sprays. Well, some sprays, I guess, but not most."

"It's all organic," Lois said. "That's why we're under-staffed and overworked and underfunded. We have a continuing grant for the next four years. We're six years into this project."

The apartments they were approaching were very ugly, institutional ugly, with aluminum windows and doors, no porches or even stoops. There were eight doors.

"No one's staying in them now," Lois said, leading the way to the end door. "They're all due for painting, refurbishing. Thorough cleaning. The usual summer mainte-nance. This one was David's."

She opened the door and they walked into a cramped, L-shaped living room with a kitchenette; one door to the right opened to a bath, and another straight ahead to the bed-room. There was only one narrow bed, but the room had been designed for two; two chests of drawers, two chairs, two desks were crowded into the space. Constance nodded. Exactly like the one she had shared with another student many years ago. By the end of summer they had been ready to throttle each other.

"Of course, nothing of David's is still here," Lois said, standing near the door as Charlie and Constance looked over the apartment. The spartan rooms were stripped to such essentials they looked uninhabitable. The apartment felt loveless and gray.

They returned to the living room where they all sat down on plastic-covered chairs with very little padding. Charlie regarded Lois steadily and asked, "Do you believe David took drugs? That he took an overdose?"

Miserably she looked down at her hands. "I don't know. I didn't. Then the sheriff said he must have done it. I just don't know."

"Okay. Tell us something about him. Good student?"

She nodded. "Good, but not brilliant. He was idealistic. His plan was to get his degree and then go to some third-world country and teach. He could have done that."

"Why don't you just talk about him. How he got along with the others here. Who his friends were. Anything that comes to mind."

The picture she painted of David Levy in halting words, with pauses and hesitations, was that of a shy young man with few friends among the other graduate students. He was not asocial but he didn't do the same kinds of things they did, and he was an outsider. He didn't dance, or like rock music, or drink anything alcoholic, or do drugs. He was a strict vegetarian, a health food advocate. He got along with everyone, as far as she had been able to tell but he wasn't intimate with anyone. When the school year ended only two other graduate students remained and they lived in an apartment in the village. They both had been away that weekend.

"So he was over here by himself?"

"Yes."

"How did he appear to you the last few days before he died?" Charlie asked.

Lois shrugged helplessly. "I didn't notice anything out of ordinary. We were working very hard, seven days a week usually, and he was as busy as I was. It isn't as if we had much time for socializing."

"Okay. What about the day he died. You found him?"

68

She took a breath and nodded. "We have two hundred cloned trees that need daily tending. Saturday, Sunday, it doesn't matter. It was David's job to see to them early every morning, and that Saturday he didn't show up. Over the weekends it was just for a few hours, but it had to be done, and I had other work to do myself, and after a while, about ten or ten-thirty, I was becoming angry that he wasn't there, I'm afraid. I assumed it was the usual kind of thing; you know, the clock didn't go off, or too late a night, something of that sort. Anyway, I started to come over here." She paused. Her face was pinched looking, strained. Now she looked nearer forty than the thirty she had seemed at first glance. "I saw one of the scientists here, Tom Hopewell. I asked him to come with me. It occurred to me that if David was in bed, it would be embarrassing for him if I showed up."

Charlie nodded encouragingly at her.

"We both came to the door. I knocked, and called David, and tried the knob. It turned, and I opened the door, but Tom actually entered. I stood in the doorway and he went on into the bedroom and found David."

"Did you go into the bedroom at all?"

"Yes. I couldn't believe . . . I thought . . . I don't know what I thought. I just ran across the room and to the bed. I . . . He was dead."

"Okay." Charlie studied her for a moment; she was pale and strained, too tight, but in control. Too controlled? "Dr. Wharton," he said then, "was anything out of the ordinary that you could tell?"

"I don't know what would be ordinary," she said, shaking her head. "I never had been in here before. It was very neat. David was fastidious, nothing out of order, nothing out of place. I didn't see a glass or a bottle or anything like that. The sheriff asked."

"What happened next? You saw him. Was he covered by the blanket or anything?"

"Yes. I touched his cheek. Then . . ." She paused again.

"I'm really not sure. I was standing at the sink, holding onto it while Tom was on the phone to the police. I kept thinking, he intended to make an omelette. I remember thinking that he wouldn't have his omelette. I was crying," she added in a low voice, her eyes downcast.

"What made you think of omelette?" Charlie asked. "What did you see at the sink?"

She shook her head helplessly. "I don't know. I was crying, and holding on, and hearing Tom on the phone saying he was dead. I must have been in shock for a minute or two."

Charlie caught a signal from Constance, nothing she said, nothing she did, no motion she made, nothing that would have been discernible to anyone else on earth, he knew, but there it was, almost like a hand on his back, fingers digging slightly into his spine. He held the next question. Constance stood up and went to Lois, took her arm.

"Let's go to the sink, the way you were then," she said.

For a moment Lois resisted the pressure, but then she got to her feet and walked slowly across the room to stand stiffly at the sink. It was dull metal with little dents here and there. Water had discolored a trail to the drain. A few inches of the same dull metal made up drain boards on both sides. A three-burner stove was to the right, a tiny refrigerator to the left.

"I think," Constance said, "you should move closer, hold it the way you did that morning."

With obvious reluctance Lois moved closer and grasped the edges of the sink and bowed her head.

"Now, close your eyes and see what you saw that morning," Constance said, as if this were the most natural thing in the world.

Lois obeyed, and after a second or two she said, "There was a yellow rubber dish drainer on that side, with a small pot in it. Two eggs were on the other side, and a piece of cheese. And a glass. His vitamins were on that side, too. Several containers of vitamins." She lifted her head and looked startled. "I smelled orange juice," she said. "I forgot that before, and the eggs. I forgot them. There was an omelette pan on the burner." Her startlement increased. "Dear God, there was a towel, wet." She spun around and looked at the room. "A chair was right here," she said indicating the place in the tiny kitchenette. "There was a towel draped over it. He must have been swimming. He swam every morning before breakfast. We had to walk around the chair to get to the bedroom."

They waited, but there was nothing else. She had not seen bathing trunks, but she had not gone into the bathroom. After Tom Hopewell called the sheriff's office they had gone outside to wait.

When they were finished in the apartment, Charlie stood just outside the door looking around. The units had been placed close to the boundary of the grounds. Behind the structure the experimental trees started. From the door nothing of the greenhouses or the quonset hut was visible. Trees were in the way, and the trees continued down to the lake. He studied the layout unhappily. David's apartment could be entered without anyone on the farm seeing a thing. For these few seconds that he looked over the grounds, Lois stood silently also.

"It just won't work, will it?" Lois said in a very quiet voice that seemed almost resigned. "He wouldn't have gone swimming, had his juice, and then take anything like quaaludes. He wouldn't have taken phenobarbital before his chores were done."

"No," Charlie agreed. "It won't work."

CHAPTER 6

Tom Hopewell got to his feet and brushed dirt off his knees when Charlie and Constance approached him at the edge of one of the corn patches. A few feet beyond him there was a twelve-foot-high fence made of posts with netting. Beans were starting to spiral up the lines. Hopewell was just as ragged-looking as Charlie remembered.

"Dr. Hopewell," Charlie said, "would you mind answering a couple of questions?" He introduced himself and Constance, who was eyeing the bean trellis thoughtfully.

"About David Levy?"

Charlie raised his eyebrows.

"Well, what else?" Tom Hopewell said with a shrug. "First Lois, now me. I thought that whole matter was handled a bit fast."

"How will you pick them?" Constance asked then, still studying the trellis.

Hopewell glanced at it, then back to her, and grinned. "We hire very tall workers." When she grinned back, he said, "Actually we want the biomass more than the beans.

For compost. And we need the windbreak. Those are scarlet runner beans, not even a true bean. They'll cover the netting, with any luck, and pollen from the corn down past the peas won't blow this far and mess up this stand." He shrugged and added, "We're working with very limited space here, I'm afraid."

Charlie waited patiently as Constance asked another question or two about the farm, but when it appeared that Tom Hopewell intended to take her away on a tour, Charlie cleared his throat quite loudly. Constance smiled at him.

"Another time," Hopewell said to her. Then to Charlie he said, "And you want to know about that morning, I guess."

"Yep. But first, how well did you know David?"

"Hardly at all. I was down in Peru all summer, their summer that is, and came back in April with seeds. Corn seeds. I was on a collecting trip. We're looking for better strains, more resistant, hardier, faster to yield, more yield. And perennial strains, of course." He was like a little boy who wanted to show off a new kite. When Charlie cleared his throat again, he looked apologetic. "Yes, David. Anyway, I met him in April, and we worked together a little, not as much as you might think, though. Lois had him pretty well tied up. Properly so, I might add." He grinned suddenly. His grin was infectious and made him look too young to be off in Peru collecting seeds, too young to be a doctor of anything. "We're always trying to snare each other's grad students, of course. Free labor, and God knows we can all use more help than we have. Early on I tried to lure David, to get him to put in a few extra hours. No dice. That was probably the only time I ever really talked to him, more than passing the time of day, I mean. Anyway. I hardly knew him."

"Who's actually in charge here? Who was around that weekend? Besides you, I mean."

"In charge," Hopewell said. "That's Dr. Clarence

73

Bosch, the head of the farm here, our boss. His daughter got married that weekend. He took off on Friday and got back Monday. There were the hired helpers, locals for the most part, but not that early on Saturday. A couple of them were due at ten, for half a day. They were mine. The other two grad students were off for the weekend. All the rest had already left for the year. School's out, off they scoot, credits in their grimy little fists."

"Okay. So that morning, what happened?"

His expression became sober. "That morning. I got here after eight or eight-thirty, I guess. I don't wear a watch, you see, and I didn't check the time anywhere. After I'd been busy for a bit, Lois called me, and I met her near the apartments. She was sore and didn't want to go in herself." He glanced from Charlie to Constance and said ruefully, "Levy had a crush on her, although I don't think she knew that. But I did, and I didn't blame her for not wanting to go in and catch him in his underwear or anything like that. Anyway, she knocked and tried the door, but I went in first. She followed me inside, but just inside the doorway. I found him in bed. Then she came on into the bedroom. We went back to the other room where I called the sheriff's office. Then we waited outside for them to get there."

Charlie nodded. "Let's back up a step. When you went into the bedroom, she was standing at the door. Was she still there when you called her?"

Hopewell's face tightened. "The sheriff asked me if she could have removed anything, and I told him no. The way the apartment is set up, it's a straight line from the door through the kitchen space and into the bedroom. I saw him, and looked back at her instantly. She hadn't moved. I said some dumb thing, like there's been an accident. Something in my voice made her run into the apartment, straight through to join me by the bed. She reached down and touched his face, that's all. Then I took her arm and moved her to the sink. Frankly, I was afraid she might upchuck or even pass out. She went dead white, and she was crying. I

74

kept an eye on her while I made the call. She just stood there hanging onto the edge of the sink. Then I took her outside. I was watching her every second."

He had not seen a container for the pills, had not seen anything out of the ordinary, accepting that he had no way of knowing what was ordinary. "I never had been in his apartment," he said. "Like I said, I hardly knew him."

"So you have no way of knowing if he did drugs," Charlie said.

"Exactly. But I'd guess not. He just wasn't the type. Now, *my* grad student Preston Heywood, that's different. But he left in mid-May. And he was in Peru with me, so he knew Levy even less than I did, I guess."

"Maybe he could have sold something to Levy," Charlie suggested hopefully. "You don't have to be bosom pals to deal."

"Not unless it was coke. I said he was in Peru with me."

He had started to fidget restlessly, and glanced at two workmen who were standing several hundred feet away under a tree, apparently waiting for him.

"One more thing," Charlie said, dissatisfied. "Do you know the Zukals?"

Hopewell looked surprised. "Sure. To be neighbors with them is to know them. So?"

"You ever go up to their place?"

"What the devil does that have to do—? As a matter of fact, when they bought that mill, they closed down one of the favorite lovers' lanes hereabout. But I haven't been up there for a spell, not since last summer, at least."

"They came down here?"

"No. I saw them by the lake. Look, I really do have work to do." His impatience was turning into real irritation. He waved to the waiting men and started to edge away.

Charlie might not have noticed his growing restlessness. "Did they have the dog with them?"

Hopewell looked at him angrily. "No. I've got to go now."

They watched him take a couple of steps. Then Charlie called after him. "What did you do when you found out that your student had smuggled coke into the country?"

Hopewell was caught in midstride. He wheeled about, palefaced. "I didn't say he did."

"What did you do?" Charlie repeated softly.

"I fired him. Are you through now?"

"Oh yes. See you around, Dr. Hopewell."

They watched him stride away quickly. He looked stiff.

"Well," Constance said. "If you wanted to get his goat, you succeeded."

"I did, didn't I?" He took her arm. "Let's go see the sheriff."

Sheriff Greg Dolman was grayer than Constance remembered, and a bit stouter, but his smile was just as wide, just as false as it ever had been. His eyes did not know the rest of his face was smiling.

"Charlie! You're looking great. And, Constance, prettier than ever. Come on in and sit down. How are you? How's the little plantation? What can I do you for?"

He ushered them into his private office in the county courthouse and stood beaming at them until they were seated in the two wooden chairs. Then he went around his desk and took his own seat.

"It's about David Levy, Greg," Charlie said. "His father came to see us."

"Poor guy," Dolman said, shaking his head in sorrow. "Walking dead man. Only son. You know how that goes."

"Uh-huh. Fill us in, will you? About the boy."

"Nothing there, Charlie. Like I told the old man. Just nothing there. Kid takes an overdose. What're you going to do? Can't supervise them all their lives."

"I'd like to see the reports," Charlie said, just as amiable as the sheriff, his eyes just as hard.

76

"Charlie, the case is closed. Did the old man hire you? What with? He doesn't have two dimes to rub together."

"The reports, Greg. Medical examiner's report, you know. He hired me. Got to earn my keep. You know how it goes."

Dolman regarded him flatly for a moment, then smiled his expansive smile again. "Sure, Charlie. But I can wrap it all up in a couple of sentences. The kid took methaqualone and phenobarbital together. A real bad combination. Real bad. Took them with orange juice, on an empty stomach, the worst way. Took all he had. We did an analysis on everything in that dump, vitamins, aspirins, juice. Not a trace of anything. He took them all, probably flushed the paper they were in. Then he went back to bed. Just not a good morning for him, I guess." He smiled again. "Frankly, Charlie, between you, me, and the woodwork, I don't give a shit if the dopeheads go out that way."

"That sounds exactly like what we've been hearing," Constance said. "Poor Mr. Levy. It won't take more than a couple of minutes, I think, to make copies of the various reports. Then we can write our report for his father. Poor man."

Dolman looked at her suspiciously before his smile returned, but she was as innocent as dawn. "Yeah," he said finally. "Why not? There's just nothing there."

Fifteen minutes later they were back in their Volvo, Charlie driving. "Pretty slick," he said. "I take it you wanted out of there."

"Damn right," she said. "He's worse than ever."

Charlie chuckled and rested his hand on her thigh. "Let's go home and do some reading."

Years before, when they bought the house in the country, long before they could spend much time in it, Charlie had said in a burst of exuberance, "When we retire, it's fifty-fifty, kiddo. We take turns with chores, okay?"

"Like what chores? I say we hire some things done, like snow plowing."

"Maybe. I meant in the kitchen. You cook, I cook, tit for tat."

"Wonderful," she said, laughing. "And, Charlie, I won't forget, you know."

And she hadn't. If either of them was really crushed for time, that was different, but generally it was tit for tat. But with a new case on their hands, Charlie was thinking at the kitchen table, maybe they could discuss it again.

Constance broke into his thoughts. "Charlie, I'm glad we worked things out in advance, cooking, things like that. It could be awkward on a day-by-day basis, couldn't it?"

He examined her carefully; her clear, pale blue eyes were guileless, her expression serene. He sighed. "Fish on the grill," he said. "Later."

"Wonderful, darling," she murmured. "Look, here's the list of the stuff they examined in David's apartment. He was a real health-food addict." She continued to read as the orange cat, Candy, sidled up to her nonchalantly and sneaked onto her lap, as if hoping she would not be noticed and sent off to Siberia. Constance adjusted to the cat and stroked her absently. Candy began to purr. Constance was reading over the shopping list they had found, more of the same: tofu, yogurt, black beans, lemons, herb tea. . . .

He sat opposite her at the table and started on the medical examiner's report. For a long time neither spoke. Candy got bored and flowed out of Constance's lap like a sluggish mass of syrup. Brutus stalked in and glared at them, stalked out again twitching his tail. Constance was skimming the early letters from David Levy to his father. When she got to April she began to make a few notes. Charlie was making notes too.

They would both read it all, and then discuss everything. But Constance was having a harder and harder time with the boy's letters to his dying father.

Finally she put one facedown and stared out the screen

door to the backyard. The early bulbs were all finished and now irises were making a show, and baby's breath had come into bloom, making the irises appear to rise from white clouds. Yellow, orange, bronze marigolds, calendulas in lemony colors, some almost white. A cardinal flitted past, then two chickadees. All too pretty to introduce such ugliness into, she was thinking. Peaceful, bucolic even, the air alive with buzzes and hummings, the twitter of birds, a song now and then—

"Tough going?" Charlie asked. He reached across the table and covered her hand with his.

"He didn't kill himself," she said quietly. "He didn't do drugs in any form. He was murdered."

"I know. And we'll find out who and why. I'm going to start the grill."

She set the table on the patio, and now the three cats prowled between her and Charlie, who was cursing softly. The grill never seemed to work exactly right without starter fluid, and he was opposed to using a chemical in his food, not even one that had long since burned off. He danced around the cats and cursed fluently and finally had a bed of coals, not ready yet, but coming along. When he backed away from the grill with a satisfied nod, she put a glass into his hand. He tasted and nodded more vigorously. Gin and tonic.

The fish was delicious, the salad superb, the wine chilled just right, potatoes crisp and brown and tender. They sat with coffee as the first stars began to appear in the post-card-blue sky.

"Okay," Charlie said then. "Okay." He leaned back in his chair. "'Star light, star bright, first star . . .' You do that when you were a kid? Make a wish on the first star?"

"Absolutely. '. . . I see tonight. Wish I may, wish I might, have the wish I wish tonight.'" She closed her eyes a moment and when she opened them it was to see him regarding her with a soft expression.

"Bet I know what you wished," he said.

After a second she nodded. "I think you do."

"Enough of the mushy stuff," he said. Then very briskly he went on. "The way I read it, David Levy got up at six that morning and went down to the lake for his swim. He went back to the apartment and had orange juice and his vitamins. He got the eggs and cheese out but he wanted a shower before breakfast. He showered, shaved, shampooed, and dried off and put on his shorts, but by then he was feeling sleepy, or dopey, or something and he crawled back into bed and fell asleep and died. Death between eight and nine at the very latest."

Constance poured more coffee. The tiger cat Brutus was stalking the grill, planning his attack. Charlie had given them fish already, but with cats *enough* was a meaningless word. "I can see why Greg had a problem," she said after a minute.

"Yep. They opened the vitamins, all what they said they were—A, B complex, E, C, mineral supplements, there's a long list. Not many of any one of them, but all okay. Containers okay, no trace of anything other than the legitimate contents, all as they should be. The juice was okay. All the food okay. Nothing in the aspirins but aspirin. One missing from a container of twenty-five, expiration date last summer. The kid just didn't take things. Period. And unless Lois Wharton Wollander or Tom Hopewell removed something, there was no container for any other drugs. But they had to come from somewhere. And if he did unwrap them and flush the paper, that means he did it himself. And there's no way we can prove or disprove a thing."

"He could have had company," Constance said after a moment. "Someone else could have made the juice and fixed a glass for him with the dope in it, and then washed it out again."

"I really hate that a lot," Charlie said, frowning. "It's the damn time element. That junk had to be in his system by six-thirty. He comes in from swimming and someone says, here's your juice, and he drinks it and goes to shower and comes back out in his shorts. That someone must have been a good friend, and he didn't have good friends at the farm. Okay, he could have had a robe on, and could have taken it off again to go to bed. He wasn't expecting company for breakfast—two eggs only. I just hate that a bunch."

"Were any of the vitamin containers empty?" she asked after another minute or so.

"Nope. Our friendly sheriff is an asshole, granted, but he's thorough. He thought of that, too. A few of this, a few of that, and so on, but something in each of them, and no container in the trash. He was running low, but the new supply must not have arrived yet. He ordered them from a mail-order company." He sighed. "Your turn."

"Not much we don't already know, I guess. It's pathetic, how he wrote to his father pretending nothing was wrong, that his father wasn't a dying man. He must have told his dad everything there is to know about the work he was doing. There's a lot about Lois Wharton. He really did have a crush on her. He mentioned Tom Hopewell's arrival and Hopewell's fight with the other student, and he told his father when the bees were delivered. He told him about cloning the trees, and a fight they all had over space and priorities. Apparently they are really strained for space. He referred to a time when they all thought Lois might approach her husband to buy the mill and the grounds there for her work with the trees. The other scientists begrudge her the space that trees take. He didn't refer to it again. I guess it was a just a wish on their part. I haven't got much further. The Zukals are due, that's when I stopped reading."

"That damn cat," Charlie muttered, and then yelled wildly. Brutus was on his hind legs, straining to see the top of the grill. He dropped to all four feet and streaked away. Ashcan slunk off into the bed of irises, and Candy crouched near the door, her eyes enormous, her hair standing up like a razorback hog's, her ears flattened. Charlie went to the grill and closed the lid; when he turned toward the door, Candy bellied away from him. "Let's get back to that stuff," Charlie said cheerfully. Any time he had all three cats buffaloed at once, he thought, he had earned his Brownie points for the day.

"You'll give them all traumas," Constance said.

"Good. I'll take the coffee, you bring the cups."

It was nine-thirty when Lois got home that night, so tired that she felt numb. Until she had a replacement for David it would be like this she had told Warren. The metabolism tests had to be done within a limited time period or they would be meaningless. Even a week made such a difference . . .

"He said you knew," Mrs. Carlysle said helplessly when Lois asked where Warren was. "One of those committee meetings."

Mrs. Carlysle was a kindly woman in her sixties, white-haired and a bit overweight. She had been with Warren for twenty-eight years. Now she said, "I'll make you something to eat. You must be starving."

A few minutes ago Lois would have agreed that she was starving, but now she felt only her fatigue. "Just a sandwich," she said. "I can do it." She started to walk through the hall toward the kitchen, Mrs. Carlysle close behind her.

"We have ham, and there's some tunafish, of course. Cheese. You just tell me what you want and I'll make it. You look so tired."

Lois stopped at the wide staircase and felt her shoulders droop. "Tunafish would be fine," she said. "And milk. I'll go up and soak in the tub for a few minutes. Thanks."

When she called to tell him she would be late, he had not mentioned a meeting, she felt certain. She would remember that. But she had forgotten that tonight was Jill's night to go to Sebastian's meeting. Every Wednesday night they did chants or something. She tried to relax in the warm water, tried to remember what Warren had said, but nothing came. Nothing. He hadn't said anything. All this week she had been taking her car to work because she no longer had time for the leisurely stroll over to the farm, and then back again. And this morning she had left before Warren was up. Had he been too abrupt on the phone? Or had she? It had been a short conversation. "I'm sorry, but I'll be late. Go ahead without me and I'll have something when I get home." Had she said more than that? She shook her head irritably. What difference did it make? He had a meeting, and he had forgotten to mention it.

But something was wrong, she thought. Something was slipping away and she didn't even know what it was, or how it was happening. The poison-pen letter he had received had something to do with it. He had refused to tell her exactly what it said. Lies, all lies, was all he would say about it. And then he forgot to mention a meeting. Or she forgot that he was going out. Wearily she climbed out of the tub and toweled herself dry, put on her gown and robe and went to the bedroom, where Mrs. Carlysle had left a tray. A sandwich, salad, milk, coffee. Even a bowl of strawberries. Lois found that she could eat little of it. All she wanted was to lie down and stretch as far as she could and close her eyes.

She would hear him when he came upstairs, she thought. She always heard him in the next room, moving around, opening a drawer, opening his closet, his bathroom door. Water running. He would come in to tell her goodnight, kiss her goodnight. She turned onto her stomach.

Three years ago when she tried to explain why they should not marry, she had said, "I have this work to do. I don't mean that it's something I just would like to do if it's convenient. I have to do it. I can't explain it any other way."

"And you don't have to explain it any way at all. That's one of the things I love about you, your determination, your unswerving march to your own goal. I promise I'll never get in your way. I won't ever try to get between you and your work. I love you very much, Lois. More than I know how to tell you."

"People will say I married you for your money. Your own daughter will think that."

"Now you listen to my secrets," Warren had said soberly. "Two years ago I had a heart attack. Not serious, just a warning, the doctors told me. Jill doesn't know. She was in Paris with her mother. I went on a cruise to think and rest, and I decided that all my life was a lie. I lied to myself and to the world, pretending I was doing public service. Public disservice is more like it. You've read how a person changes when death comes too close? Believe it. I changed. When I came back, I began to sever ties, to disengage myself. It's been slower than I'd like, but I'm still working on it. I don't know what I'll do with the rest of my life, but not what I've been doing. People who look up to me look up to an illusion, nothing more. You think I care what they say about you, about us? Jill's mother married me for money and it killed her. Addicted to everything that money can buy, she died of money. She was respected because she was from a good family, and she sold herself like a common whore. You would do me great honor if you will marry me. I know I'm rushing you, but I'm afraid of time. Maybe I see salvation through you. Don't say anything else now. Maybe we've both said too much for one evening. I'll take you home."

Lois rolled to her side and breathed deeply, remembering. Salvation. But now with a grandchild on the way, with reconciliation between him and Jill, everything had changed. It was like looking into a kaleidoscope that had been still for so long that she had forgotten how swiftly the pattern could change.

This was ridiculous, she told herself as she slipped into sleep. He would come in to kiss her goodnight. She would remember that he had mentioned a meeting. She would get a replacement for David and not have to work such long

84

hours. And they would walk hand in hand in the garden again.

This way! This way! he called, and she ran toward the sound of his voice, up there, past a gate, running without effort. Then she stopped in terror. All around were ghost trees, pale and stripped of leaves, rising from drifting sand. The sand made a whispering sound as wind stirred it; nothing else moved. The trees had been denuded of smaller limbs, and those that remained were stilettolike, gleaming in a light without a source. She backed away, but was mired in sand; when she dragged one foot loose, the sand whispered. *This way!* His call again. All the trees were gray, silver, unmoving, the trunks too thin to hide anyone, but she could not see him, could only try to follow the sound of his voice. Her legs ached with the effort and when she would have fallen, she found herself unable to touch one of the ghost trees for support, staggered instead to her knees, and had to work desperately to stand up once more.

Now the sand started a slide, and she was caught in it, dragged along downward, twisting and turning to avoid the sharpened tree branches, breathless with fear. Below was the sapphire lake, unreal, painted-looking, but then churning with motion. *Alive,* she cried out in her dream, laughing and crying at once, eager to finish the slow-motion slide. As she watched the boiling water, a figure emerged, upright. David! His hair swirled about his face, then was plastered to his cheeks, across his open, staring eyes. He rose as far as his shoulders, and began to sink again as she gazed with horror.

This way! No! She tried to scream, and the sound was no more than a moan as her slide toward the lake continued. The water was subsiding, becoming still again, unreal again.

Standing in the open doorway between the bedrooms Warren watched her toss and twist. The sounds she made were unintelligible; her thrashing and her moans reached a

85

crescendo and for a moment he thought she would surely wake up, but instead she sighed deeply and then became still. In the dim light he could see a sheen of sweat on her forehead, her cheeks. Silently he backed into his own room and closed the door.

When she woke up it was six in the morning.

CHAPTER 7

O kay," Charlie said on Friday afternoon. "We're stymied until we get the report on the dog. Right?" Constance nodded. They had learned so much in the past few days, she thought, mildly surprised again by how much of everyone's lives had been recorded, filed away, remembered by unlikely people. Clarence Bosch, in charge of the experimental farm, world-famous for his introductions of various vegetables, bigger and better tomatoes, better peppers, earlier melons . . . Jill Wollander, a wild girl in years gone by, now respectable, married to a millionaire . . . Lois Wharton, brilliant in silviculture circles, introducing a new tree that would grow twenty feet in a season in the north . . . Warren Wollander, power behind the visible power. The reason no one could construct any of them, Constance knew, was because there were great gaps in all of their lives. Jill had flitted back and forth between mother and father for many years. What had she done in those years in Europe with her mother, who apparently had been in and out of sanatoriums for the last ten years of her life, addicted to alcohol, drugs, who knew what all? Even Clarence Bosch. He had sued Warren Wollander for a million dollars fifteen years ago, charging malicious slander. It had been dropped, but the mystery persisted. What had that been about? Lois Wharton. She had appeared with a Ph.D. in hand and had been hired on at the farm out of nowhere. Six years of her life a blank. Nothing on record for those years. And Sebastian. Con man? Preacher? Enlightened? Just suddenly there in the picture, looking into buying the mill for a school, or possibly a temple. Or something. They had found nothing yet about Sebastian.

There was no point in calling Wilbur Palmer, the pathologist who had dug up the dog Sadie. He would simply snap at them and hang up until he was ready. There was little they could do until they had his report. There might be little they could do even after they had the report.

Charlie's thoughts were equally gloomy. This was the kind of case he had hated back when he was a New York City detective. Pointless deaths. No direction to strike out in. No direction for questions except the obvious one: Did you kill that boy? He had dumped out the contents of the box Mr. Levy had left with them, and morosely moved stuff around. Such a pitiful little pile of stuff. A few bills, a checkbook, postcards. . . . He had lived on practically nothing, had no extravagant habits, damn little to show for having lived at all. He put it all back inside the box.

"When David came to talk to you," Constance said then, "he didn't know who killed the dog. So, if there's a connection, something must have happened in the next day or two to make him suspect he knew. Or maybe he did know by then. But, Charlie, no one would commit murder to keep something like that hidden."

"A nut might."

She rolled her eyes. He had more faith in crazy people behaving in crazy ways than she did, he knew, but nuts did nutty things all the time; they earned the title. And killing David Levy seemed to be in the category of nuttiness.

"So, let's make a case," he said, tapping his fingers on the table. "Someone wanted to buy the mill property, but the Zukals got there first." She made a noise; not an interruption, she never did that, but still. . . . He paused, waiting.

"Maybe it wasn't that someone wanted to buy it, just that someone didn't want the Zukals there," she said. "For a lot of reasons. Starting a furniture factory, trucks maybe, traffic, noise. All those grandchildren at play, Sylvie and Al themselves yelling. Or maybe for a reason we can't even guess—a treasure buried on the grounds." She spread her hands. "There's so much we can't even guess about."

Charlie nodded. "I know, but let's assume a scenario, that someone wants them out, for whatever the reason. So someone decides to drive them away. First the dog. Give them a scare. Then David catches on, and he has to go." He looked at her and shrugged. "Won't play in Baltimore, will it?"

"I wouldn't buy it."

"Me neither. Let's go to to Sebastian's service tomorrow."

Sebastian had private, invitation-only meetings every day for one thing and another, they had learned, but on Saturday he had open services.

"We'll have to sit on the floor," Constance said. Charlie made a face.

Lois watched Jill and Warren climb the bank from the lake that Friday evening. For days she had been unwilling to go near the brilliant water; even glancing at it filled her with dread. Jill and her father were talking and laughing. All this time, Lois was thinking, how she had wished they would be close again, father and daughter, friends, loving, confiding in each other. The kind of relationship she had yearned for with her own father, who had died too soon for it ever to happen. Warren's first wife Shelley, and then Jill, had hurt him so much; Lois had ached for him, and now he had his daughter back. She knew she should be rejoicing, but her stomach felt leaden and her head throbbed with a persistent pain. She sipped her wine and forced a smile when they drew near.

"Al Zukal has come up with a fantastic scheme!" Jill said. "He's going to put in a beach at his end of the lake. Limestone. He's planning to ship it in from Tennessee or Kentucky. It'll look like snow!"

Lois looked past Jill and Warren. From up here she could see only the upper end of the lake, but now Al and Clarence came into sight. They were strolling back in the direction of the mill, their heads lowered. Limestone? She felt a rising excitement as she considered it. Every rain, every snow would dissolve some of it. How much would it take? Maybe if they did their beach over. . . . She looked at Warren; he averted his gaze.

"I've got to change and meet Stanley's train," Jill said as she hurried to the house. "I made a reservation for us at Hazeltine's, but we won't be out very late."

As soon as she was gone, Lois said, "Warren, what's wrong? What's happened?"

He shook his head. "I'm just a little tired. I'll lie down before dinner."

Her hands were shaking. Carefully she put down her wineglass and took a step in his direction. "Something's happened, hasn't it? Warren, what is it?" Her voice rose and she stopped abruptly as he walked past her.

"We have to talk about it," she said, controlling her voice so much that it sounded strange to her own ears. "Whatever it is, we have to talk about it or this weekend will be hell for all of us."

He paused and turned finally to regard her. "I'll be here when you want to tell me what you're hiding." He entered the house then.

She sank into one of the lawn chairs and stared blindly at nothing. For a long time she could not track any single thought from start to finish; they merged and blended, and disconnected things joined one another haphazardly. Last night Warren had pressed Jill for an explanation of exactly what it was that Sebastian taught, exactly what she meant by enlightenment, by the rapture of nothingness.

"Nothingness," Jill had said hesitantly, "has to be by choice. But if you choose, you are actively involved, and that can't be real nothingness. But it can't be simple mind-wipe fatigue, because that's negative, and it has to be positive." She had thrown up both hands. "I can't explain. You have to ask Sebastian."

"It sounds exactly like my problems with algebra back in the good old high school days," Warren had said, smiling. "I followed the teacher's explanations, watched the steps on the blackboard, and each time I thought I had it finally. It was so clear, so simple, logical. Then I would tackle the homework and it was all gone again."

Jill had set her mouth stubbornly. "It's not like that."

Lois had left them to return to her quonset hut and the metabolism studies she was trying to finish. Now, thinking about that conversation, about nothingness, she felt that she had come back from nothingness herself, and it had not been enlightening or rapturous. The shadows had lengthened perceptibly and the only thoughts she could recall had to do with nothingness. Tired, she rose and walked into the house. She told Mrs. Carlysle she would not be home for dinner, collected her purse from her room, and left.

Much later she was still staining one slide after another, studying it under the microscope, making the cell count, and recording it. Her eyes burned and her headache was like the surf—pounding, receding, pounding.

"I taught you well, didn't I?"

She dropped the slide she was holding and spun her chair around. "What are you doing here? Get out!"

"Just wanted to see for myself." Earl Malik was slender, wiry, with black hair untouched by gray. His eyes were very dark, and bloodshot at the moment. His eyebrows nearly met and were bushy, much too heavy for his thin face; they gave him a made-up look, like a performer inept with the tools of his trade. He leaned against the door frame, looking about the lab with contempt. "They're going cheapo, all right," he said.

There was her workbench with the microscope, the tray of slides, notebooks, a computer with figures in columns on the monitor. Behind her station were two more workbenches, sinks, shelves of flasks, burners. . . . Many high schools were better equipped.

Lois stood up and pushed her chair aside. "Get out of here, Earl. Now. I don't have any more money. I don't have anything at all for you. Warren suspects you're around, and if he finds out for sure, he'll make a lot of trouble for you. Just get out and leave me alone."

"But, Lois, I'm your collaborator, remember? I taught you everything you know, and that's my work you're messing around with. Let's be reasonable. I don't want your money. I want us to work together like we used to."

"You've been drinking," she said with disgust. "How did you get out here?"

"Took a little walk, not that far, couple of miles. I waited for you last night, and the night before, and tonight I said to myself, old friend, she's not coming, so you'd better get your ass over there and see why not. So here I am."

"Earl, listen to me. I don't have any money left. I don't have access to his money, and even if I did, I wouldn't give any to you."

He shoved himself clear of the door frame and stood swaying. "We'll work together, Lois. Like before. So you won't mess up again. I'll check things out this time."

She went to the computer and saved what was on the screen, turned it off, and began to stow away her materials on the workbench.

"Too early to stop now," he said. "Couple more hours, finish up here. My work, Lois. Remember that, it's my work."

"It isn't!" she cried, suddenly furious with him, with herself for not knowing how to get him out again, furious with the whole bloody mess, she thought. "You botched it once, remember? You botched it. I started over from scratch, and this is my own work and it's damn good work. Now get out of here!" She was screaming at him, trembling all over. She drew in a deep breath. "If he does find out, I'll tell him you're blackmailing me, Earl. I will! He'll put you in jail!"

He smiled and took a step toward her and she rushed at him and shoved him backward, back through the open door to the outside. He staggered, caught himself, then fell into the hydrangea bush, cursing hoarsely. She grabbed her purse, flipped the light switch off, and pulled the door closed and locked it. He was scrabbling in the bushes, still cursing, when she ran to her car and got in and locked the door. Gravel flew as the wheels dug in and spun before the car jerked away and she raced up the drive to the road.

"What the hell are you doing?" Al Zukal demanded Saturday morning. Sylvie was bustling around the kitchen as if preparing a holiday dinner, and it was just eight-thirty.

"Apple kuchen," she said with a withering look. Any idiot could tell that much if he just took the trouble to look.

"Yeah, yeah, I seen that. What for?"

"Stanley might like a bite of something. You ever seen anyone turn down hot apple kuchen?"

"He ain't coming for no breakfast. This is a business meeting, like I told you."

"He don't eat none, the kids'll polish it all off later. Won't go to waste."

"Yeah, yeah." Flora was due with the children by noon. This weekend Bobby was tied up at his job. With only two more weeks there he was trying to clean up things, not leave his boss in a lurch. Good guy, Bobby. Considerate like. Al looked at the table and groaned.

He had spread brochures and folders all over the kitchen table, but he knew he was out of his depth here. Stanley had sent the stuff ahead of time to give him a chance to look over the various proposals, and Stanley would be here before nine to review them with Al, but so far none of the stuff had made any sense at all. Insurance come-ons, certificates of deposit, trust deeds, treasury notes, equity loans. He understood none of it. Sylvie put two pans in the oven and a strong whiff of cinnamon drifted across the kitchen. He'd end up doing whatever Stanley thought best, Al had already decided. It was like a game with Stanley, Monopoly or something. See how much money you could make with money, watching it every second, keeping track, knowing when to move, when to sit still. And it was a headache bigger than the house for Al.

When he heard a car in the drive, he went to the door to watch Jill come to a stop near the turnaround at the garage. The new station wagon was still parked outside the garage, but maybe this week he'd get to work hauling the junk out, hauling it away. Stanley got out of the car and crossed in front of it to stop at Jill's side. He leaned in and kissed her and then stood watching until she made the turn, headed out, and disappeared at the first curve in the driveway. When he turned so that Al could see his face, he was grinning like a kid with his own strawberry jam pot.

He started to walk toward the house, then veered in the direction of the station wagon and went to it instead. Mystified, Al watched him pull open the back and then scream hoarsely and throw both hands up over his face, backing up, screaming.

"Jaysus!" Al ran out of the house, crossed the yard and came to a stop. Stanley had fallen down and was rolling over and over, and clustered all over him were bees, hundreds of bees. Stanley convulsed suddenly, his back arched; he shrieked and went limp.

CHAPTER 8

Ellis Street was lined with venerable maples that met overhead and made a tunnel with diffused lighting. Parked along the street that morning were two Cadillacs, one Continental, one Saab, several Volvos, and half a dozen other cars far less remarkable. Charlie found a parking space and pulled in. When he got out he noticed that their three-year-old Volvo needed a good washing. He took Constance's arm and they strolled back to number 1242, a neat, well-kept two-story frame house with a postage stamp-sized lawn closely sheared. On the porch they were greeted by a pretty, slender woman in white pants, a white silk shirt, and a blue sash at her waist.

"Welcome," she said softly and opened the door for them. They entered to find a closed door on one side of a foyer, and open double doors on the other. Many shoes were lined up in the foyer. They added theirs and went into the meeting room where a dozen other people had already assembled.

An assortment of cushions was at the end wall. They selected one each and looked around for a place to settle.

The others in the room were in many attitudes, some lotus position, but not many. One woman was kneeling. Most of them were cross-legged or had their legs sprawled out. Charlie felt a touch of relief at that. He knew damn well that he could not sit cross-legged for more than a few minutes, and as for lotus, forget it. He indicated a place that would allow him to see the double doors, as well as a single door in the back of the room, and they sat on their cushions and waited.

At the far end of the room was the only furniture—a tier of long tables covered with white cloths held many arrangements of flowers. Like a funeral, Charlie thought gloomily. On the floor in front of this was a red cushion on a white rug. A pagan funeral, he added. The windows were covered with white drapes that admitted light. On each side wall were two pairs of gold sconces with tapered lamps in them. The floor was covered with straw mats. Very simple, very soft sitar music drifted in from somewhere; there was no other sound except for the occasional rustling movement of one of the other attendees.

Already present, and seated, were eight women, four men. Most of them were simply dressed, in white or pastels. Most of them were waiting with their eyes closed, breathing evenly, some so deeply that it appeared they were in a trance state. Charlie recognized Jill from many newspaper photos when she entered. She was in white, a jumpsuit of some sort with a scarlet sash. She sat down cross-legged, bowed her head, cradled one hand in the other, and did not move again.

Sebastian's entrance was so underplayed that it would have been easy to miss it. He glided into the room and took up a lotus position on the red pillow; the sitar music ended abruptly. Most of those gathered bowed, some touched the floor with their foreheads, and then they resumed their silent, unmoving positions.

"The student came to the master and said, 'In my village is a very powerful man, a very rich landowner who tells me

I must finish my studies quickly in order to return home and enlighten my fellow villagers and thus lead them to a happier life more quickly.'" Sebastian's voice was pleasant, low-pitched, and conversational. He seemed to be making no effort whatever, but his voice carried throughout the room. He looked totally relaxed, his expression both serene and eager as he gazed at his listeners, first here, then there, including everyone in a very personal way that was engaging. He was dressed entirely in white, even his sash.

When his gaze lingered on Charlie, the effect was strangely unsettling. He had the gift, Charlie thought then, the same gift that carried politicians into high office, that made evangelists draw thousands to their television sets, to stadiums where they preached. Myopic, Charlie told himself, that accounted for the peculiar staring quality of the man's eyes, but he knew it was more than that. Sebastian liked him personally; he liked everyone in that room personally. They all felt it and responded. That was the gift he possessed, the ability to project such warmth, such acceptance, liking, even loving the other, the stranger. Uh-huh, Charlie thought, and watched as Sebastian turned his myopic blue eyes here, then there.

"'What should I tell this powerful landowner?' the student asked. The master laughed delightedly and raised his staff and whacked the student across the head. 'Just this,' he cried. 'No more, no less.'"

Sebastian smiled widely, as if he shared the master's delight. "What a beautiful story," he said. "What a beautiful man was this master, how fortunate this student. But let us examine this student. A student is one who is receptive, who comes empty, yearning to be filled, who comes with no thought of what he has left behind, but only of what is before him. The student must sever his ties to the past, because the past shackles him to his ignorance, to his preconceptions, his false thoughts. . . ."

Charlie's legs were going to sleep. He glanced at Constance who had taken her aikido position of sitting back on her heels, her hands loosely joined before her. She looked as comfortable as Sebastian; she looked as if she could stay that way for hours. He had tried that position once, only to find that after ten minutes he could not straighten his legs at all. He had hobbled for an hour, he remembered bitterly. He knew she was thinking, *I told you we'd have to sit on the floor.* He refused to look at her again, but began to ease one leg inward, thinking if he could just bend that knee a little, then work the other leg in a little. He caught a glance from one of the women, and stopped moving temporarily.

". . . can have but one master. A student can have no thoughts for those he left in his village, whether family, friends, lovers, whoever . . ."

He had not even got to the rich man yet, Charlie thought, and began to ease his leg again. Across the room a woman went from lotus to simple cross-legged. When he realized that no one gave her a glance, he drew in his right leg. Several people looked at him, their concentration broken.

"How long had this student been harboring this burdensome problem that he evidently brought with him to the ashram? Lost time, every second of it gone, never to be recaptured, and he would have to start . . ."

Jill had not yet moved. How could she do that? Her head was turned so that he could see only the tip of her ear, a bit of her chin. Too thin, much too thin. Anorectic, like most young women, he decided, especially most rich young women. Why did the ones who could afford to eat anything so often choose to eat practically nothing?

". . . did not say young man, or old man, a wise man or a fool, a good man or an evil man. No, he defined him in the simplest terms available, and the most untrustworthy: a powerful rich man and a landowner . . ."

Charlie looked at Sebastian with awe. He was still going on about the student. But it seemed he intended to slop over to the landowner any day now, any month now . . .

And he, Charlie, was going to die right here, gangrene would set in, both legs would fall off.

Suddenly Warren Wollander stood in the doorway looking at the group. Charlie recognized him, too. There was a flutter of stirred air, as if his presence affected the charge, and molecules were rushing back and forth in a dither searching for equilibrium again. Warren spotted Jill and went to her quietly, whispered into her ear, took her arm, drew her to her feet and took her away.

Sebastian's voice faltered less than a second, then he resumed his analysis, although most heads had turned to watch the exit of father and daughter.

Charlie jumped to his feet as soon as Warren led Jill out of the room, but one of his legs really had fallen asleep, and he would have plunged headlong into his nearest neighbor if Constance had not caught and steadied him. Leaning on her heavily, he hopped from the room, dragging his useless leg.

They reached the porch in time to see Warren depositing his daughter in the passenger seat of a Buick that he then entered and sped away in.

"I'll be damned," Charlie grunted. "Now what?"

"I don't know. Wait here and I'll get the car. Flex that leg to get the blood running again. Be right back."

"I can make it," he protested.

She was already moving. "You hold onto that rail and exercise. I'd rather get it alone than carry you down the street."

She hurried away and he bent his knee, straightened the leg, bent it again. He was now getting pins-and-needles, and they were all red-hot.

She drove to the curb moments later and he walked to the car, determined not to limp or hobble. "Fine," she said, grinning. "Where to?"

"Let's just drive past the Wollander house, and Al's place. See if anything's stirring."

Actually they didn't get farther than Al Zukal's house,

99

and it was clear that whatever had happened, had taken place there. The sheriff's men were on the road, waving traffic on, and a medic unit was pulling out when Constance drew near.

"Make a U-turn, back to the farm," Charlie said, craning to see something besides the traffic cops. The medic unit had left without its siren blaring, meaning no one inside it would benefit by being rushed to a hospital.

He slouched down in the seat. First the poor dumb mutt, then the boy next door, and now what? Al? Sylvie? He remembered Al's words: "You sure didn't do him no good." Christ, he thought then, there was another possibility they had left unexamined: What if Al or Sylvie was really the target of the murderer? But who out here could want either of them dead? He scrunched down in the seat scowling.

Constance made a turn and headed back. She pulled into the driveway of the farm, and there was another police car with an officer leaning against the door.

This officer's instructions had been simple: keep those people at the farm until the sheriff got through up at the mill. Nothing about keeping anyone out, or stopping anyone from talking to anyone else. He didn't interfere when Constance parked and she and Charlie got out of the Volvo and entered the building.

"What's going on?" Charlie asked Tom Hopewell, who had opened a door to peer out when he heard them enter.

"Come on in," Hopewell said, and swung the door open farther to admit them. "Clarence, Mr. and Mrs. Meiklejohn. Private investigators. Dr. Bosch," he finished, and closed the door again.

They were in a small office cluttered with too much furniture and too many file cabinets. There were also three computers and monitors, all working with blinking lights and ever-changing columns of figures. Clarence Bosch was standing at the window when they entered, a slender, pale man in his sixties, with thin gray hair that did not quite cover his scalp, and oversized glasses with dark frames. He seemed confused by their presence.

"What are you investigating?"

"David Levy's murder," Charlie said.

Clarence Bosch sank into a chair behind the desk, staring at him. "Good God!"

"What's going on up at the mill?" Charlie demanded. "Why are the cops here?"

Bosch shook his head helplessly and Tom Hopewell said, "I was hoping you could tell us. All I know is that Lois went tearing out about forty-five minutes ago, and soon after that the cop outside arrived and said we should hang around and wait for the sheriff." He spread his hands and shrugged, then sat down at one of the computers and gnawed on his finger, watching the numbers scrolling past.

"Come on," Charlie said to Constance.

"But we're supposed to wait," Bosch said.

"Wait then. See you later."

They went through the hall, out the back, past the rows of tagged and tented vegetables and on to the quonset hut. Charlie stopped and looked at the gravel scattered on the path, on the single step that led inside.

"He said she left in a hurry," Constance said.

"Twice. Come on."

They continued to the path among the tagged trees, and a few minutes later they emerged onto the mill property. They had almost reached the house before one of the deputies spotted them and escorted them to Sheriff Greg Dolman, which was where Charlie wanted to be at the moment.

"How the hell did you get in here?" Greg snapped.

"Just out walking in the woods and came to call. What's up?"

They were near the driveway where the station wagon was parked at the side of the garage. Half a dozen deputies were standing well back from the station wagon. Squinting, Charlie could just make out the box inside the wagon. And

101

bees seemed to be everywhere, zooming back and forth purposefully.

"We're waiting for the guy who owns the hives," Dolman said. "He knows how to get that hive out of there. We're not about to touch it."

Charlie nodded. "Who opened the back?" he asked grimly.

Dolman gave him a quick look and nodded. "You read it right," he said with a sigh. "Stanley Ferris. Dead. And old man Wollander's after someone's scalp for this."

It took several seconds for the name to register. Ferris, Jill's husband, Wollander's son-in-law. He exhaled softly. "Boy oh boy, Greg. You've got a hot one this time."

"Yeah. Punk kids did it, trying to tie a can to Zukal's tail, get him out of here. Pothead friends of that Levy, I bet. Got high, thought, what a gag it'd be. And now Ferris is dead. I'll get them, Charlie. You better believe."

"How are the Zukals?"

"Real shook up. Pretty bad. She told me about those letters. Guess they're getting a message all right. Goddamn punk potheads!"

"I'll go see how they are," Constance said in a low voice.

Charlie squeezed her arm slightly and she left them standing near each other regarding the hurrying bees. She went to the kitchen door and peered through the screen to see Al and Sylvie at the table, both voices going.

"Damn it, it's getting in my eyes."

"I can't help it. You're hot as a firecracker. Ice melts soon as it touches you. Hold still."

"Let me have that."

Constance entered. Al had been stung too. His face was puffed on one side, and both hands were blotchy with red welts. Another one was on his neck.

"Did someone take the stingers out?" she asked over their voices.

"Miz . . . Miz . . ."

"Just Constance. Did the medics treat him?"

"Yeah. They used tweezers and got the stings, and they said to keep ice on them, but he won't sit still."

"I'm sitting still, but it's running down my neck and in my eyes. Damn it, Sylvie, watch it."

She had turned to speak to Constance and was jabbing a cloth with ice cubes wrapped in it against his ear.

"What my mother used to do," Constance said, "was use baking soda. You have any?"

Sylvie nodded toward the cabinet, and presently Constance had a paste made and began to dab it on the stings. "How about some vodka?" she asked.

"You want a drink?" Sylvie asked in wonder.

"No. Just another trick from the old country."

Sylvie went out and returned with a bottle of vodka. Constance put ice cubes in two glasses and added an inch of vodka to them and swirled them around a few seconds, then took them both to the table and handed one to Sylvie, one to Al. "Aspirins?" Al lifted his glass and downed the vodka in a gulp, and after a second Sylvie drank hers.

"Aspirin in the bathroom, down that hallway." She kept smearing the baking soda paste on Al.

Constance found the bathroom, and aspirins in the cabinet, along with cotton balls, and brought both back to the kitchen. "Another thing she did," she said, mashing a dozen of the tablets in another glass. "The paste dries out and falls off. Makes a real mess, I'm afraid. But when it did, she would swab off the sting with this solution, clean it, and then put more paste on." She poured vodka on top of the aspirin granules and stirred it. "Helped us. How are you doing?" she asked Al kindly.

"I'll live," he muttered. Some of the paste on one of his hands was already flaking off. Constance dipped a cotton ball in the vodka-and-aspirin solution and cleaned the sting, and then reapplied the soda paste. Al's wrists were very hairy.

One of the deputies appeared at the door, wanting keys for the station wagon. The bee man had moved the hive, he reported, but he wanted to move the wagon away from the area because the bees kept going back inside it.

A few minutes after that Charlie appeared at the door. "I'm going down to the farm with Dolman. Won't be long. How are you, Al?"

"Not bad. Not bad. Constance knows a trick or two them medicine men could use."

"I bet she does," Charlie said, grinning, and trotted off.

Sylvie cleared all the brochures and pamphlets from the table and brought the apple kuchen over along with the coffee.

"See," Al said, as she moved back and forth arranging things, "Stanley, he was a genius with money, and he was coming to be my advisor. What he said, my advisor. Early, before the kids get here making a whoop and holler all over the place."

"They're coming pretty soon," Sylvie muttered. "I don't know, Al. This just about does it for me. You know what I mean?"

"Yeah, yeah. I know. So he's coming over, like I said, and Jill drives up and turns around, and he gets out and smooches her real big through the window and off she goes. And I'm thinking now he's coming on in, but he turns to the station wagon and pulls the back open and the bees are all over him. Just like that. He's yelling and throwing his hands over his face trying to get them off, and he falls down, and by then I'm going out there, and I'm trying to get them off him and pull him away. I tried artificial resitation. I took a class once, but it don't do no good. He's a goner even before I reach him. Bees on his face, even his eye, all over his arms."

"And I'm right behind Al and I seen him fall down and I run back in and call that emergency number wrote down on the phone book and the bitch goes you gotta stay on the line and I go, no way, I gotta call Wollander, and he shows up about the same time them near doctors get here in their truck and when he sees that Stanley is a goner, he goes tearing out for Jill."

Sylvie dabbed more paste on Al's cheek, and they all ate kuchen and drank coffee and Sylvie and Al talked about staying here, or going back to the city, or getting a hotel room for a few days, and about installing a real professional security system on Monday, and maybe trying another dog. And finally Charlie came back with Greg Dolman.

The sheriff's tone was solicitous. "You doing better now?" His eyes were as hard as ever. Al nodded, and he said, "Look, if you get any more letters, give me a call, will you? And if you decide to go somewhere else for the next few days, let me know where I can find you. Wouldn't blame you for leaving for awhile. But we'll get them kids. We'll get them."

He started to leave, then paused. "My guys have been holding the reporters off, but when the word gets out that it was Stanley Ferris, they'll be thicker than fleas out here. I'll leave someone to hold them off while I go talk to Wollander. Another hour, hour and a half." He nodded to them and went out the door.

Wordlessly Sylvie got up and poured coffee for Charlie. She examined the paste on Al's stings and cleaned off a couple of them. "What'll we do, Al?" she asked then, subdued. "That sheriff ain't going to do us no good."

"Yeah. I don't know. Maybe we'd better just take off."

"Al," Charlie said gravely, "your station wagon still has some bees hanging out in it. The beekeeper plans to come back after dark, after they're all back in the hive, and take the hive back down to the farm. Meanwhile some of the bees seem confused and keep homing in on the wagon."

Al shuddered and Sylvie made a moaning sound so deep in her throat it sounded inhuman.

"Our car is down at the farm," Constance said. "After your daughter comes and you send her back home, you can

105

go down through the trees and take our car. You can go to our house and wait for us. Do you mind cats?"

Charlie blinked at her, then nodded slightly.

"Cats?" Sylvie asked uncertainly. "Your house? Where's that?"

"We'll give you a map," Constance said. "Three cats. They'll hate having you show up in our car, and they may even just take off and sulk. Don't worry about them. You can relax and try to decide what you want to do without any reporters bugging you. We'll wait until the beekeeper comes back and clears them all out and then join you."

Al and Sylvie looked at each other, then looked more closely at Constance and Charlie, and in the end they nodded and began to talk about what they would take with them. "Not too much to lug through them woods," Al said, and she said, "Three, four days of clothes. Is the suitcase in the attic or the basement?" When they began to talk together, Charlie leaned back in his chair and grinned faintly at Constance.

"Well?" Constance asked later, when she and Charlie were alone in the house. The daughter and grandchildren had come and gone, the Zukals had left. The reporters had not landed yet.

"No one knows when the hive was taken. It could be one that was put under the trees in April when the trees were blooming. They're checking now. You can move a hive at night, no problem. Probably it was done overnight. The sun heated up the wagon and the bees got mad when they couldn't get out and tend to business. And that's about all. No fingerprints on the hive, or the wagon."

"It's so ugly," she said after a moment. "What if one of those children had opened the station wagon first?"

"Everyone's thought of that," he said quietly.

She told him the story Al had told her. He didn't know why Stanley Ferris had opened the station wagon. There wasn't any reason for him to go near it that Al knew. He and Sylvie had used it yesterday and there wasn't anything in it, nothing that should have been of any interest to Stanley.

"They know it was meant for them," she said matter-of-factly. "They're taking it a lot better than I would be doing."

Charlie nodded. He knew he would be out with a gun looking for someone to shoot along about now.

The reporters came to the porch and Charlie got rid of them. He didn't know where the Zukals had gone, he was house sitting for them, he didn't know anything about anything. That was the station wagon, and it still had bees in it; if they wanted to go get pictures, fine. They left. Constance straightened up the table and put the baking soda away again, put dishes in the dishwasher, and stood looking at a can of dog food left in one of the cabinets. Sylvie's green kerchief was on the counter, and the stack of brochures that Stanley had sent them. She sighed and turned to the door as someone knocked. More reporters, she thought.

But it was Lois Wharton Wollander. She was very pale and had been weeping; her eyes were inflamed and puffy.

"Oh," she said uncertainly when Charlie opened the door for her. "I came to see how Al is."

"He'll survive," Charlie said. "Come in. How's Mrs. Ferris?"

Lois shook her head. "It hit her pretty hard. She . . . she miscarried. The doctor has her sedated now."

"Hospital?"

"No. She was only a few weeks pregnant, he said that physically it shouldn't be too serious. She just needed calming down for now." Lois sank down into one of the kitchen chairs. "Have Sylvie and Al left for good?"

"Probably not. They're tough, and once they get over the shock, they'll be ready to fight back." Charlie studied her thoughtfully, then asked, "Were you interested in buying this property?"

Startled, she shook her head. "What for?"

"Your work, maybe. For the school, maybe. I don't know."

"That's a crazy idea. It never occurred to me."

"What's the cause of the hard feelings between Clarence Bosch and your husband?"

She flushed. "I don't know that there are hard feelings."

"Mrs. Wollander," Charlie said, drawing out a chair and sitting down, "murder has been done here twice now. A lot of questions are going to be asked, and if they aren't answered, a lot of digging will be done anyway. There aren't many secrets that will stay under wraps from here on out. If there's something between Bosch and your husband, it'll come out."

"Ask them," she said sharply then. "Why are you asking me things like that? Ask them."

"I will. And I'm asking you because you're here. There's been a death in the family, your stepdaughter's had a miscarriage, your husband must be devastated by such tragedies, and you're inquiring about a neighbor you just met recently. I'm surprised you're not over at your own house holding someone's hand, or making tea, or answering the phone. You know, rallying around."

She rose stiffly. "I was on my way to lock up the lab. I won't be in it for days, of course. I just stopped in to see if Al was all right. I'll be going now." She went to door and paused. "The sheriff is calling Stanley's death accidental. Some boys were playing a prank on Al Zukal and it got out of hand."

Charlie nodded. "I know what the sheriff is saying, but I'm still investigating murder, Mrs. Wollander."

She walked out, and he watched her return through the yard toward the break in the fence. She had just reached the area where trees and unruly undergrowth would hide her when Tom Hopewell and Clarence Bosch emerged from the tangle. The three scientists stood together talking for a few minutes. Lois turned and headed toward the mill and the swinging bridge. Hopewell watched her go out of sight, then he and Bosch continued to the house.

"Reporters," Tom Hopewell said with disgust when they entered. "They're getting a human-interest story from some of the workers. We decided to duck out until they're done."

"Did Al and Sylvie get out before they arrived?" Constance asked, ushering them both into the living room. The furniture was very good in here—two sofas, comfortable chairs, and pleasant lamps; all subdued colors, ivories and tans with green and blue accents. One of Sylvie's scarfs was on the sofa, a beer can was on an end table, a child's toy vacuum cleaner stood in the corner. A window seat at a bow window was completely covered with children's coloring books and crayons.

Tom Hopewell nodded. He seemed about to say something, but held it back. All the friendliness that he had shown them earlier was gone now. He looked angry and upset.

"Al said you would be up here until dark, and I thought this would be a good time. I wanted a word with you," Bosch said. "You made a serious statement earlier. You said David Levy was murdered. Why, Mr. Meiklejohn? On what basis?"

Charlie shook his head. "Let's just say it's what I believe. Why were you feuding with Wollander?"

Bosch groaned. "This is what I was afraid of," he said. He was perspiring and took off his coat. He had on a short-sleeved shirt, open at the throat. His arms were tanned up to the edge of the shirt sleeves, and when he moved, the white above the sleeve appeared and vanished. "Questions. The past dug out and aired all over again. That's old history. It has nothing to do with the present."

"If anyone knows, I'm bound to find out," Charlie said reasonably. "Why not let me have the real story?"

When Bosch hesitated, Constance said, "I can see the

tabloid headlines now: ATTACK OF THE KILLER BEES. OLD
FEUDS SETTLED AT LAST." She looked at him kindly. "You
know that's how it will be treated."

"I know. It's just a silly thing, sordid and unpleasant, but
not relevant. And I know you're right, it will come out
again. Back in the seventies, you remember all the turmoil
on campuses, everywhere. It was here, too. Wild kids, re-
bellious, experimenting with LSD, magic mushrooms,
whatever came down the road. They got out of hand here,
too. I threatened them with expulsion—there were eleven
graduate students, supposedly young adults, too old to re-
quire supervision. Anyway, there were parties, and people
from around here were upset because some of the local
kids got involved. I had my students in and warned them
that at the next party I'd call the sheriff and round them all
up. And I did. One of the locals who got hauled in was Jill
Wollander. A kid, fifteen, sixteen. And Warren threatened
to have my head. He said things he shouldn't have said and
in self-defense I got an attorney and slapped him with a
suit. To shut him up, stop his threats. It worked, and he
hasn't spoken to me since."

"What kind of threats?"

"What you might expect. He would close down the farm
here, or have me removed, things like that. Called me incompetent, said I provided the atmosphere, and maybe
even the drugs, let things get out of hand. It was ugly."

He looked grim, his mouth set in a tight line. His soft,
slender appearance had been deceptive; now with his coat
off, his arms revealed wiry muscles when he moved, and his
expression was obstinate. He would take on Wollander
again if he had to, Charlie thought. A tough old bird who
would fight city hall and all the king's men, whoever got in
his way.

"And now your bees kill his son-in-law. Oh yes, it will be
aired again, I'm afraid." Charlie regarded him with com-
miseration. "Tell me something about the bees. Could any-

110

one have gone in there and just picked up a hive and walked out again?"

"Walked out, maybe. But our night watchman says no one drove in or out after Lois left at ten-thirty. The sheriff practically accused him of lying about it, falling asleep on the job, or something, but I believe him. He's a good man, and he's been with us ever since I've been there, twenty-one years. There's no reason for him to lie."

"How heavy are the hives?"

Bosch glanced at Hopewell and shrugged. "Seven, eight pounds. They're lightweight, meant to be carried out to fields or berry patches. And if it was the one left under the trees, it didn't have to be carried far."

"If you don't think it was neighborhood kids, who do you suspect?" Charlie asked softly then.

"I didn't say that," Bosch protested. "I'm just saying they didn't drive in with a truck and collect a hive. And if the hive was up in the trees, they wouldn't have had to drive in. Maybe they spotted it earlier and knew it was just a few feet from the fence. That fence is down here and there, has been for years. Harry wouldn't have seen them necessarily if they had gone in that way, through the trees, but he would have seen a truck. There wasn't one. That's all I'm saying."

"What happened to Jill after the cops collected her?"

Bosch shook his head. "I don't know. I think Warren packed her off to live with her mother. Maybe they put her in a convent. Where she belonged in those days. With a high fence topped with barbed wire. The next time I saw her, four, five years later, things were different here. That crazy phase had ended."

"Does she speak to you?" Charlie asked.

"Sure. She's been over a time or two to bring Lois mail that the rural delivery woman leaves over at the house. Jill is as friendly as a pup. But Warren will never forgive or forget."

111

Tom Hopewell was getting restless, tapping his fingers on the arm of his chair, crossing and recrossing his legs. Charlie glanced at him. "Anything you can add?"

"Nope. I agree with Clarence about the truck. Actually, what I suggested we do is inspect the fenceline and see just where the breaks are, and if there are traces someone might have left. And we decided that we shouldn't do it ourselves, alone, I mean. We thought maybe you would come along." He stood up and began to move about the room.

"You really don't want the sheriff to pursue the truck idea, do you?" Charlie murmured. "Afraid of a blot on the reputation of your watchman? What is it?"

Bosch looked more obstinate, more irritated than before. "That's partly it, of course. We don't want a blot, not now. I'm due to retire the month after our grant runs out, three years, six months, nine days. And I don't want to get into another fight with Warren. He could start a lot of trouble, talking about dangerous, uncontrolled bees, that sort of thing. He couldn't shut us down, but it would be a nuisance that I frankly just don't have time for. But more than that. You said that David Levy was murdered. Presumably you have your reasons. Lois said the dog was poisoned. I assume she has her reasons for believing that. And now, the bees. Someone obviously has launched a campaign of terror directed at the Zukals with the possible intention of driving them away. And it's just a matter of time until the rumors start flying that one of us at the farm may be behind it." His voice had gone very dry, his words precise and clipped. "It is no secret that I tried to get our board to buy this property on two different occasions. The second time it seemed a possibility, but then funds vanished and there simply wasn't enough money to make it feasible. But that's the sort of thing people will be saying if this doesn't get cleared up quickly. And if the sheriff is off searching for an illusory truck, it won't be cleared up quickly or any other way. I told him about the fence being down and he sent an

112

incompetent to have a look, but that was the extent of his interest. I thought you might be more interested, if you are seriously looking for a killer."

Charlie nodded. "I think we should go look at that fence. How I heard it was that when Lois Wharton married Wollander, it was assumed that she would add the mill property to the farm."

Bosch shook his head vehemently. "Rubbish. Warren would be just as likely to cut off his arm and present it as a gift. Let's go inspect the fence."

Tom Hopewell had been standing at the bow window gazing out; abruptly he swung around. "Wait a minute," he said. "You know where rumors like that lead. If it wasn't bad kids playing bad jokes, it must have been an outsider, someone who tried to move in on the old families by marrying one of the big shots. They sure don't need you to suggest any such thing, Meiklejohn. They'll think of it all by themselves. Come on." He strode from the room, out of the house, and led them to the break in the fence. "I found it on one of my rambles years ago," he said. "There's another section down nearer the road, and of course the one at the lake end. Everyone knows about all of them."

"We talked about fixing it at a board meeting," Bosch said dryly. "But it's mill property, not ours, and there's just no money for anything extra."

On the mill side of the fence there were fine old maple trees with a thicket of straggly new shoots that competed for light and room. Closer to the fence there were sumacs and a few blackberry brambles. The break wouldn't be noticeable to anyone not aware of it. Then the ground was too rocky to support even that underbrush, and here the fence had been bent over. The break could have been used recently, or not; it was impossible to say.

"Deer do it getting down to the lake," Bosch said, surveying it. "Snow piles up, they walk over it. Comes a thaw, it's low enough they still walk over it, or maybe jump over it. Two, three seasons and it's all the way down."

113

They stepped over the fence and kept to the rocky ground for fifteen or twenty feet where more sparse undergrowth struggled, and then they were among the experimental trees.

"Where was the hive?" Charlie asked.

"I don't know. Lois's chart will show where it was placed. But you can see that I was right, no one had to drive in. No one had to carry the hive more than a couple hundred feet."

Charlie nodded slowly, and said even more slowly, "I see. And you're right, it would have been easy for anyone who knew the hive was up in the trees here, and who knew there was a broken section of fence, and who knew his way around in the dark, and who didn't mind leaving a car or truck parked somewhere and walking in nearly half a mile. Doesn't sound a hell of a lot like your typical teenagers. How I hear it is that they won't walk to the mailbox if they can help it. And probably not your typical transient from Toledo."

Bosch returned his skeptical gaze steadily. "Warren probably knew all those things. He's a good walker, and he knows every inch of all this area, dark or light."

CHAPTER 9

What do you think?" Charlie asked a few minutes later. He and Constance were walking at the edge of the lake on the farm grounds. Across the lake the woods had ended at a grassy slope; the upper part of the Wollander house was visible, as if rising from an emerald carpet.

"I think that if our culprits are neighbor kids, the sheriff is in a much better position to find them than we are."

"Granted. What about Bosch?"

She knew that Charlie had a lot more faith in instant analysis than she did, and that he believed implicitly that she had the ability to peer through all layers of masking to see to the core. She had disputed this too many times to try yet again. Instead, she said slowly, "He's driven to complete his work, of course. I plant half a dozen vegetable varieties that he developed and introduced. Tomatoes, peas, some peppers. He's done very important work in horticulture. I can imagine the fights he's had just to get where he is, spending the last ten years of his professional life doing exactly what he wants. The bureaucracy probably put up roadblocks all the way, but he won. I wonder what really lies behind his hatred for Warren Wollander."

"You don't believe the story about the bust, about Jill being caught in the net?"

"Oh, certainly. But I suspect he knew ahead of time that she would be. Maybe that's why he called the police," she added thoughtfully. "It really isn't how the system works. You have to see the university as a clan; those who wear the tartan keep the problems at home, keep the family secrets hidden away, they don't call in the police and get their own into that kind of trouble. They just handle it in house, the way Tom Hopewell handled his student. Nothing on the record, no police, no bust, matter ended. And Clarence Bosch has been a clansman his entire life, as a student, then a teacher; it's the only world he's ever lived in. He wouldn't have done that unless there was something else behind it. And it seems to me that Warren must have overreacted to the incident if Jill just happened to be one of several. But if she was a target, then fifteen years of hostility isn't so excessive, is it?"

Charlie nodded, and gripped her hand tighter. That hadn't occurred to him, and he believed every word of it. See? he wanted to tell her. See what you can do without any effort at all. He said nothing like that because they had had that debate too many times, and it was one he couldn't prove or win. But he knew. He nodded toward the general view before them.

"Pretty, isn't it?"

On this side the ground sloped gently to the lake, with knee-high grasses, waist-high in spots, and wildflowers in bloom. Butterflies and bees were everywhere, but here they seemed benign, a piece with the setting. On the other side the grass was clipped, and the slope was steeper and higher. They had drawn even with the small beach, a length of golden sand twenty feet wide, fifty or sixty feet long. It looked as artificial as it was, but it, too, was pretty, uncluttered and clean. How much value did Warren Wollander place on this serenity, this privacy, this quiet? Charlie tried to imagine the lake filled with loud-mouthed youngsters, and Sylvie and Al's voices raised in warnings, and radios blaring, bonfires blazing, hotdogs burning. Paradise lost? Maybe, he decided. Maybe.

Yet the thought was swiftly followed by another; he preferred the chaotic imaginary scenes he had conjured. Knowing the lake was beautiful and dead, that the water flowing into it brought only more death tainted the beauty; unbidden, unseen, unidentified evil had insinuated itself into the pristine valley and now owned the dead waters. Silver wind ripples played on the surface, a mockery. He forced his gaze from the lake.

"What I'd like to do is walk to the end, see how hard it might be to cross the stream up yonder. Game?"

She nodded. "I suspect what you'd really like to do is walk across the water and beard the lion in the den," she murmured, her expression calm, her eyes busy taking in the landscape.

He grunted, and they walked on toward the end of the lake.

It would be hard, he had to admit a few minutes later. The lake narrowed until it became a swift stream that ran ten to twelve feet down a rocky gorge. Not wadable, he decided, unless you didn't mind rock climbing, and getting soaked, and then what was the point? You might just as well swim across the lake itself.

"You know," he said, "there might not be a connection, and that's why we can't see it. Like the little man on the stair."

"Three murders—if you count Sadie, and I do—and no connection? How likely do you suppose that is?"

"Not very, but possible," he said grumpily. "And I'll be damned if I can link them. A dog that's trained not to take food from anyone but the owner, poisoned. A boy who doesn't do drugs, overdosed. The wrong schmuck opens the car door, dead of bee venom."

"You agreed to look into the death of David Levy," she reminded him. "Just that."

"Yeah, yeah. But the other two tag along like kids from the first marriage. What does David's death have to do with forcing the Zukals out of here? Why on earth would anyone here want to kill the Zukals? What kind of nut would kill someone just because he saw him toss bad hamburger to a dog?"

"Maybe someone whose reputation is extremely important to him," she said after a moment.

"And we don't have anyone around here like that," he grumbled. "Just a few world-famous scientists, a presidential advisor, and a guru."

She laughed softly. "You're just hungry. Al and Sylvie will eat our food, we eat theirs. Let's go see what kind of food they provide."

When they reached the break in the fence that Lois always used, they saw a woman waiting for them. She was middle-aged, with gray hair, wearing a simple skirt and blouse, and sandals; the sort of woman, Charlie thought, whom you saw in supermarkets and discount stores clutching coupons and comparing prices, and whom you forgot instantly.

"Mrs. Meiklejohn? Mr. Meiklejohn? I'm Carla Mercer, Mr. Wollander's secretary. He would like to talk to you this afternoon, if it's convenient."

She did not offer to shake hands, and got no closer than ten feet. Charlie imagined that she could type up a storm. He nodded. "Fine. We were hoping to get to talk with him, too. When?"

"He suggested three."

"We'll be there. Up through the woods okay? The station wagon has been invaded by bees and we're on foot."

"It's the best way," she said seriously. "I'll tell him."

They watched her cross the swinging bridge, staying well in the middle, not looking down at the water at all. Holding her breath, Charlie thought; when she reached the other side, he heard Constance exhale softly. He chuckled and took her elbow. "Food. And I don't care what it is as long as it's soon."

Lois sat in a small room they called the flower room, a solarium, sun-drenched in the winter, filled with greenery and blooming plants that got carried out to the patio at the start of summer each year. The room was white, with tall windows, and window seats; although it looked stark now without the greenery, in winter it was a cheerful haven from the often-bitter cold, and it was her favorite room. She held a book in her lap but she had not read any of it since entering the room; it was a shield, to be used only if someone came in. She did not expect anyone to come in.

Now and then she heard herself say under her breath, "Poor Jill." But it was mechanical, as if someone else were saying it. Dissociated, she thought, remembering an article she had read. One of the stages of schizophrenia was dissociation, in which the person saw herself as if she were an actress in a play. And that was exactly right. She kept seeing herself at different stages of her life, herself as a child, as Earl's bride, as a student, facing her committee. Warren's bride. It was strange that the figure she saw was so identifiable and yet so distant.

Her mother screaming at her father: "Don't you see that she doesn't want you pawing her like that?" Her father drunk, trying to draw her close, his arm around her shoulders, swaying and leaning on her more and more heavily. "You love the old man, don't you, sweetheart? You know I don't blame you, don't you?" Until then she hadn't even considered that he might blame her for anything; until then she had loved him, although she tried to avoid him when he was drinking because at those times she was afraid of him. The fear was too general to have a real basis, she knew, but it was there, strong, pounding, making her shrink away from him then. At that moment she had realized that she was to blame for his failure; if she had not been born, then

119

maybe he would have become the scientist he yearned to be, not the junior high school teacher he actually was. Her fault, she accepted, and she shrank away from him because he might have to punish her for destroying his life, and finally the fear of his drunkenness had a cause.

Ten years later, her father long since dead, her mother insurance-rich, she had been confronted by the ghost of the past. Earl, drunk, weaving back and forth, lurching against a door frame, clutching the table for support, cursing the committee that was persecuting him. And she shrank away from him because she was afraid of him. She could say nothing, because anything she did say would provoke a tirade aimed at her; he would lash out, once he even swiped at her and fell heavily onto the couch when he lost balance. And the next day he would forget, or pretend to forget, all of it.

Now the ghost was walking again, had entered her life again, and it brought the same fear as before, the same helplessness. She could see the twelve-year-old child pleading with God to make it not happen, to make it stop. "I'm sorry," the child whispered into her pillow. "I'm sorry." She could see herself at twenty-two: "I'm sorry. I should have checked everything closer. I should have double-checked. I shouldn't have been so trusting, so confident. So stupid." That time she whispered into the dark in their bedroom while Earl crashed around in the living room beyond the locked door.

Last night, when he crashed into the bushes outside the quonset hut, her fear and helplessness had been exactly the same as the child's many years earlier. Nothing had changed.

She stared out the window at an oak tree unmoving in the sunlight and wished for a storm, a hurricane, a volcano to erupt, a tornado to wipe everything away, a flood, anything. Exactly the way a child wishes for a catastrophe, she thought wryly, and turned to see Warren standing in the doorway. How long he had been there she didn't know, but she had the feeling that he had been watching her.

"I have to tell you something," she said then, surprised at the steadiness in her voice. "Earl Malik is hanging around. I tried to pay him to go away again, but I don't think he will."

Warren shook his head, as if trying to recall who Earl Malik was, or why she was bringing this up now. She felt a wrench at the sight of him; for the first time she realized that at sixty-two he was starting to look old.

Before he could say anything she went on, "I wasn't going to tell you. You were right, of course; I did have a secret. I didn't want to worry you with my old problems, but with so much other trouble now, there can't be anything like this getting between us. I'll handle him some way, Warren. I don't want you to get involved with him."

"Maybe he's behind all this trouble," Warren said. "That would explain it."

She shook her head. "Not Earl. He wouldn't do anything like that. He just wants money, and recognition, and . . . I don't know what all he wants, but he wouldn't deliberately harm anyone. He isn't dangerous that way."

"You're still protecting him," Warren said harshly, sending a shock through her. "Why, Lois? What's that man to you now?"

She put down the book she was holding and very carefully walked across the room, trying to quiet her shaking hands, trying to control her breathing. She felt as if there wasn't enough air to go around, that he could breathe, or she could, but not both of them. He moved aside as she drew near the door.

"I was trying to protect you," she said finally. "And maybe myself. I don't care if Earl Malik is alive or dead."

She walked past him stiffly, out into the broad hallway, and stood still, no longer knowing where she could go in this house, where she could feel safe, not like an intruder, an unwelcome guest who had lingered beyond decency.

Half an hour later she was pacing in her room, back and forth, to the window to gaze at the wide expanse of lawn that looked painted, back to the door where the wood grain revealed a multitude of faces, some in profile, some full view, one grinning, one leering, back to the window again. She watched Carla Mercer scurry up from the woods and cross the lawn, and envied her. A break from her work, then back to mind-numbing details. She yearned for her own work, her tiny laboratory and the endless slides to examine and catalog. She was at the window when Warren tapped on the connecting door between their rooms.

"It's open," she said, not turning around.

"Lois, I'm sorry."

She looked at him then. He did not move into the room. She waited.

"Too many shocks, too fast," he said hesitantly. "And I'm a fool."

Slowly she crossed to him and then reached out her hands. He took them and drew her to his chest and held her. After a moment he said, "My first reaction was to call the sheriff and tell him to look for Malik. An easy out, I thought. But I didn't. Then I called Diedrick and asked him what he knows about Meiklejohn, and he called back to say we can trust him. He's discreet and he's thorough. I sent for him. We don't have to tell anyone else. Let him find some answers. If Malik isn't involved, that's that. And if he is . . . We'll go on from there. But, at least, there won't be publicity."

It didn't occur to her to wonder when he had found time to call Diedrick, his attorney, when Diedrick had found time to learn anything about the private detectives, when he could have sent for them. She felt only a great relief as she stood sheltered in his arms, secure again, safe. Not until they were in the study with Charlie and Constance did she realize that this must be why Warren had been searching for her in the solarium, to tell her that he was bringing in private investigators. And by then she had already told them about Earl Malik.

They were in Warren's study, with its good old cherry furniture, green-leather upholstered chairs and sofa, floor to ceiling shelves with neatly arranged books. Very nice, all of it. Charlie had glanced around with obvious approval, then said bluntly, "Why us, Mr. Wollander?" Wollander's retainer check was on the desk; Charlie had not touched it yet.

Warren Wollander was equally blunt. "I don't want anyone to make any connection between those unfortunate occurrences and this house. My . . . resources . . . would surely establish an interest on my part. I want someone to be very discreet. Since you are already on the scene asking questions, you seem the obvious choice."

"What is the link you want to keep under wraps?" Charlie asked. His voice was bland, his eyes as hard as obsidian chips.

Warren studied him for a moment, glanced at Lois, then said, "My wife's former husband has been hanging around—a stranger in these parts. And we all know a stranger is the likeliest suspect if there's trouble. I want that to stay unpublicized. Unless, of course, he is actually involved. But we doubt that he is."

Charlie looked at Lois, who now had two patches of high color on her pale cheeks, as if rouge had been applied hastily; it gave her a look of vulnerability. She held her head up and sat with her back straight; only her hands, clutching one another, betrayed her nervousness.

Briefly she told them about Earl Malik. When she was finished, Charlie shook his head at her. "You know we want more than just stripped facts. Is he the one who knocked over bushes outside the quonset hut last night?"

The color left her cheeks and her hands clutched spasmodically. She nodded. "He came there and I ran out. I drove around a while to calm down and then came home. But he wouldn't have moved the bees. He couldn't have known anything about them or the station wagon, or anything else up there. Besides," she finished in a very low voice, as if she had cause to feel shame, "he was very drunk. He wouldn't have been able to carry out anything. I . . . he used to go to sleep and not wake up for ten or twelve hours when he was that drunk."

She didn't know, she said, what time she had left him; after ten was as close as she could come. She didn't know what time she had arrived home; she had driven around to calm down, and had stopped at a diner somewhere for a sandwich first. This morning she had not seen him and the lock had not been disturbed on the quonset hut. When she finished, she leaned back, visibly relieved.

"What does he expect of you?" Charlie asked. "Did he mention buying the Zukal property, having you buy it?"

"Of course not," she snapped. "That's a ridiculous idea."

"I agree," Charlie said, nodding. "But so is blackmail when you come down to it. You've paid that man over twenty thousand dollars, you say, just to get him away from here, and yet he hasn't gone. How much more does he want? How much more are you willing to pay? Is it going to be a monthly annuity for him? For how long? You say he showed up in April. Before anyone knew the Zukals were interested in the mill. Why not consider that he might have wanted it for his work, his and yours? You see, the problem is that you don't usually pay blackmail to someone simply because you don't like him. In that case, you sic the dog on him, or call the cops, or tell your husband, who takes steps. When did you tell your husband, Mrs. Wollander?"

At that moment everything fell apart again, and the pieces shattered into dust, and the dust was in her mouth. She realized that Warren had sent for Charlie before she had confessed that Earl was in the area. With a startled look she turned to Warren, who was gazing out the window

124

as if none of this concerned him, and she knew that the security she had felt in his arms, the safety she had found there was an illusion, that this large, important, self-assured man whom she had thought so wise was a stranger.

She swallowed painfully, and said in a steady voice, keeping her gaze fixed on Charlie Meiklejohn, "I didn't tell him until today. I knew he would do something, just not what. And I knew that Earl would go to the press and betray me. If Clarence learns that I have been involved with Earl in the past, he will let me go. He made Tom fire his student a month or two ago. He won't keep me either if I become a liability. It's his project; he pushed it through the administration, through the committees, he wrote the grants and got the money. It's all his, and he has the power to hire or fire. He saw to that. No tinge of scandal is to be allowed, or the entire operation might be suspect, and it's important work. I don't blame him. I might do the same in his place. It is very important work."

When Charlie spoke again his voice was gentle. "The trouble with paying blackmail is that sooner or later you run out of money. Have you considered what you would do then?"

Tiredly she shook her head. "I told him I don't have any money, not the kind of money he's talking about. I have my salary. I gave most of it to him already. I told him that Warren and I signed a prenuptial agreement that I had insisted upon. I can't touch Warren's money. Earl chose not to believe me. And then, I don't know what I will do. My salary, as long as that satisfies him. I don't know. I haven't thought ahead that far."

It was interesting, Charlie was thinking, how at the beginning of this conversation she had glanced again and again at her husband, as if for reassurance, support, something. And now she was apparently oblivious of him. As she might as well be; he was as remote-looking as the sphinx.

"Why did you confess this now if you don't think there's

125

a connection with the trouble at the Zukals' property?" he asked then.

She felt her muscles go stiff in her effort not to look at Warren. "There were some letters," she said, "sent to Warren. One about me. I don't know what was in it, but obviously someone must have seen me with Earl, or something. And if someone knows, no doubt, there will be talk now. The sheriff may learn about it. I thought if there are questions, we should both be prepared."

Charlie turned to Warren Wollander. "May I see the letters?"

"I burned them." He continued his fascinated study of the great outdoors.

"Uh-huh." Charlie got up from his comfortable chair and crossed the room to the desk, where he lifted the check made out to him. "Mr. Wollander, presumably you want an investigator who won't ask embarrassing questions, and to whom you can lie. I'm not that man, sir. Sorry."

"What the devil are you talking about?" Wollander swung around.

"I mean, what's the point of hiring me and lying to me? There are letters. There were other letters that the Zukals received. There are links and cross-links all through this crazy case, and you burned the letters you got. Fat chance, Mr. Wollander. I rather think you handed copies of them over to your lawyer, or those other resources you mentioned earlier, and at this very minute someone is trying to find the author. Or has someone already found the author? You think you can hand out a smidgeon of information here, another smidgeon there, another to the sheriff, and when we all bring in our crumbs you can piece them together and make a cake?" He looked at the check regretfully and then tore it in half and let the pieces fall to the desk. "I'm already hired, you know. So I'll just keep on asking questions here and there and do the best I can."

Well, he thought, he hadn't whacked him over the head, but he might as well have. He certainly had Wollander's

126

attention. Suddenly that attention was diverted and Wollander was on his feet, deep concern etching his handsome face.

"Jill! What are you doing up? You should be resting."

She entered the study to stand by the door. "I called Sebastian," she said. "He said he came and they stopped him at the gate. I want to see him. Call them and tell them to let him in."

"Jill, baby, you need to rest. I told Duane I'd call him when you woke up. He's standing by."

She shook her head. She was very pale, with the waxy unnatural look of a gardenia; the long dressing gown she was wearing was pastel green, so little tinged with color that as she moved it went from a suggestion of green to silver. The green reflected from her skin eerily. Her hair was mussed as if she had been tossing and turning quite a while. "No more of your cronies. No more of the good old boys. No Duane or Richard or Herman. I wouldn't let Richard touch me with his fat pink fingers and I don't want Duane talking about his fat pink God. No more. His God took my mother and my baby and my husband. No more. I want to talk to Sebastian. Call them."

"Honey, you're hysterical. Just lie down and rest—" He moved to her side and she flinched away from him, shaking her head. Her eyes were wide and too bright, the pupils pinpricks.

"I wouldn't let him touch me but I took his pills and I dreamed. I was showering Mother with money, tons of money. Crisp, green, like lettuce leaves, so pretty in the sunlight. Up to her knees, her hips, and she was spinning around with her hands out, laughing, trying to catch some of it. Then I woke up. I know what it means. I have money now. More money than I ever dreamed of. I can go anywhere, stay anywhere. You can't stop me. I would give it to her if she were alive. God, to see her happy like that! I could do it. And I can see Sebastian. Here or at his place in town. You can't stop me, Father! Call them at the gate!"

"For God's sake, Jill. This is shock, hysteria. You don't need company." His voice had become peremptory, harsh. "I'm going to hire a nurse. You need nursing care, bed rest."

Now Constance got up and went to Jill. "She isn't hysterical," she said briskly. "But she's doped to the eyes. I think you should call and tell them to admit Sebastian. She certainly can't go out this way."

Jill looked at her gratefully, and when Constance took her hand, she did not resist. Neither did she allow herself to be drawn from the room. She watched Warren Wollander, who finally went back to his desk and lifted the phone; he spoke to his security people. When he replaced the receiver, Jill turned and walked out with Constance.

"I'll stay with her until Sebastian arrives," Constance said over her shoulder.

For a time no one in the study moved. Lois looked frozen in her chair, and Warren stared at the open door blankly. Charlie had not left the desk. When he stirred, Warren glanced at him and then seemed to remember where they were, what they had been saying and doing.

"Sit down," he said. His voice was flat, tired. "The letters are in my safe-deposit box. I'll get them on Monday. No, Tuesday. Funeral's on Monday. In Bridgeport."

Charlie nodded and sat down. "And the report on Sebastian."

Lois looked surprised, but Warren merely nodded, almost absently. "That, too. I couldn't leave it around here because Jill would have found it and been angry." Again he seemed to make an effort to collect himself, and more briskly he opened the desk drawer and withdrew his checkbook.

Charlie got the address where Earl Malik was staying. He asked a few more questions, but nothing of consequence, and when Warren pushed a new check across the desk, he took it without comment. "I'd like to walk around the house and grounds a little," he said. "And when Con-

128

stance comes back, we'll leave. I'll see you on Tuesday, around two."

Warren Wollander nodded, and now Lois was watching him with concern. Charlie was anxious to get out of the room, out of the house where it felt as if an impossibly heavy weight had descended. And Warren looked like a man shell-shocked, he thought, as he began his stroll. He corrected himself. Warren Wollander looked like a man who had only this minute realized how passionately his beloved daughter hated him.

Jill's room was spacious and all over the same pastel green that she was wearing, and gold and white. A white, fluffy rug was mashed down in a regular pattern, from window to bed to bathroom, as if she had paced miles around and around. The bed was a heap of sheets and a satin spread, a pillow on the floor. Jill stood in the center of the room and seemed to shrink, to become a child in front of Constance's eyes.

"He always does that," Jill said. "Says do this, do that, stop doing this, stop doing that . . ." She felt her hair, glanced down at her gown. "Excuse me." She went into the bathroom and closed the door.

On a white-and-gold table flanked by two white and gold chairs there were magazines, fashions and decorating, one of them French, and a number of pamphlets and booklets, all spiritual material. One of them had a smiling Buddha on the cover. A large music system lined one wall; another had a portrait of a beautiful woman. Constance studied it. Jill's mother, she decided, dressed almost exactly the way Jill was dressed now, in a flowing gown of silvered green, a large emerald on one finger, her eyes almost as green as the gem.

Jill returned and stood at her side. "Isn't she beautiful? How could he treat her the way he did? She loved light and gaiety, dancing, music, everything alive, and he wouldn't leave this mausoleum. Never. He treated her like a hired prostitute, made her sign an agreement never to leave him, never to even ask for a divorce, never to demand anything more than their contract allowed." Tears were streaming down her cheeks as she gazed at the portrait of her mother; she seemed unaware of them. She continued to talk rapidly about her mother, life here, life in France and Switzerland, as if all these words had been stored in a container too tight for them and, now that it had been opened, the words were not to be denied.

Constance moved away from Jill and went to the bathroom where she wet a washcloth and wrung it out. She glanced swiftly over the counter at twin gold basins, hastily opened both cabinets and looked inside, then returned to Jill, who had not moved and was still talking in that out-of-control staccato. Constance didn't miss a word, and when she gently wiped the girl's cheeks with the cool cloth, Jill seemed as oblivious of her as of the tears.

Jill was talking about the parties, about the house they had had outside Paris. "And she was so ill, so much of the time, but she never let anyone know. She was so brave. When she was too sick to stay home, I came back here and she went to a rest home in the country. And then she got better and called me and I flew back. I hardly even needed an airplane. She could have had any man in Europe, but he wouldn't release her, and she had nothing. Nothing. And so sick so much of the time. And she had to take care of me. I tried to make her leave him anyway, and she was afraid. What would become of us? Of me? Always it came back to that—what would become of me?"

Suddenly she stopped talking and snatched the washcloth from Constance. "Oh, God, look at me!"

She dashed into the bathroom and turned on the water.

"Let me brush your hair," Constance said, following her. The brush was gold and very heavy. She began to pull it through Jill's hair. "Are you bleeding very heavily? Perhaps you really should see a doctor."

Jill drew in a shuddering breath and held the washcloth

130

to her eyes. "It isn't that bad," she said dully. "Lois talked to her gynecologist. He told us what to watch for, made an appointment for me, in a few weeks, I forget when. I'm all right."

Constance finished with her hair; it was silky, with a slight wave. "Well, come sit down for now, and keep the cloth on your eyes."

A minute or two later, when there was a tap on the door, Jill was composed. Constance opened the door to see the housekeeper and Sebastian. He ignored her and went straight in, and before the door closed, she saw him kneeling at Jill's chair, taking both her hands in his.

CHAPTER 10

As soon as they left the lawn and walked behind enough trees to hide them from the Wollander house, Charlie stopped and caught Constance up in his arms. He nuzzled her hair, and kissed her, and then kissed her a second time.

"Well," she said. "Well."

"Touching base with reality," he said, grinning, and took her arm, steered her toward the path back to the mill. "What happened?"

Dreamily she said, "I think that could catch on. Sharing reality. Your reality or mine, baby? What do you think?"

He pinched her bottom.

"Oh well," she said. "Beautifully furnished room, lots of white and gold and pale green. If she sat still in that dressing gown she would melt right into it and be invisible. No books. A few magazines, some religious material, booklets. One on meditation, one titled *Unwinding the Universe*. Stanley was a hypochondriac, lots of prescription medications, more over-the-counter do-it-yourself nostrums. Stomach, bowels, muscle tone, hair loss, you name it, he

132

was probably treating himself for it. Plus heavy-duty sleeping pills, chloral hydrate, a prescription. And high blood pressure medicine. And allergy medications, ointments, pills, Caladryl lotion and tablets, and a sting kit still sealed."

"Good Lord," Charlie said when she paused. "You were gone ten minutes."

"I know," she said regretfully. "If she hadn't talked so much I probably would have had time to snoop around a little. Let's see, what else did I intend to mention? Oh yes. A portrait of her mother. Remember that scene in *Tales of Hoffmann* where Beverly Sills plays the girl who sings a duet with her dead mother? I always forget the names of the various women, but you know the one I mean. The father either is or has been dealing with the devil, and it's time to pay up. Anyway, it reminded me of that. Jill looks very much like her mother, and of course the mother is highly idealized in the portrait, great tragic eyes, honey silk hair, boneless hand draped beautifully over her pale arm. Dressed in a pale green satiny thing with lots of highlights. I guess it's too late for me to have a portrait done, isn't it?"

Charlie dug in his heels on the path and brought her to a stop for a second time. "The biggest mistake I ever made was in packing you off to learn self-defense. Otherwise I would threaten to toss you over the hill into the lake. What did she *say?*"

"I was just getting to that," Constance explained. "It was all about her mother. That's why I prefaced it with the portrait, you see, just so you would have a basis for underst——" She broke it off to say warningly, "Now, Charlie. It seems that her father kept her mother on a very short leash for a very long time. He had her sign a prenuptial agreement, and if she insisted on it, Jill didn't mention that. The agreement stated that if she left him, divorced him, she would take only what she had brought to the marriage, an inheritance of ten or fifteen thousand. He would pay for the education of any children and their maintenance, but not a penny alimony. If he broke it off and got a divorce, an arbitrator would settle the financial terms. He had an obsession, Jill said, about no divorce, the need to keep a good public image of an intact family, just in case he decided to run for office himself instead of pulling wires from behind the screen. So they all lived here when she was a young child, and then the first Mrs. Wollander split for France and never came back. In and out of hospitals, boyfriends, drugs, alcohol, the whole Fellini bit. When she was too disabled, she sent Jill home, but she never stayed more than a few months at a time, and then back into the party with Mother. She died a little over four years ago, and Jill married Stanley a few months later."

"Wow. And Wollander has a clean image, electable by a landslide."

"I'd say so. It's quite an in thing to admit to dependency treatments, attempts at cures. And he stood by her through thick and thin." Her voice had become detached and too thoughtful, too professional, as if she had Warren Wollander on a slide and was interested the way a doctor might be interested in a bacterium. "I wonder if the current Mrs. Wollander really believes the idea of a prenuptial agreement was altogether her own." She paused, then added, "Something came up today that shook her. Remember? It had to do with when she told him that her ex was in the neighborhood. She changed completely after that."

He remembered clearly. Now they had reached the place in the path where they had to walk single file, and he stood aside for her to go first. He liked to watch her move, liked the way the low sun was filtered through the trees to touch her hair again and again, the way her hair changed from brilliant to pale. The path was a pleasant walk, never steep, and, except for this one stretch, comfortably wide. Here the trees had funneled the trail to a scant two feet, and even that was nice, the fact that they had let the trees have their way. She looked very nice here among the trees in the

soft dappled sunlight. When they emerged from this section, the lake was visible again. Constance turned to reach
for his hand, and paused at the look in his eyes.

"Another reality check?" she murmured.

"You're a wicked woman. And it's not too late to have a
portrait. By God, it's not!"

This time she kissed him.

The beekeeper came and Charlie watched closely, but
there was little to see. The man looked inside the station
wagon and nodded in satisfaction. It was not altogether
dark, but the bees had had it for the day, apparently. He
simply picked up the box by handles on each side and put it
on his truck, and that was the end of that. "Italian strain,"
he said. "They're real peaceful if you treat them right." He
got in the truck and drove away.

When they got home, after winding through several un-
familiar roads to make certain they were going home alone,
they found Al and Sylvie in the television room playing gin.
The television was turned on too loud, and they were arguing, and Al was holding Brutus in his lap. Brutus barely
acknowledged Charlie and Constance.

"I'll be damned," Charlie muttered. "Perverse beast."
Brutus hated strangers, had always hated strangers, and
wasn't too crazy about people he knew.

"This one's a pussy cat," Al said, stroking the cat.
"Aincha, tiger? The others ain't showed up."

"He thinks he's back prowling city streets," Charlie said,
and Sylvie said at the same time, "Betcha you're starving,
aincha? Me and Al, we snacked some but we ain't ate.
Thought it'd be polite like if we waited. We got Polish sausages and potato salad and a couple other things. We seen
this little store on the way over here and stopped and we
got plenty lost when we come out again, got real turned
around, but then we got on the right track again."

Al's stings were all but gone now, no welts, not even an

135

itch, he said proudly. "Some tricks," he said to Constance. "What we thought," he said then, "was that while Sylvie's finishing up supper, I'd show you the stuff we wrote down today. Everything we can think of that happened with David after Sadie kicked. Ain't much, but who knows?"

"That's right," Sylvie said. "Who knows?"

They all went to the kitchen to keep her company and Charlie looked over the notes they had made while Constance set the kitchen table.

Sylvie talked disparagingly about her cooking, and Al talked about the security system he had in mind, the kind where if someone moves without you doing nothing the lights come on and an alarm, and she said that they would just shoot out the lights, and he said that would be a signal too, they could fix it like that.

Charlie found it hard to read what they had written down. Sylvie capitalized every noun, and Al capitalized nothing at all. Neither seemed to have much use for periods.

Sylvie was a superb cook and dinner was too good to talk through; it was late by then and they were all very hungry. Sausages and potato salad with a sweet-and-sour creamy dressing like none that Charlie had ever had before, with bits of green onions and olives chopped up in it. She had made a green bean casserole with mushrooms, and a tossed salad that had shredded raw beets and carrots and even pine nuts. He sighed his contentment when he finally pushed his plate back half an inch, his signal that another bite would do him in.

Constance made coffee and Charlie brought in brandy; they all cleared the table and sat down again, and this time Charlie actually read some of the items they had written down.

"Them with checks," Al said, "that means we both seen him together."

Charlie went to the beginning of Al's paper. David had come to the mill to see how things were going on Monday;

Al began to talk about the work being done in the mill, and with great concentration Charlie managed to blank out his voice and read on. Thursday of that week David had dropped in briefly to visit with Al while Sylvie was shopping. Now she talked about Betsy, the lady with the new antiques, whose son made them and made them look old by torturing the wood. They don't torture it, Al said, they just torment it a little, make holes in it with a drill. They worry it, that's what they do. Charlie looked up helplessly and found Constance following their talk with very bright eyes and not a trace of a grin. Betsy might even show some of the furniture Bobby made, Sylvie continued, pointedly ignoring Al, but not pretend it was antique, and Bobby sure wouldn't think of torturing good wood.

Charlie gritted his teeth. On Friday David had brought their mail in; that was confirmed by both of them. He stayed for a glass of milk and a couple of cookies. Sylvie talked about how thin he always had been. That night they agreed they had him for supper.

Sunday he brought her head scarf, found it on the beach or somewhere. Filthy. Past washing. She had got used to wearing them when she cleaned offices in the city. No one had any idea of how filthy some doctors and lawyers could be. Maybe out here in the country she would get out of the habit, but her head felt naked . . .

Monday, Sylvie told David about the poison-pen letters, and he had got real upset, she said soberly. Al nodded. Thursday, the day after he had talked to Charlie, although they didn't know nothing about that, but it was just like him, anyways, he had asked Al exactly where the dog died, where they had found her. Sylvie said he stood at the grave and looked real troubled, and he walked around the mill, troubled real bad. Al nodded again.

"We figured that maybe he was trying to come up with his own answers," Al said. "And maybe he did."

"Next day," Sylvie said, "we both seen him tossing sticks in the water. He looked just like the little Robin boy with

137

his teddy bear. You know how they stood on the bridge and threw sticks in the water? Only he wasn't playing no games. He looked worried and bothered, and then he walked down the side of the lake and we didn't see him no more."

"Sticks?" Charlie said faintly, and put down the papers in defeat. He would read them tomorrow.

"Little sticks. Twigs, like." Al measured about three or four inches with his hands, then adjusted them a bit. "Little sticks. Charlie," he said, leaning forward, "something that we both seen. Everything bad that happened was always on a Saturday. You see that? Sadie dies. Then David dies, and now Stanley dies. Always on Saturday."

Charlie nodded. "I noticed."

Al looked disappointed, then brightened again. He and Sylvie exchanged a meaningful glance and she nodded. Al said, "Something else, Charlie. Me and Sylvie, we think you want to be more careful. I mean, if there's a high school kid out there with ants in his pants, that's one thing, but if there's a nut out there, you want to be careful. You're too trusting, Charlie."

"How's that?"

"Well, like you let us come here and we coulda robbed you blind. You don't know if I'm a nut or a thief or what have you. See what I mean?"

"It goes both ways, Al. We could have robbed your house."

"She wouldn'ta." Al nodded toward Constance, who nodded back emphatically.

"Well, she's the one who invited you to come here, if you'll recall." And *she*, he thought, a bit disgruntled, didn't pipe up to say he wouldn'ta, either.

"You wouldn'ta axed us?"

"Not on my own, probably."

Al nodded in satisfaction. "That's okay then."

"I told you," Sylvie said.

"Something you might be able to tell us," Charlie said

then. "How did David get over here to see me that day? Do you know?"

"Sure," Al said, and Sylvie said at the same time, "In Lois's car. He borrowed it."

"Then probably everyone at the farm knew he was going somewhere, even if not where. And maybe at Lois's house, too. She could have mentioned it, I guess."

"Gonna buy us a gun or two," Al said suddenly, making an abrupt right turn in the conversation without warning.

Charlie groaned. "Do you know anything about guns? Ever do any shooting?"

"Nope, but all them punk kids in California know, and just about everybody on television. Even the president's wife had a gun, you know? Can't be that much to learn, even if she did say it was just a little tiny one."

"You'll kill yourself, or Sylvie," Charlie muttered unhappily.

"You think we should go back there without no protection at all?"

"Why don't you take a little trip? Just a few days, a week. Go to Atlantic City and play the slots or something for a few days."

Sylvie screeched something and Al said something, and altogether it added up to no. They weren't going to be driven out of their house after all these years. Sylvie began to talk about her grandparents who had come from Poland, and Al talked about his father setting up a butcher shop, only to be burned out, and now they were trying the same with him and Sylvie. . . .

"Okay, okay," Charlie said, shouting over both of them. "Let me go over the security system when it's in place, will you? Before you go back, I mean."

"Sure," Al said agreeably.

"My grandmother had a stove like that," Sylvie said, pointing to the wood-burning stove that wouldn't be used again until fall. "And one of the places we seen, they had a stove like that. Remember, Al? The place with the horses?"

139

"Yeah. Horses. Never get them stables smelling like roses in a million years. You know horses, Charlie?" he asked with a thoughtful look. "Big. Real big."

Helplessly Charlie nodded. "Yes, Al. I know."

"We gotta go now," Sylvie said, standing up. "We called a hotel we seen on our way here, and if you'll just point us in the right direction, maybe we can find it again." She sounded as if she doubted it. "It sure is dark in the country, you ever notice?" she asked Constance. "Real dark. You'd think they could put in a street light or two, for appearances or something."

They both talked and Charlie went out with them and pointed directions and then rejoined Constance inside. "Well," he said, "watcha think?"

"I think they're swell," she said judiciously. "And I think we had better catch that nut who's keeping them from enjoying their new fortune."

While Constance finished straightening up in the kitchen, Charlie went through the house turning off lights. He was carrying one of Sylvie's headscarfs when he came back; she had left it in the television room. All three cats were prowling around the kitchen now to see if any interesting tidbits had fallen, and Candy was complaining bitterly, her hoarse voice very like Sylvie's. Charlie watched the cats approach to investigate the scarf, which he had draped over a chairback to be returned the next day. He was thinking of Sylvie cleaning offices, Al butchering for a supermarket, four girls growing up in a small apartment, all four of them getting educated, and he agreed with Constance. They should be allowed to enjoy their place in the sunshine, their place in the country. Candy kept getting closer to the scarf, then backing off suspiciously, and she kept complaining. He felt certain her raucous words were very obscene.

Constance flicked off the light at the sink; he put his arm around her waist, and they went upstairs, leaving the cats to decide if the green scarf was friend or foe.

140

CHAPTER 11

Sunday was a bust, Charlie decided in midafternoon. They had read all of David's letters, and the papers Al and Sylvie had left with them. They had gone over David's other belongings and there was nothing new. He had been pitifully poor, saving for three months to buy a new pair of running shoes, doing without a new watch when his old one quit, making do. Just making do with what he could afford, and writing letters week after week to his father. His checking account had bottomed out each month while he waited for his scholarship money, but he never was overdrawn. He had done without instead of bouncing checks. It all made Charlie grouchy and on edge.

Constance brought in peas and asparagus from the garden and he prowled around the house and yard, making the cats uneasy. They kept starting at noises he couldn't hear, and staring at objects he couldn't see, and casting swift, frightened glances over their shoulders at nothing at all. After dinner Charlie announced that he wanted to see a movie.

"What movie?"

"Any movie. Preferably a western, with lots of shooting and frantic riding around on the prairies and deserts."

"Oh, that kind of movie." She found the weekly local newspaper and scanned the two ads for coming attractions. It really didn't matter which movie he saw when he was in this state, but if she had to sit through something with him, and if there was a decent choice, she preferred to make it herself. When Charlie said any movie, he meant it. He might see it, or maybe not, or maybe some of it. It was as if at times he had to have something taking place before his eyes in order to let his brain get on with its own business of making sense when no sense was apparent. Later, he might walk endlessly. Other times he might play solitaire, but now it was a movie that he needed.

She drove to the theater in Woodbury, ten miles away, and they entered to find a Woody Allen movie already started, full of New York scenes done in sepia. Charlie settled down contentedly with a bag of popcorn, and she watched the movie. When it was over, she had to nudge him with her elbow.

They went out and walked the half block to the Volvo and she got behind the wheel again. Halfway home, he grunted, and said, "Where are the damn vitamans?"

"Didn't the police lab destroy them when they were looking for drugs?"

"I mean the new package," he said softly.

She thought, recalling David's belongings, and then said, "Oh! Of course."

In just a few minutes they were back inside their house, with David's personal effects once again spread on the table. Charlie found the police report and the list of vitamins they had destroyed: A, E, B-complex, C . . . Constance found the other list of what the sheriff's men had taken, and later had returned to David's father. No new package of vitamins. She picked up the catalog that David had ordered from and began to look for a price list, an order form. It had been torn out. But there had been a

142

check made out to the company, she remembered, and now looked for that in the register.

"He ordered a three-month supply on May twelfth," she said a few minutes later. "And before that, back in February. Orders spaced just over three months, one hundred of this and that. It's an in-state company, wouldn't take more than a few days for the order to be processed and delivered."

Charlie made a noise that wasn't really a response. He was comparing the catalog to the list from the sheriff's office of destroyed vitamins. "Four of this and five of that," he murmured. "You'd think with one-a-day type vitamins, the numbers would be the same. And he was almost out of them. As close as he was with money, if the new supply hadn't been delivered before he died, they should have been in the next week while the police were collecting his mail."

"Four of some, five of others? But, Charlie, if the drugs had been in vitamins, there'd be some trace, wouldn't there? I mean, Greg Dolman uses a good lab technician, surely. And who could count on David's taking the drugged ones? That's just too chancy."

He nodded. Then abruptly he read down the list again. "I'll be damned," he muttered. "The fives are all capsules, the fours tablets."

Constance waited, trying to reason it out, drawing a blank.

"Try this," Charlie said at last. "You see that there are a lot of small containers, each one with five vitamins, and you take away the ones with capsules. You replace them with identical containers of capsules that have been tampered with. It doesn't matter which ones he takes of the capsules, they're all poison, but they'd look normal, and still have the right smell. Then, after he's taken the doped capsules, you return the containers with the harmless vitamins, and there are still five in each of them, but only four in each container that held tablets. Tablets are too

143

hard to duplicate, but capsules are a snap to empty and refill. No trace of drugs would be found, obviously, since none of these ever had drugs in them."

Slowly Constance nodded. "Someone could have taken the new package, his new supply, and tampered with them, thrown away everything afterward." She began to study the catalog list again. "Some of those capsules would have been awfully big—a thousand milligrams of C, with rose hips, for instance, in a time-release form. That means hundreds, even thousands of little individual bits, like beads, to dissolve over eight hours or so. That begins to get pretty large for a single dose. Some of these are in the mega-vitamin category, really big, but would there have been enough of the capsules? Enough space for a lethal dose?"

"I don't know. We'll have to get some and see."

"Oh!" she said then. "Look, he ordered cod-liver oil. A lot of drugs could have been dissolved in it, and the taste and smell would hide just about anything."

Charlie looked over the list of things the sheriff had tested; no cod liver oil was there.

"Maybe he was just going to start it," Constance said.

"We'll sit on it for now," Charlie said. "I want to get the damn pathology report on the dog. But I think we've got this link. And it sounds a lot more plausible than a six-in-the-morning visitor."

"Just one more thing," Constance said then. "This other price list. Did you notice it? I thought at first it was more of the same, but look." She held up a list and pointed to the top margin, where words had been scrawled: *The list I promised. S.*

Charlie looked from it to her and shook his head. "So?"

"It's a different company altogether," she said. "And he could have saved nine dollars by ordering from this one. And who do you suppose *S* is? And why didn't David order from this company instead of the higher-priced one? They seem to be offering nearly identical items."

"S," Charlie said then. "Sebastian? Remember David's

144

letter about the party at Wollander's? They talked about bees and about vitamins."

"I know."

"Well, well," Charlie said then. "Interesting, isn't it? No matter where we toss our net, the same fish keep swimming into it. I told you I wanted to see a western movie."

She suppressed a groan and he started to put everything back into the box.

Early Monday they found the address Lois had provided for Earl Malik; it turned out to be a trailer court, Hunt Acres. The manager's name was Petey Wilson, and he looked like a wrestler, with great bulging muscles and a neck that was the same diameter as his head. His head was shaved and it was deeply tanned, as was the rest of him. He was wearing an undershirt, cut off jeans, and sandals. Even his toes appeared muscular. His eyes were bright blue and clear.

"Earl? Sure. Third trailer from the end, left. But he's not here."

"Say when he'd be back?" Charlie asked.

"Man, he hasn't said anything for days. Haven't seen him in nearly a week. His tough luck. He's paid up in advance; I should worry. If he isn't back by the end of the week, I'll clean out his junk and rent the unit to someone else. I could care less."

Charlie nodded and surveyed the trailer park. Ten trailers were visible and probably there were others beyond them in a grove of trees. A gravel drive wound around them all. At the moment the whole complex seemed almost empty, but in hunting season, he suspected, it filled to overflowing. A blond woman in pink short shorts was sweeping her two steps endlessly, watching them. She was heavily made up, as if for a performance.

"You live out here, too?" Charlie asked Petey Wilson.

"Yep." Petey pointed toward the road and the first trailer in the place.

"So anyone coming or going would have to pass right by your place."

Petey looked somewhat disgusted and shrugged. "If they come in this way they do. There's a back entrance in from Huntaker Lane. Lots of them use that one. Closer to Spender's Ferry that way."

Charlie was eyeing the third trailer from the end, not yet moving toward it, but evidently intending to do so. Constance said, "Haven't I seen you on television? Wrestling? Or was it football?"

Petey peered at her suspiciously, then nodded. "It's been a long time."

"But you've kept in such good shape! You look as if you're ready to go back to it right now, this minute, if you wanted to."

He flexed his biceps. "Could. Pays to keep in shape. You watch wrestling?"

"Pretty often in the past. It's not the same now, for some reason. I knew the minute I saw you that you were familiar. Did you ever get hurt much? It always looks so cruel."

"Naw. We learn to take it, that's all. Nobody watches it much anymore. All fake now. Not like it used to be."

She nodded sympathetically, then turned to Charlie. "Why don't you take that stuff to Earl's unit? I'll wait for you here." Then she looked at Petey again. "Mr. Wilson, is it really true that those matches are all decided in advance?"

Petey glanced from her to Charlie and back, then he shrugged slightly. "Now maybe, but not in my day." Charlie left them talking.

The door was locked, but even a kid on his first solo burglary could have opened it. Charlie slipped his plastic card in and opened the door. The trailer was hot, and smelled foul—too many spilled drinks, too many fried onions and hamburgers, too many cigarettes, never enough air. It was dirty and messy, with clothes scattered about and magazines and newspapers everywhere, and a thick coating of greasy dirt on the window frames and the back of the stove. There were many books, science books, biographies, books about trees, plants . . . The refrigerator smelled even worse than the apartment, but there were steaks and apples, milk, butter, eggs. A broken egg had dried on the bottom of the refrigerator. On the only table was a notebook opened to a page of numbers and cryptic notes. It looked like the same sort of thing that had been scrolling on the computer monitor back at the farm. A stack of computer printouts with more of the same was by the side of the notebook. Earl Malik was keeping up, apparently.

There were two unopened bottles of bourbon, one of gin, three bottles of beer, some collins mix, and a trash can filled with empties. Charlie was hurrying, trying to get a picture of the man, and the picture was too uneven. A pig, but a smart pig was the best he could do. A tiny chest of drawers held a few shirts and socks; two drawers were empty, and a pair of slacks and a jacket were in a small closet. All the pockets were empty. He ran his hand under the mattress on the sagging bed, and he looked under the cushions on the sad-looking sofa. Nothing. He picked up a crumpled map near the table and opened it. Then he folded it and tucked it inside his pocket and stood surveying the place for another second before he left. A real search by experts might turn up something, he thought morosely, but he doubted it.

Constance was still in an intent conversation with Petey when he rejoined them. The woman in the short shorts had stopped pretending to sweep; she was simply watching them now. Constance looked at Charlie brightly. "You wouldn't believe some of the tricks they use now to fool the audience!"

"I'd believe," he said. They all looked toward the road as a siren blared nearer and nearer, then passed. Medical rescue unit, Charlie thought distantly. The road was hidden by trees.

"Well—" Petey started; he stopped again as another siren wailed, approaching.

"Let's go see," Charlie said, taking Constance by the arm. "When Earl comes, tell him we'll be back. Just say Charlie. Okay?"

Petey nodded, following the sound of the sirens. A third one was approaching.

Charlie drove back up the gravel driveway to the county road, and waited there for a sheriff's deputy to pass with the siren screaming. His face was without expression as he watched it go by. He listened briefly, then pulled out after it.

"The farm!" Constance exclaimed a few minutes later.

They were waved off the driveway to the front parking lot, but no one stopped them when they entered the admin building and hurried through and out the back door. Charlie was nearly trotting as he led the way past the rows of plants to a group of people near the quonset hut. They were farm workers and a few others that Charlie had not seen before. Tom Hopewell was with them, his hands jammed into his pockets, his shoulders hunched. Everyone was watching the activity at the apartment units, although deputies were keeping them all well back.

Tom Hopewell started, then nodded to Charlie and Constance when they reached him; a deep frown lined his face, aging him many years. "My God," he said. "My God!"

Charlie looked past him. Several of the apartment doors were wide open, one unit had windows broken out. Greg Dolman was near it, but no one, as far as Charlie could tell, had entered.

"What the hell?" he muttered, and then he got a whiff of gas. He gave Constance's arm a slight squeeze. "Wait here," he said, and strode toward Greg Dolman.

A deputy moved toward him, to intercept him probably; he ignored the man. "Greg, what the hell is going on?" he called.

148

Dolman scowled at him and motioned the deputy away. "Gas," he said unnecessarily. "Place was full of it when the painters opened the door. Thank God, no one tossed a cigarette or match in."

Charlie nodded. "Someone's in there?"

Dolman's expression turned suspicious, and Charlie said irritably, "For Christ's sake! What are the medics waiting for if there isn't someone in there?"

"Just to haul him away," Dolman muttered. "He's been in there a long time apparently. Too long. Bosch took one of my guys up to the main building to try to find a fan. But that sucker in there, won't matter to him."

Charlie's hands bunched up into fists, and he stared at the apartment, every muscle taut now. Another one, he kept thinking. Another body.

The fan was produced; someone had to go find an extension cord, and finally it was working to air out the apartment. Bosch was the color of wet newspaper, and said not a word. He stood near Charlie watching the apartment as if he expected to see fireworks. He looked as tightly wound as Charlie was.

When Dolman approached the apartment, Charlie followed. No one seemed to notice. He entered, sniffing first just to make sure, and then stood well out of the way, keeping his arms tightly crossed, observing. A dead man with dark hair, dressed in jeans and short-sleeved shirt, running shoes. On his side in the kitchen area. Bedroom door closed, bathroom door closed. The technicians— death technicians, he thought bleakly—did the usual things; some took pictures, then more pictures, while others dusted for prints here and there. Dolman prowled around purposefully, and finally they turned the man over and there was blood-soaked hair matted on that side. Charlie left.

Bosch had joined Constance and Tom Hopewell. "Who is it?" Bosch asked. A little color had returned to his face, but he still looked bad. A tic jerked one eye again and again.

Charlie shrugged. "They didn't find any ID. It may take a while to identify him. I never saw him before." He looked at Tom Hopewell, included him in his question, "What happened?"

Bosch said quickly, "I was in the admin building when I heard people yelling, running for a telephone."

Tom Hopewell was looking everywhere, and likely seeing nothing. His gaze flitted here, there, somewhere else too fast for anything to be registering. Charlie touched his arm and he jumped. Very quickly he said, "I was in the field. One of the painters opened the door, and, thank God, he had enough sense to yell for me to turn off the gas. I looked in through the window, and saw that someone was in there. That's why we broke the windows. I covered my face with my shirt and went in, but there wasn't any point to it. So we waited for the sheriff to get here."

"Did you touch anything?"

"No! Just the body, and only enough to make sure he was dead." He looked like a man who had only this minute finally come to believe in the irreversible fact of death. And he looked like a man lying in his teeth. Charlie wondered if he had become this pale, this ancient when he found David's body, if he had looked this guilty then. Would finding a third body finish him off entirely?

Greg Dolman came to the small group. "Why don't you folks go back to the main building. I'll want a statement when we're through here, and a list of everyone who's been around the last few days. You could get it together while we're finishing up."

Charlie lingered as Bosch and Hopewell started toward the building. After a glance at him, Constance followed the two scientists. Tom Hopewell was moving so fast she would have had to run to keep up.

"Any ID?" Charlie asked Dolman then.

150

"Nothing. Transient. I think this wraps it all up, Charlie."

"Is that how you're going to play it, Greg?"

"That's how it is," Greg Dolman said flatly. "A bum moved the bees. Who knows why? Then he went out in an accident. Finis."

"Was there a bottle in there? I didn't see any."

"No. Why?"

"Wondered, that's all."

"Well, stop wondering. I don't give a shit about a bottle. I say it's complete as it is."

Charlie shook his head. "It won't work, and you damn well know it won't."

"Butt out, Charlie. Just butt the hell out." He turned away abruptly and strode back to his men still working in the apartment.

When they reached the admin building, Clarence Bosch sent Tom Hopewell to talk to the rest of the staff, and get the list of employees. "If those two people show up for interviews, tell Wanda to keep them in the front office. I'll get to them as soon as I can." He busied himself with making coffee. "Something about coffee," he said absently. "I think it's just something to do, keep the hands busy, that's why we always think of it."

Constance agreed; she studied the room they were in. Apparently this had been the original kitchen of the house that had been turned into the administration building. There was a sink, some cabinets painted brown with the paint flaking off, and a refrigerator, but there were also file cabinets, a computer and work station, and an array of test tubes and flasks on two of the counters, also a coffee maker. A box of latex gloves was on the table, and a metric scale.

"Ever since the Zukals came," he said, stopping in the

151

middle of measuring the grounds into the basket. "It's as if they brought a bad wind with them. Nothing but trouble."

"That piece of ground is so small, just fourteen acres. It's hard to believe anyone could want it so desperately as to cause all this trouble."

"No one wanted it for more than ten years," he said, and finished measuring the coffee, plugged in the machine. "Frankly, I was glad to see someone buy it, maybe put an end to the lovers' lane reputation it had. Ever since I can remember, since I was a boy, it's been that, a place to rendezvous."

"You grew up here?"

"I, my wife, Warren, his first wife . . . all kids together." His gaze was distant, as if he were looking into the past. "We used the mill, too, in those days," he said with a faint smile that was so fleeting it might not have appeared at all. "Things were different, though. No drugs, a little beer, maybe; now and then a little booze. Then we all grew up and went our own ways. Warren to Harvard, I to Penn State. Warren got Shelley, and after a few years I got Barbara. And we were all grown up."

"I understand that Jill's mother was very beautiful."

"Oh yes. Every one of us wooed the beautiful Shelley, and Warren won. Or lost. Who's to say anymore?"

He turned his back on her and began fishing around in cabinets, pulling out a cup here, another there. Constance knew she was pushing it, but she kept up the questions as if she simply wanted to pass the time with him, distract him from the gruesome business at the apartment units.

"Was she really as wild as rumor has it?"

He laughed harshly. "Rumor can't even touch the reality," he said, and counted the cups he had assembled, went back to rummage for more.

"And was Jill like that?"

He stiffened and stood motionless for a second or two, then turned to regard her carefully. "I've been rather naive, I'm afraid," he said. "You're working, aren't you? I forgot."

"I'm working," she admitted. "Dr. Bosch, the present doesn't exist independently of the past. The gun that was loaded thirty years ago sometimes is fired in the present, but the question remains: Why was it loaded at all?" She had heard Charlie enter the building, but he was not coming into this room yet. She sensed that he was on the other side of the closed door, listening, letting her carry it for the time being.

"Our past has nothing to do with the troubles going on now," Bosch said almost primly. "Believe me, it doesn't."

"Probably you're right, but there are such big blanks. You called the police and turned in Jill Wollander when she was an adolescent. There are many ways to interpret that action. Revenge. Hatred for the Wollanders. Hatred for Warren in particular, striking at him where he was most vulnerable." Clarence Bosch's face looked frozen, his eyes unfocused. Very gently Constance said, "And another way to interpret it is to wonder if maybe you were trying to save Jill. You knew what her mother had been like, and you could have seen a chance to prevent the daughter's following that path."

He closed his eyes for a moment and shook himself slightly. He looked down at the cups on the table and moved one, then another aimlessly, keeping his gaze on them. "I . . . loved Shelley very much. Most men did. And she taunted me when she became engaged to Warren. She said he would do anything she demanded, and that he had money and position, things I didn't have. I was going to be a teacher, a poor teacher. She laughed at me. And suddenly I hated her. Just like that. Later, I pitied her, I think. And then Jill was slipping across the lake at night, meeting the students in the mill, in the apartments. I don't know. She was so young, so ignorant. I told my wife, and she tried to talk to Warren, but he . . . he wouldn't hear a word

153

against Jill. I called the police, knowing he would have to pay attention, be aware. I knew the price I would pay, that we all would pay, but she was so like Shelley in those days. Barbara, my wife, agreed with me, that we should at least try to help her, even if it meant scandal and hostility and an end to our relationship with Warren." He looked up finally and shrugged. "As you see, it has nothing to do with what's been happening around here."

Constance nodded. "I think your wife must be a very fine person."

He blinked in surprise. "Of course. The coffee smells done, don't you think?"

He was pouring coffee when Charlie entered the kitchen. Constance watched Charlie make a swift survey of the room, and she knew that later, if necessary, he would be able to list proportions, contents, windows, everything about it. Training, he said; she called it magic.

Bosch looked at Charlie with an expression that was almost pleading. Charlie shook his head. "The sheriff will be along in a couple of minutes. We'll take off before he gets in. Just a question or two first, if you don't mind."

Bosch ran his hand through his thin hair. "Go ahead."

"Right. When will Dr. Wharton return to work?"

"Tomorrow."

"And you're interviewing her applicants for her? Will you hire them, or one of them?"

"No, of course not. I told Lois I would simply determine if they are qualified. It would have been best to contact them both and put off the interview until tomorrow, but with the weekend, and they were already on the way . . ."

"I understand. Dr. Bosch, when this project is finished, you'll retire, won't you? And Tom Hopewell? What will he do?"

"You'll have to ask him. I imagine he'll cast about for another position where organic methods will be approved. It's far enough in the future that we haven't really discussed it."

"And Dr. Wharton, she would have to start a job hunt, too?"

This time Clarence Bosch shifted uncomfortably. He sipped the coffee he had been holding and paying no attention to. "I really don't know. Her situation is different, of course. A commitment to trees is a commitment to time itself. A lifetime is really too short."

"You haven't discussed it with her?"

His discomfort increased and a flush of color tinged his pale cheeks. "We talked about it," he said. "She said at the time that she didn't know what she would do."

"Did she discuss the possibility of continuing her work without the sponsorship of the university?"

"She didn't, but I did. Not on the mill property, not on fourteen acres. But damn it!" he said with his first show of real passion, "Warren owns over four hundred acres, much of it in pasture, there's a big apple orchard, open land. Good land. I suggested that she could work at home, and she was adamant about not doing that. That was the end of the discussion."

"Do you know that the organic project will end at the ten-year mark?"

"Absolutely. They'd like to phase us out now, if they could. The high-tech bio engineering people can't wait to get in here. That's already in the planning stage."

Charlie cocked his head, listening, then said quickly, "Just one more thing, Dr. Bosch. Who would know if a liquor bottle was found anywhere on the grounds over the past couple of days?"

"I'd know," Bosch said, looking bewildered. "The grounds keeper reports to me. If anything unusual had turned up after the bees were taken, I'd know. Believe me, everyone's on full alert, a bit late maybe, but they are now."

"Thanks," Charlie said. "You've really helped, Dr. Bosch. We'll be on our way." He took Constance's arm and hurried her through the hallway out the front of the building as Greg Dolman entered the back.

"Are we on the lam?" Constance asked, seated in the Volvo, with Charlie behind the wheel.

"Not yet," he said, engaging gears. He waved to the deputy, who waved back, and drove out the gravel driveway to the county road.

"Was it Earl Malik's body?" she asked after a moment.

"Probably."

"And did you mention that to Greg?"

"It didn't come up."

She nodded slowly. "Eventually he'll find out that you suspected it was Earl Malik and that you deliberately withheld the information. How long do you suppose it will be before we *are* on the lam?"

Charlie chuckled and patted her thigh, and then let his hand rest there.

CHAPTER 12

Today no cars were parked along Ellis Street. The postage stamp-sized lawn was just as immaculate as it had been on Saturday, but when Charlie knocked on the door, the young woman who answered was wearing jeans and a T-shirt.

"We would like to see Sebastian," Charlie said.

"I'm sorry, do you have an appointment?" She looked sorry to the point of tragedy. She was a pretty young woman with very long dark hair held off her face by a blue ribbon, no makeup, no jewelry. Her eyes were a lovely clear brown. She looked as if her sorrow might lead to tears momentarily.

"Just tell Sebastian that I am a private investigator employed by Mr. Wollander, and I would like to talk to him."

Her eyes widened and her mouth made a little O; she withdrew and closed the door. Charlie glanced at Constance and winked.

"Ten seconds," she said gravely.

It was no longer than that before the door opened again,

157

and this time Sebastian appeared. He motioned for them to enter.

"You were at the lecture Saturday," he said.

"Indeed we were," Charlie said agreeably. He introduced himself and Constance. "This won't take long. I know you must be a very busy man, what with services and lectures and private counseling and house-hunting, and all."

Sebastian smiled and shrugged. "My office," he said, and opened a door in the foyer. The office was small and had no desk. It was painted white, with a soft gold carpet, and soft gold draperies. There was a rack of books and pamphlets on one wall; Constance recognized titles that she had seen in Jill's room. There were many cushions piled along the opposite wall, and between the two walls were several upholstered chairs. Still smiling, Sebastian motioned them to chairs.

"I noticed that you found the seating arrangement not altogether satisfactory the last time," he said.

"Very observant," Charlie said, as he and Constance sat down in chairs. Sebastian stood near the window. "Are you still looking for a place to buy?"

"I have not looked at all for a place to buy, much less still." His eyes bulged slightly, and his lank hair fell continually into his face. He used both hands to push it back again and again. The slight smile did not waver.

"Ah. I understood that Mrs. Ferris was showing you the mill property a few weeks ago."

"Many people show me many things, Mr. Meiklejohn."

"I bet they do," Charlie murmured. "Mr. Pitkin, there have been several deaths in and around the mill, as you well know. We can play games, or you can level with me and I'll go away."

"Please, just Sebastian. And believe me, I want very much to help in your investigation. I'm afraid I have a small problem, however. I don't quite understand exactly what it is you are investigating."

158

"The murder of David Levy. And the death of Stanley Ferris."

He sobered at the words, and now looked sorrowful. "Murder? David? Surely not. I met him only one time, I'm afraid, so I have no knowledge of his usage of drugs, but I assume that when the authorities decide a death by self-administered drugs is accidental, they have sufficient grounds to make that assessment."

"Murder, Mr. Pitkin. You gave him a list of vitamins. When was that?"

"Vitamins? Oh, yes. I remember. We talked about vitamins at that cookout. Weeks ago, the same day Jill escorted me through the mill. He was paying far too much. That company is without a conscience, I'm afraid. I did tell him he could buy less expensively through the company I recommend to my own people, and a day or two later I gave the list to Jill to pass along to him. She said she would give it to her stepmother who would actually give it to David. I heard nothing more of the matter."

He looked so self-satisfied, so *superior,* Charlie thought, that he wanted to give him a swift kick. "And you said that evening that a person with the right attitude wouldn't get stung by bees, didn't you?"

Sebastian shrugged, and his hair fell into his face; he pushed it back. "It's possible I said that, of course, because it is true. But I confess that I don't recall saying it."

"Is it also true that if you have the right attitude you won't get bitten by a dog?"

"Of course. You see, Mr. Meiklejohn, you are the bee, and you are the dog, and the tiger, and the snake." The cadence of the words, the rhythm suggested thinly disguised mockery. "Naturally there are many quite self-destructive people who haven't grasped that yet, and they are at risk, but with understanding and acceptance, there is no longer any danger with anything of nature."

Constance had been watching him intently, but now she left her chair, as if bored, or perhaps simply restless. She

159

moved about the room and came to a stop at the books and pamphlets. At first Sebastian watched her movements with annoyance as she strolled farther and farther from Charlie, forcing Sebastian to turn his head from side to side to include both of them in his sweeping gazes. When she began to examine the various books, he seemed to give up and concentrated on Charlie, only now and then glancing at her as she browsed in the reading material as if unconcerned with the questions and answers.

"Uh-huh," Charlie said, ignoring Constance. "If you aren't looking for property to buy, what were you doing at the mill with Jill Ferris?"

"Looking." He held up his hand and shook his head. "Don't be angry, Mr. Meiklejohn. Your questions are difficult because they carry so many presuppositions, so many assumptions. Why is it, I wonder, that you ask only questions that you already believe you have answers for? Anyway, at one of our discussion meetings here, the matter of a school came up. I did not bring it up myself, but it was the subject of discussion once it did arise. It was suggested by one of our people that if we had a school, a large enough building to accommodate sleeping space and lecture rooms, that then some people could use it for a retreat, immerse themselves more fully in study and meditation without the interference of pressures of the outside world. A cloistered retreat seemed idyllic to many of us, I admit. But I have no money and I did not pursue the idea. Since then, several people here have offered to show various properties that they had reason to believe might be suitable. Jill made such an offer and I accepted. Not with any intention of buying, however, because I can buy nothing."

Charlie regarded him for a moment, and then said, "And if one of your people takes you on a tour and you find the ideal place, and if that person then says, 'Hey, don't sweat it, I'll buy it for you,' then you're in like Flynn. Neat."

"There are many paths to enlightenment, Mr. Meikle-

160

john. That may well be one that one of our people will follow."

"How long has Jill Ferris been coming here?"

Now Sebastian shook his head, in sorrow as deep as his receptionist's had been. "You know I won't talk about any of my people, Mr. Meiklejohn. I came here in March this year, and I met Jill Ferris soon after that. She never offered to buy a building for me, or to help me financially to purchase one, and that's all I intend to say on the subject."

"I see. Was she driving all the way out from the city, just to attend your meetings? When did she become a regular?"

Sebastian shook his head again, harder, sending his hair flying out both sides. "You will have to ask her."

"Oh, I will. Do any of your . . . what do you call them? Parishioners? Disciples? Students? Do any of them ever stay here in this house?"

Sebastian folded his hands before him. "Exactly what are you implying now, Mr. Meiklejohn?"

"Just curious. You got here in March. Jill turned up for her prolonged visit in April, I understand, and yet she's become quite an adept in meditation. Makes me wonder how she had time to advance so fast."

"Some people are ready to progress rapidly. Others never are able to see beyond their own noses. I really must go now, Mr. Meiklejohn. Is there anything else?"

"One thing," Charlie said, rising lazily. "Why did you agree to see us at all? You had no intention of telling us anything, did you? And did you notice that I asked not a single question about where you're from, how you got into the soul business, your qualifications to counsel troubled people. Nary a question. No doubt, that sort of thing will be neatly wrapped up in Wollander's report on you. If I see that I need more, I'll come back."

Sebastian did not move, but his stance changed subtly, his hands became tighter in their grasp, one of the other. "What report are you talking about?"

161

"Did you really think you could set up camp in his back-yard and not be investigated? Now that is really naive. Especially where his daughter is concerned. I haven't asked you about your movements over the past couple of weeks, last Friday night particularly, or if you've been over to the farm, communing with the bees, your alter egos. We'll see how much of your time is already accounted for."

"I have nothing to hide, and nothing to fear from any investigation," Sebastian said with tight lips. He strode across the room and yanked the door open, then stood aside for them.

"Thanks for your time," Charlie said good-humoredly as they went through the foyer to the front door. "Be seeing you around, Mr. Pitkin."

Sebastian's lips tightened even more, and his eyes looked strange, more bulging than before, as if suppressed rage was pushing on them from behind. A high flush was on his cheeks now. He said nothing.

Charlie opened the door and let Constance go out first, then pulled the door closed hard. He did not let go, however, and did not allow it to latch. Silently, with an amused expression, he counted to seven and then pushed the door open an inch or two in time to hear Sebastian's voice:

"Goddamn son of a bitch! If they come back tell them I'm in Poughkeepsie! That bastard Wollander!"

Silently Charlie pulled the door closed again, this time releasing the knob. Grinning, he took Constance by the hand and they went down the front steps.

"Made you mad, did he?" Constance said softly.

"Damn right. But I made him madder. What was that with the books?"

They reached the car and got inside. He turned the key and then waited for her answer.

"All his own work. I was just curious. Jill's reading matter seemed a bit odd—high-fashion magazines and spiritual material. I guess he hands out the pamphlets and articles, or sells them, to his people."

"His people," Charlie snorted. He started the car, began to drive. "I'm in the wrong racket. Nobody ever bought me a school or a church, or even a house."

"You could grow a beard and wear a serape, or a ruana, or even a simple blanket—go barefoot, of course—and talk about taking the right road, scorning the wrong road, not being distracted by enticing signs, like luncheonettes, or anything that. . . . Where are we going?"

"You know damn well we're going to have lunch and mull things over."

She smiled slightly.

"What I want," Charlie said in the Spender's Ferry Coffee Shop ten minutes later, "is a roast beef sandwich with lots of gravy." Constance cleared her throat, and he added, "But what I'll have is the tuna salad with tomatoes and dressing on the side." He looked at her balefully. "Okay?"

"Very good," she said, and ordered the same. "And coffee right away."

"We need a spy," he said, and fell silent until the waitress poured coffee for both of them. As soon as she was gone, he continued, "I want to know the minute that crew gets home over at the Wollander house."

"Charlie," she said, a little shocked, "they're at a funeral!"

"I know. Jill can hightail it to her room if she wants. But you can count on it that Greg Dolman won't waste any time in telling them the whole thing's settled. They've got their bum, in the best possible condition as far as Greg's concerned. He sure as hell isn't going to deny anything. So, case closed with even better speed than he managed when he closed the case of David Levy. The county's clean and all's well with the world. I want to get there first, that's all."

She nodded thoughtfully. Not the Zukals, she decided. They were probably still at the hotel. Not anyone at the farm, too many unknowns concerning all of them. Not anyone. "I could hang out at the mill. I wonder if you can see enough from there?"

"No way. Not you."

She looked searchingly at him then. No trace of amusement was visible on his face.

"Honey, there's a real killer loose in that neck of the woods. Someone as opportunistic as hell and pretty damn smart. And desperate by now, I expect."

"Can Greg make a case for Earl Malik? Will it stick?"

"Not if I can help it. They'll find a high alcohol level in the blood, no doubt, and Greg will think that cinches it, but he can't have it both ways. If Malik was drunk enough to fall down and bash in his head, he was too drunk to be lurching around the woods carrying a beehive. They didn't find a bottle, remember. He didn't sober up and then start drinking again. And there weren't any prints on the stove. Whatever was on the doorknob was messed up by Hopewell when he opened the door. No prints. So Malik goes in the apartment and turns on the gas, and wipes off his prints, and then obligingly falls down and knocks himself out. Won't work."

"Then he must have seen whoever got the bees, and that's the motive for killing him."

Charlie nodded. Their salads arrived and neither said any more for the next several minutes. "What they'll do," Charlie said then, "is mill about for a while after the funeral, more than likely. Say they start for home again around three. Be back by seven. I guess our best bet is simply to be on hand and wait for them."

"We'd better go through the mill property," she said. "The security people probably won't let us in the front gate."

"Right. So we go home and brood about that damn dog, and light a fire under Wilbur Palmer if he hasn't got his report ready yet."

"You brood. I intend to freeze peas and speak encour-

164

agingly to the tomatoes." She had left most of her tomato on the plate. It was picture-pretty and tasted like plastic.

When Charlie called the animal pathologist that afternoon the report was ready. "One of the organophosphates," Wilbur said. "More than a dozen trade names for the stuff—insect sprays, dusts, that sort of thing."

"A smart dog would eat something like that?"

"Charlie, the word smart is relative, right? So the dog's smarter than a possum, what's that mean? You mix this stuff with some canned dog food, and watch."

"But if it was insect spray, she could have got into it accidentally."

"If there's a store of it around. There was a lot in the body. Still is. I doubt that even a pretty dumb dog would lap up that much unless it was mixed with something. Oh, maybe some fruit got sprayed heavily, but dogs sure don't eat many apples or pears, now do they?"

Charlie thanked him and hung up and then stood at the patio door watching Constance move about in the garden. She picked a pea pod and ate it and continued with the chore of picking enough for the freezer. Hers was an organic garden, no poisons. You could go out there and eat whatever struck your fancy, he thought, and shuddered at the idea of the meal that had been fed to that poor dumb dog. "But how?" he muttered to himself. How had anyone managed to get her to eat it?

Someone out there was an opportunistic and smart killer, he thought again. Too smart. Taking advantage of every opening to get whatever the hell he was after. Or she, he corrected himself. First the dog Sadie, feeding her poison when she was trained never to take food from anyone but her owners. Then David Levy with drugs when it was known that he did not do drugs. Then the attack on the Zukals with the bees. If Al were allergic, he would be as dead as Stanley. One of the grandchildren, both of them

165

could have been killed. And now the man he was certain was Earl Malik. Each one killed, using materials at hand, leaving no trail, hitting and vanishing in good terrorist form. Kill and run. If Greg announced the end of the mystery, the closing of the case, then whoever was responsible could strike again, and again, until . . . until what? he thought bleakly. Who next?

The phone rang in the kitchen as he stood watching Constance. He took the call before the answering machine got its act together. It was Al Zukal. The sheriff had called, he said, and they could go back home. The crazy killer was dead.

CHAPTER 13

Lois felt like an interloper, an intrusive guest who was always in the way, no matter what she did. Coming home from Stanley's funeral, Warren had held Jill as if she were a small child, her face against his chest, his arm protectively around her shoulders. One of the security men, Robert something, had driven the Buick, and Lois had been superfluous. The Ferris family had virtually ignored her, and again she was superfluous. That family's grief was so consuming, so overwhelming that even Warren and Jill had felt excluded somewhat; no one had suggested they linger after the funeral services, after the obligatory wake that had been cut short when Mrs. Ferris left the room on the arm of her husband. "We'll go home now," Warren had said, and they got in the Buick and Robert drove them home. No one had uttered a word during the drive.

Worst of all, Lois thought, gazing at the landscape without recognition, she had gone blank. She tried to think of work and nothing came. Two people to be interviewed, she reminded herself, and forgot them again. Where had she stopped the metabolism studies Friday night? No answer came. Had she put everything away on Saturday? No answer. Would Clarence think to check the moisture level of the cloned trees in their pots in the greenhouse? Would Tom? When the Buick stopped at the front of the Wollander house, she seemed to come up from a trance state that left no memory.

Mrs. Carlysle admitted them to the house and Jill started up the stairs silently. She was deathly pale, and looked as if she had lost five pounds in the last day or two. Should she be made to see a doctor, be examined? When Lois had asked hesitantly if she was bleeding heavily, if she needed anything, Jill had simply shrugged. "I'm all right." Lois saw again how she had looked Saturday in the brilliant white jumpsuit, with the blood-red sash, and blood running down the legs. Jill had looked mortally wounded. At the stricken look on Warren's face, she knew he was seeing that same image again. She wanted to take his hand, but their new awkwardness permitted no such intimacy now.

"Mr. Wollander," Mrs. Carlysle said in a soft voice that was almost fearful, "there is a message from Mr. Meiklejohn."

"For God's sake! Not now!"

"I'm sorry, sir. He said to tell you it's extremely urgent, that it can't wait. He left a number to call." She held out a slip of paper, but Warren pushed past her and went into the study. Lois took the message, and Mrs. Carlysle looked relieved and grateful. "Thank you," she whispered, with a frightened glance toward the study. "He said it's vital and even told me what to write down, or I wouldn't have brought it up now."

Lois watched her hurry away down the broad hall toward the kitchen, and then opened the folded paper. *I have to talk to you both immediately. It's about Dr. Wharton's former colleague.* There was a telephone number.

She watched the paper start to shake, and realized that

she was trembling all over. She closed her eyes and took several deep breaths, and then went into the study.

She offered the note to Warren, who was standing at the window looking out toward the front of the property. He ignored the slip of paper.

"I'm going to call him," she said.

"Leave it alone until tomorrow. My God, that man knows we've just come from the funeral!"

"I know he does. That's what makes it frightening." She went to the desk and dialed the number, watching Warren's back all the while. He was suffering, she knew, losing his son-in-law, his grandchild, maybe his daughter . . . being brought face to face with his own mortality again. Charlie's voice sounded in her ear.

"I got your message," she said. "Can't it wait until to-morrow?"

"No. Tell your security people to let us through. We're at the mill property. We'll be there in five minutes."

"But what's hap——"

"Five minutes." He hung up.

"They're coming from the mill."

Warren's shoulders seemed to hunch as if he were bracing against a cold wind.

"I'll go meet them," she said. She started to leave, but stopped again and said pleadingly, "Warren . . ." He didn't move. She left the room after a moment to wait on the patio.

They never had needed security before, she was thinking distantly. She had felt as secure as a child in her parents' home, protected, safe from the world and everything it might threaten her with. And now there were men on duty to keep out reporters, sightseers, curiosity seekers. Killers? Maybe even that. And the more security they hired, the less secure she felt. She felt as if the threat existed at her elbow, not out there at all. She started to walk across the

169

expanse of manicured lawn, feeling more exposed with every step.

She waved away one of the guards when Charlie and Constance emerged from the woods. They were an odd couple, she thought, still with the distance that seemed to be her self-protective armor. He was so dark and bearlike, she so tall and slender and fair. Lois liked the way they looked at each other. One plus one made a bigger one, she thought then, and thought of them that way, bigger than one, but still one. She felt a rush of envy, and she had an impulse to warn them that the cleaver could fall, even on them. They wouldn't believe her, any more than she would have believed such a warning just a few weeks ago.

"What's happened?" she asked, as soon as they were in range.

"Let's save it for you and your husband," Charlie said. The crinkles at the sides of his face were gone, and deeper lines etched his features now.

Her fear returned, redoubled; she nodded and led them inside the house. They went straight through to the study where Warren was now seated in his favorite chair, with a drink in hand, an invisible wall all around him. It started at his eyes; they were cold and hard. He nodded curtly at Charlie, and ignored Constance altogether.

"This shouldn't take very long," Charlie said. "Today another body was found in the apartments at the farm. The sheriff will be around either this evening or in the morning. I wanted to get here first."

Lois went paper-white and sank down into a chair, her eyes wide and staring. "My God," she whispered. "Who?"

"Unidentified at the moment."

"Earl?" she whispered. "Was it Earl?"

"I never met him or saw a picture of him. Hard to say for sure. But I think so."

Warren's eyes had narrowed and he looked different; he looked dangerous. This must be his political face, Charlie thought. Briefly and succinctly he told them what he knew about the body in the apartment, watching them both closely. Neither moved until he finished.

Charlie caught a motion from the corner of his eye and glanced at Constance who was moving toward the study door. She opened it. Jill stood there.

"Come on in," Charlie said. "You heard enough to know what's happening, I take it." No name had been mentioned, he knew; Lois's whisper *Earl* could not have carried to Jill. What she had heard would be broadcast news, and it made no difference. The interesting part was that she had learned it this way, by eavesdropping.

She had changed her clothes and was wearing jeans, a black shirt, and sandals. She looked childish and ill. She went to the sideboard and poured gin, added tonic and ice cubes, and sat down without a word. She looked too young to be drinking anything but a Coke or juice.

Lois stirred finally and said, "I'm sorry. Do you want a drink? Sit down please." She looked at Charlie and Constance in turn, but without real invitation behind the words.

"You were right to tell us first," Warren Wollander said then. "A man without ID. Died the same night that the bees were taken. He probably did it himself, then. They may never find out who he was." He looked steadily at Charlie as he spoke in a very deliberate voice.

"They'll find out," Charlie said just as deliberately.

"Meiklejohn, I hired you to do a job for me. I find now that I made a mistake. Keep the retainer, but you're no longer in my employ. I think that's all we need say. Our business is concluded as of this moment." He lifted his glass and drank, and set it down on the table by the side of his chair.

"Dr. Wharton," Constance said then, "we have to talk, you know."

"My wife is under no obligation to talk to either of you," Warren said coldly.

"Mrs. Wollander may be protected by your name and

171

your position and your wealth, but Dr. Wharton is at grave risk," Constance said.

Lois was watching her, pale down to her lips now. She glanced at Warren, who returned her look, stony-faced. Suddenly Jill jumped up, knocking over her glass that she had put on the arm of her chair. Everyone ignored it.

"Look at you!" she cried, facing Lois. "Mrs. Wollander will obey! I always envied you, did you know that? I did! Your degrees, your brains, your work, your freedom. Your freedom! You could tell the world to fuck off if you wanted to. But you're just like the rest of us! One look from him and you're just like the rest of us. I thought someone finally would say no. That's all, just *no!*" Tears were streaming down her face by now. She wiped at them with the back of her hand. "Shit! I'm going down to the lake." She ran from the room and a moment later a door slammed, the sound muffled by distance.

"What do you want to know?" Lois asked. Her voice was harsh, grating.

Of them all, Charlie thought at that moment, only Constance appeared unruffled by the scene Jill had made. And Constance had a thoughtful expression—her professional expression, was how he thought of it. And since it was her show now, he waited for her to go where she was heading.

Constance nodded to Lois, but turned to Warren and asked, "Why didn't you ever run for office?"

He started at her question. Jill's outburst had affected him deeply, it was apparent; he looked very tired, and very old. After a second he said, "I don't even know her. She's like a stranger over and over." He took a breath. "I'll get you both a drink. Lois?"

He busied himself at the sideboard, handed out gin and tonics, and then said to Constance, "I thought I could be of more service in the background." He stood at the sideboard watching her.

Constance sipped her drink, then put it down again. "Thank you," she said. It wasn't clear if she was thanking

172

him for the gin and tonic, or for responding. "And in the background there would be no public scrutiny, no inquisitive press hounding your every movement."

He shrugged. "That too, but I have nothing to hide, nothing to fear."

"Maybe not personally. But what about the first Mrs. Wollander? What would have come up about her?"

His jaw muscles tightened noticeably, but he controlled his voice so much that it was flat, expressionless. "It was never an issue."

"I want to tell you something about your daughter, Mr. Wollander, but first you must tell me something. Why didn't you divorce your first wife? What was her hold?"

Charlie tensed, then made himself relax again. Wollander looked murderous, but he was not moving, not threatening. And if he did, Charlie thought, Constance would flatten him like a pancake. He waited.

When Wollander remained silent, Constance said gently, "She was a lovely young woman, much sought-after. She could have had her pick, and she accepted you. She made demands that you were happy to concede to. And the demands were binding long after the time when you would have divorced her if there hadn't been a hold. Isn't that right, Mr. Wollander?"

He was regarding her with disbelief. "Who told you any of that?" He rubbed his eyes suddenly and left the sideboard where he had been standing, took his chair again, and looked at nothing in particular. "You have it pretty much as it was. I agreed to sign over the property here to her, in the event that I ever divorced her. I agreed that no illegitimate child could inherit the estate. We were drinking champagne, celebrating her acceptance, laughing, joking. I thought we were joking, playing a game. I agreed in advance to a divorce settlement that seemed as remote as Mars. Divorce was the last thing on my mind then. I was deeply in love with her, crazy in love, I think the expres-

173

sion was in those days. I doubt that she could have suggested anything I would have balked at."

"I thought it must have been something of that sort," Constance said, still gentle and thoughtful. "You see, Mr. Wollander, your daughter believes that your prenuptial agreement bound your first wife financially in such a way that if she sued for divorce she would be penniless. Did Jill have any money of her own?"

He shook his head, looking baffled now. "Just an allowance. But that's a preposterous idea." His expression changed, became harder. "Shelley did it deliberately, to turn her against me. She had an instinct for that, finding the sore spot, knowing how to turn people against people. She told Jill a half-truth; if she sued for divorce, she would have been comfortably fixed, but without power over me. She wanted me to start the proceedings and I wouldn't. That explains so much. I knew she lied to me about Jill, I just never considered that she also lied to her about me. I didn't think of that." He turned to Lois. "That's what she meant, that she was envious of you. It didn't make sense. But if she thinks I held her mother in bondage—"

"And now me," Lois said. She looked at Constance in dismay. "We had a talk with her and Stanley, before we announced our engagement. We told her about our agreement, and I tried to make it clear that I wasn't interested in the money or the property, that I didn't want to get between father and daughter in any way. I thought it was important for her to hear that from me. And she must have assumed that we were repeating what she thought she knew about her mother and her father." Her voice trailed off and she shook her head. "We'll have to talk to her again."

"It won't be easy to overcome a lifetime of believing something else," Constance said. "You may need help."

And now she was finished, Charlie realized, and could not have said how he knew that.

"I have copies of everything," Warren said. "She'll have to believe."

Constance shrugged and did not reply. She glanced at Charlie.

He turned to Lois. "How drunk was Malik Friday night? Staggering, falling down, incoherent?"

Lois started, and then closed her eyes hard for a moment, as if she had to clear out the present revelations in order to think back to Friday night. "Coherent," she said then, faintly, "but weaving back and forth. Unstable."

"How did you push him? Stand up, show me. I'm Malik and you're coming out."

She hesitated, and he said impatiently, "Stand up and show me."

With reluctance she stood up, still uncertain. Charlie motioned. "Here's the door. I'm blocking it, is that right?"

She nodded, and now picked up her purse and put it over her shoulder. She glanced around, at Constance, at Warren, and took a step forward toward Charlie. When he did not move, she reached out with both hands and shoved him in the chest. He took a step backward and sat in a chair. "He fell like this, straight back? Into the bush?"

She moistened her lips, nodded.

"Then what?"

"I ran to my car, it was only a few steps away, and got in and drove off."

"Did he get up?"

"I don't know. I didn't look at him again."

"How did you pay him off? Cash?"

She nodded.

"Where?"

"I met him on the road, at the entrance of the trailer court. He got in my car and I drove about half a mile to a turnoff. I parked there a few minutes and he took the money. Then I drove back."

"Where did he live?"

"I don't know. He said in the city, that's all."

"Was he using his own name?"

"I don't know. Probably."

"Did you ever enter the trailer court?"

"No."

"Did you give a vitamin list to David Levy?"

She looked bewildered and shook her head.

"Did you give work printouts, computer printouts to Malik?"

"Yes. He insisted on knowing what we were doing."

"Did you find David Levy's thermos at the farm?"

"I don't know what this is all about! What difference does it make? No. He kept it in his backpack."

"Could Malik have moved a hive of bees in his condition?"

"No. I don't know. He was staggering. Maybe if he slept a while and sobered up. But he didn't know anything about the bees or the mill property, or the Zukals. He didn't even know where I lived. He thought this house was miles away, that the only way to get here was by car. He came by train and stayed a couple of days and then left again. Then he came back. But he knew nothing about this area. No."

"Was he ever fingerprinted? In the service? Arrested?"

She shook her head. "I don't know. Not that I'm aware of."

"Did he have a family, close ties who would start a search if he stayed missing?"

"No, not that I know." She looked exhausted. She bit her lower lip when it began to tremble visibly.

Charlie looked at Warren Wollander, and without moderating his tone, he said, "Did you have Malik investigated?"

"I think I've had just about enough of this," Warren said coldly.

"It hasn't even started," Charlie said, in a voice even colder and harder. "You had him investigated and that fact will come out. This is going to blow up in your faces and you know it. When did you have it started?"

"Last week," Warren said finally. "But my men don't talk about private work."

"Last week?" Lois asked in a faint voice. "You told me you didn't believe the letter."

"I didn't believe it," he said harshly. "My God, I thought you were faithful! It never occurred to me to believe it until I saw you leave that night. The night Jill told us she was pregnant. I couldn't sleep for thinking of it and I saw you, someone, going up the driveway. I came down to wait, to speak to you, someone, I don't know what I intended, but no one came back in. When I went upstairs again, your lights were still on. What was I supposed to think? The next day I called Myers and had him look into it."

"And a few days later Malik is dead," Charlie said softly. "Mr. Wollander, you know this isn't going to stay a secret."

Lois was staring at her husband with incomprehension. "I didn't go out that night, or any other night, not to meet him, or anyone else."

He looked at her with a penetrating gaze and finally rubbed his eyes. "It wouldn't have been Jill," he said slowly. "Why would she sneak out in a black raincoat like that? She was with that man Sebastian for hours every day, no need to meet him like that. Who else? Mrs. Carlysle?"

"Show me," Charlie said then. "You were where?"

Warren went to the window and pointed. "She vanished behind the copse of birch trees. I didn't see her again. I thought I'd hear her when she came back in but I didn't."

Charlie dismissed it. "Okay. Is it possible Sebastian believed that Jill had enough money of her own to buy the mill? Did she have money of her own?"

"No, of course not. Stanley was more than generous, but it was his money. Now it's hers, of course. What Sebastian believed, who knows?"

Lois seemed to have shrunk into herself; she sat huddled in a tight mass, her arms hard about her body. She looked from Constance to Charlie, and she asked quietly, "You

177

think they will find out that dead man is Earl, don't you? No matter what we do or say, they'll learn that?"

"Routine police work usually uncovers an identity," Charlie said. "It may take a little time. Maybe fairly soon. What will you do if they bring around a picture and ask if you know this man?"

Before she could speak, Warren said, "I'm sending my daughter and my wife away for a rest. My daughter has had two terrible shocks and needs complete rest, and she needs a companion."

"No," Lois said, still not looking at him, keeping her gaze on Charlie. "I have my work to do. That won't help. Running away never helps." She moistened her lips. "Tell us what to expect."

"Right. I expect the sheriff already knows I'm in here with you, and that's enough to make him come calling this evening. He'll be polite and insist that the case is neatly tied up, the killer is dead of gas inhalation, accidental death, and that's that. But the routine will take place anyway. They like names to attach to corpses, after all. And he'll find out. That will bring him back here with more questions. And he'll find out that you've withdrawn large sums of money from your bank account. He'll find out that Mr. Wollander has had a private investigation of Malik. He already knows about the campaign to get rid of the Zukals. Probably there will come a time when he'll say to himself what if this Malik character and Dr. Wharton decided they wanted the property themselves in order to continue the work they started together so many years ago? And he'll come back with even more questions. Somewhere along the line, they'll connect material found on Malik's clothing with the bushes outside the quonset hut, and someone will remember the stones that were thrown up by tires, and someone will remember two sets of skid marks, two fast departures. Someone will suggest a scuffle between Malik and his former wife, on the night the bees were moved. Now Greg Dolman doesn't like trouble, but the way this is

178

shaping up, the Wollanders are really out of it. This is between a flat-land foreigner who is now dead, and a lady scientist who doesn't really belong here anyway. That will reassure him and he'll keep coming back with more and more questions."

Abruptly Warren snapped, "Stop this! This is nothing but speculation! It won't get that far!"

Lois regarded him very steadily, as if he were a stranger. "Why not?" she asked quietly. "You know me better than anyone else here, and you were ready to believe the worst. You still believe the worst." She turned to Constance. "I was naive. But now I understand what you meant. High-priced lawyers may be able to save Mrs. Wollander, but Dr. Wharton is doomed, isn't she? Dr. Wharton cannot survive another scandal, especially of this magnitude. Suspicion, innuendo, accusations, even if it never gets as far as an arrest."

There was a soft knock on the door and Warren strode over to open it. "What is it? We're busy in here."

Mrs. Carlysle nodded. "Yes sir, but it's the sheriff. He says he has to see you."

"Our cue," Charlie said, when Warren looked over his shoulder into the room again. "We'll leave by the back door."

"I'll show you," Lois said, rising. "I doubt that he'll want to see me at this stage." She led them out without another glance at Warren.

They went through the wide hallway, into a narrower one. Good, old-money comfort, Charlie was thinking, glancing around with approval, not new-money chic; there wasn't a trace of an interior decorator more recent than the turn of the century. Good woods, cherry and walnut, chestnut paneling, stained-glass windows here and there. Very nice.

They came to a side door and Lois paused after opening it. This was the side of the building; a short brick path led to the wide lawn; beyond the lawn was the trail through the

179

woods. The sun had set; violet, shadowless twilight yielded to darkness under the trees.

"Thank you for . . . for preparing us," Lois said formally then. "Mr. Meiklejohn, you think that all this is connected, don't you? David's death, the bees, Earl."

"Oh yes. Starting with Sadie."

"Sadie?" Momentarily she lost the tight control. She closed her eyes and drew in a long breath, and then said, "Thank you. I'd better go back in now."

Charlie and Constance walked across the lawn in silence. At the edge of the woods he stopped to look at the driveway that curved around the birch trees and vanished. The woods were close on the other side of it. It was a wonder Wollander had been able to see anyone moving there, he decided, and took Constance by the hand and entered the woods. It was getting dark fast and under the trees it was almost too dark already. Still, the trail was easy to follow.

"Charlie," she said in a low voice, "that scenario you outlined, I think Greg Dolman would buy it in a second if things get that far."

"Oh, so do I."

"And it will come out that she was friendly with Sadie. She's the only one beside the Zukals who was."

"Yep. I know."

"And she certainly had access to David's apartment."

Charlie took out a penlight and they walked single file, and then they were out of the woods at the end of the swinging bridge. They had taken only a step or two on it when bright lights came on at the corners of the mill. Charlie grunted. Al's new security system was up and running.

"If our killer decides to strike again," he muttered unhappily, "those lights won't mean diddly."

180

CHAPTER 14

They turned down the offer of dinner from Sylvie and inspected Al's security system for a second time. Smart lights that came on when anyone got within twenty-five feet, dead-bolts, sensors on doors and windows. All very good stuff, Charlie admitted, and knew that none of it would matter in this particular case with this particular opportunistic killer. He did not tell Al and Sylvie this. Instead, he merely cautioned them to be alert and not to put too much faith in the sheriff's pronouncement that the case was over and done with. Then he and Constance drove to El Gordo's where they ordered Mexican pizza with green chilies and authentic white cheese that was very like Feta, and a seafood platter for two, Vera Cruz–style.

"With a pitcher of margaritas," Charlie said firmly. "Soon."

"A whole pitcher?" Her protest was mild, without conviction. He pretended not to hear.

"Okay," he said, as soon as the waiter Rene appeared with the pitcher that was so cold it looked frosted. "All right!" He poured for them both. "You were saying?"

"Not a thing." She sipped, then took a real drink. "Charlie, what about the thermos? Why bring that up with Lois Wollander?"

"Funny that it's missing, that's all. Not listed among his things. Just wondered."

She drank again and settled back against the leather seat. The furnishings in El Gordo's were authentic—massive black tables and chairs with dark leather. The service pieces were heavy pewter that retained heat no matter how long, the diners lingered. A nice place, she thought contentedly, and the margarita was not the only reason, although it helped.

"So," she said after a moment, "he used the thermos for tea or lemonade. Not the sort of thing you would leave in it overnight, especially if the next day you planned to work only a few hours, with a late starting time. I think he was out of lemons, at least none were mentioned in the inventory, and he had them on his grocery order. You especially wouldn't leave tea overnight," she added with a grimace. "The dishes were all washed and put away. The thermos should have been put away too, or at least on the counter ready for use. Then what?"

The way she did this, voiced the thread that was running through his mind, sometimes bothered him, sometimes amused him, most of the time startled him no matter how used to it he pretended to be. Once or twice, many years ago, he had asked her to explain how she did that, and she had looked puzzled and said simply, "I don't have an idea in the world what you're blithering on about." The one time the question had taken the form of a demand, she had turned her pale blue eyes on him in a way that reduced him to a thieving boy caught dead to rights in the act. His demands had been very infrequent over the years.

Tonight he followed her reasoning with a grin and nodded when she finished. "Then what, indeed," he said. "I wish I knew. And who took a late-night walk in a black raincoat on a warm night without rain? Why? As Warren

Wollander said, Jill spent hours every day with Sebastian, no need to meet him like that. And as Lois said, Earl Malik never went to the house. I guess he didn't. I found a map with the farm marked on it, but not the house. Remember, he was on foot. That's a long walk by road, seven or eight miles from the trailer court. Just over two miles to the farm from there. That road curves and recurves before it passes by the Wollander place."

The pizza arrived and they became silent as they ate the spicy food that was piquant just to the point of pain, and drank the tangy margaritas. A couple they knew, the Martinsons, passed by their table and stopped briefly to chat. Rene brought the seafood platter and lifted the pitcher in invitation. Charlie shook his head regretfully. Rene shrugged with artistry and went away.

"Tomorrow," Charlie said, "I want to mosey over to the county board of zoning commissioners and bat the breeze a little. And I think I'd like a chat with the real-estate company that handled that piece of property. Routine stuff. No point in dragging you through it." Routine that he disliked, he thought, but did not add that. She already knew. This was the sort of thing he used to have underlings take care of. Sometimes he missed that privilege, of giving orders that would be followed without question, more or less the way he expected them to be.

"You know, your Aunt Maud's birthday is coming up fairly soon," she said thoughtfully. "And there's an anniversary present for my parents to shop for. Maybe I'll browse the antique stores in Spender's Ferry."

"Aunt Maud is an Aries," he said coldly. "And your parents aren't entitled to celebrate more than once a year, just like the rest of us. We sent them something back in March."

"But shopping takes so much time," she said. "Never too early to begin."

"Christ," he muttered. "Tell me something. Do you think any of those people are crazy?" She rolled her eyes

183

and sighed. "All right, not crazy, just demented, psychotic."

"I see. But not crazy. Clarence Bosch is determined to try to keep the project up and running for the duration of his grant. How far would he go to do that? Pretty far. Lois Wharton Wollander is determined to continue her work; she is driven by her need to accomplish good work. How far would she go to get rid of anything in her way? Pretty far. Warren is determined to protect his daughter, his property, and his wife. Same question, same answer. Pretty far. The Zukals are determined to keep that land. And so on. Crazy people? Of course not, but obsessional people, yes."

"You left out a couple," he said after a moment.

"I know. Sebastian. Charlatan, simpleton, or believer? A bit of all, I suspect. Did Jill make him a promise to buy that land and the mill? How far would he go to get it? I think the answer depends on the strength of his faith in what he's doing, and I can't judge. I haven't seen enough of him to have an opinion. Do you think he's a complete charlatan?"

He hesitated, then shook his head. Not really, he had to admit. He wanted to believe in Sebastian as one hundred percent charlatan, but not yet. He had that particular gift, and in Charlie's experience people with it usually came to believe in what they preached, to some extent, anyway. "Jill?"

Constance looked remote. "She's been twisted out of shape by too much hatred. Shelley must have been extremely clever, also twisted out of shape. I think Jill is going through a terrible time. Coming of age shouldn't be this hard, but she's waited a long time to start the process. I wouldn't like to be Warren."

"What about when he tells her the truth about the prenuptial agreement? What will that do to her?"

Constance shrugged. "Probably not what he wants. She may take it as an attempt to whitewash him, and to turn her against her mother, whom she obviously loved. She could become even more furious with him for not telling

184

her years ago, for allowing her to live the lie of her mother's invention. She could simply start running and never stop until she's back in Paris or wherever she lived with her mother. It takes a certain amount of readiness to begin the reconciliation process and I don't think Jill is ready just yet."

Charlie thought about this for a time, and then asked softly, "And what about Tom Hopewell?" It pleased him that she looked surprised.

"You've noticed?"

"Come on," he said. "Think I'm that blind?"

"I don't think he's even aware of it himself."

"Let me have a go at him," Charlie said. "He sees Lois as a brilliant, very attractive woman, exactly as I see her. Well, maybe not *exactly* as I see her, but anyway, as a colleague that he respects and admires, and he thinks that she's wasted on an old man like Wollander."

"I doubt that he's thought through any of that."

"Yet."

"But what could he hope to accomplish by driving the Zukals away?"

"I don't know. Maybe he thinks that Lois could have bought the property and they could have worked on it together."

Constance shook her head. "He's into corn, not trees."

"Right. But two other men who looked at Lois with lust in their hearts are dead, remember. Speaking of lust, let's hit the trail. I have this little proposition I've been meaning to bring up practically all day."

"The game plan," he said the next morning, slowing down in Spender's Ferry, "is that we meet at Al's place. You wait there if you're done first, or I wait. You're sure you want to hike out?"

"It's only two miles or so," she said. "Of course."

"And, honey, watch your step. I think that crazy or not, there's someone hanging around who is sure deadly."

185

"I do, too," she said.

He stopped at a corner and she opened her door, then leaned across the seat and kissed him. "I wouldn't be Lois Wharton Wollander for anything," she murmured, withdrawing. "See you later."

What the devil was that all about, he wondered, as he pulled away, and watched her in the rearview mirror. She waved, smiling softly. And he thought he knew. He began to hum under his breath. And the people she grilled today wouldn't even suspect a fire had been lighted under them.

In the first antique shop Constance compared a milk-glass bowl to a depression-glass vase, and priced a set of iron sconces. She asked a few questions and listened, and asked a few more questions. In the next shop she examined a wicker chair and end table, and listened. And so it went for over an hour. She dropped in at the bank to cash a check and met the sister of Carla Mercer, who was Warren Wollander's secretary. She remarked on the resemblance and listened some more, and moved on. Midway down the street she saw the blond woman who had been at the trailer court; today the woman had on yellow slacks and a yellow tank top. The dark roots of her hair made her look like a sunflower.

Constance nodded to her as they neared one another; the other woman paused, then stopped.

"You were out at the court, weren't you?"

"Oh, that's where we met!" Constance said in apparent relief.

"You're new around here, aren't you?"

"I'm just waiting for my husband. He has some business to take care of and I'm burning up. I was thinking of a nice cool drink. Iced coffee, maybe. Is there a place around here for something like that?"

"Sure. Coffee shop up in the next block."

"Want to keep me company? Have a coffee with me. Charlie said fifteen minutes but he's been hours already. And my feet hurt."

186

"Husbands!" the blond woman said eloquently. "Up this way."

Her name was Ellen Thurmond and her husband was canvassing the county for a national survey company. *He* had said it would be fun for her to come along for the ride, but then he parked her in the trailer court and took off every morning. *Husbands!*

It was cool and dim in the coffee shop. They sat in a booth and Constance sighed. "This feels good. That looked like a pretty nice trailer court, I thought. And that Petey! He's something else, isn't he?"

"But what? That's the question. It's a good thing your husband got there yesterday. Would have been too late by now, I guess. That Earl, he's something else, too. Flits back and forth to New York like a commuter flight or something."

"I never got to know him, but Charlie seems to think he's pretty weird."

"Weird! That's putting it mildly. A nut is more like it. Your husband a process server?"

Constance looked around, then said conspiratorially. "Something like that, why?"

"Thought so. It figures. See, Earl comes to the court and he's there alone, without a car, and I'm there all day alone without a car, and I think, well he's someone to talk to, at least. Can't talk to Petey. All he wants to talk about is Petey. So I go over to Earl's place and look in, and the place is a mess. I mean a real mess. And there's all these computer printouts everywhere. And he acts like it's national security time suddenly." She fell silent as the waitress brought their coffee. Then she leaned forward and said in a harsh whisper, "I think he's one of those hackers who breaks into the big computer systems and does them dirt or something." She sat back, satisfied with herself, and began to sip her coffee.

"Oh dear," Constance said. "I wonder if Charlie suspects anything like that. Go on."

187

"Well, the way he goes back and forth into New York City, I mean, why doesn't he just stay there if it's that important? Anyway, this morning a guy comes and says he's Earl's buddy and he's supposed to pick up his stuff for him. He has a letter from Earl and some extra rent money for the inconvenience. He says he wants to keep renting the place for another couple of months, and even pay extra just to hold it, in case Earl decides to come back and finish his work. And he even signs the register for Earl." She glanced swiftly about the coffee shop, exactly as Constance had done, as if checking for eavesdroppers, and then added, "But he spelled the name wrong. Earl Marker. That's how he signed it."

"But that's awful! I don't even know his last name. What is it?"

"I don't remember. But not Marker. Maxwell, something like that. But it's Marker now."

"It really sounds as if there's something funny going on," Constance said with a frown.

"Yeah. Let me tell you. You know how when you want to make a phone call, you put in your money and get the other person, and you talk. Right? Not Earl. He puts in his money and says a word or two, and hangs up. Then in a couple of minutes the phone rings, and he's right there, and this time he talks. We don't even have phones in those dumps. Petey's afraid we're going to run out without paying up, I guess. It's a pay phone out by his apartment. In clear view from my place. I saw him with my own eyes, twice. Like in the movies or something." She finished her coffee. "Anyways, I think he got wind that the process server was closing in or something like that. And he's skipped."

"I guess you're right," Constance said. "But that's how it goes." She listened to Ellen go on for a little while longer, but when it became apparent that nothing of interest would be added, she looked at her watch and then asked, "Would you like more coffee?"

"No, thanks. I've got to get over the store before it gets much hotter. It's a long walk home. And *he'll* come in wanting supper on the table like always. I tell him it's a long walk, but he's out in the air-conditioned car all day, what does he care about that?"

A few minutes later they stood on the sidewalk and Constance waited to see in which direction Ellen was headed, and then walked the opposite way. She dropped in at the drugstore, and looked over the racks of magazines and books, then chatted with the pharmacist while she mulled over the numbers on the sunscreen lotions and finally chose a number twenty. He approved. Skin as fair as hers needed protecting, he said. Finally she decided she was ready to start the long walk to Al and Sylvie's house. She felt her morning had been well used.

She wished she had paused to make some notes, but that would have been too conspicuous; now, since she hadn't done that, she began to review the facts. Just the facts, Ma'am, she told herself, rubbing sunscreen on her nose as she walked, sometimes in the sunlight, then in a shady area. The trailer court was only half a mile from town, not at all the long walk that Ellen had complained about. She passed it. The houses were far apart now, farmhouses mostly. The road was narrow and curvy, bordered by fields of corn, a truck garden, a small apple orchard, and some abandoned cherry trees that were gnarly and beautiful, and alive with birds eating their fill and making a raucous, joyous cacophony.

The experimental farm started, fields of corn that were planted in blocks, not like the uninterrupted fields of commercial farmers. Although from the car the farm looked like the others, on foot it was easy enough to tell the difference; there were many labels here, rope dividers, and interplanted with the corn were other crops—a block of amaranth with furry, red flowers already; squash vines sprawled; blocks of what looked vaguely like bush beans. . . .

189

When she reached the entrance to the farm, she turned in. She walked around the admin building, nodded to workers here and there, and kept walking toward the quonset hut where Lois worked. When she drew near the second greenhouse, a plump young woman in shorts came out carrying a clipboard. She looked as if she had fallen asleep in the sun. Her nose was bright red; her cheeks, her forearms, and thighs all glowed.

"You looking for Dr. Wharton?" she asked.

"Yes."

"In there," she said, pointing to the greenhouse she had just left. She hurried on to the next one and went inside.

"Thanks," Constance said after her, and stood in the open doorway peering in. Toward the far end she could see Lois Wharton and another young woman. Lois was watching this woman do something with an instrument that from here looked like a complicated hybrid of thermometer and syringe.

"Hi," Constance called.

Lois looked up, spoke to the other woman, and came toward Constance. She looked haggard, in jeans and a tank top and sneakers, her face moist, her hair stuck to her forehead here and there. There was a smudge of dirt on one cheek.

"It all comes back to me," Constance said with a smile when Lois got near. "The reason I chose psychology instead of one of the hard sciences. Actually there are several reasons, I'm sure. I never could remember to keep both eyes open when I used a microscope, for instance. I always felt that if they wanted you to use both eyes, there should be two eyepieces."

"Mostly there are these days," Lois said. She was smiling slightly now. "When your husband introduced you, he said Leidl, but I didn't make any connection with the name, I'm afraid. One of the grad students is awed, though. He's studied some of your work, he says. I'm not very good with people, associating names, remembering things that are important to others." There was hardly a hint of apology in her tone even now when it was clear that she intended to be apologizing.

"That's a strange relationship, isn't it?" Constance said. "Student and teacher, I mean. I've had students act as if they really believed I was born with a Ph.D. They sometimes seem to want to deny that we put in the hours, did the classwork, were disciples of teachers who were as difficult taskmasters as the ones they face in us. TA's, waiting for the acceptance notification, summer workshops, never quite enough money, the orals, they seem to think we skipped all that. Especially the women students," she added. Neither of them mentioned Jill.

Lois was nodding emphatically. If she noticed that Constance had started them strolling toward the trees that screened this part of the farm from the opposite side of the lake, she gave no indication. "What I was always so terrible with was the politics in academia," Lois said, her gaze on the ground before her. "Somehow I kept forgetting that everything ended up being political, no matter where or how it got started. I still do. I guess, coming out of psychology, you were better at that part."

Constance laughed with a touch of bitterness. "What I seemed to be good at in those days was butting my head against walls. Idealistic and all that."

Lois glanced at her with understanding. "Me, too."

They had reached the trees where the shade and the breeze coming off the lake were both welcome. Constance lifted her face and breathed in deeply. "I was pretty hot," she said. Before Lois could respond, she went on, "I was thinking of you last night, the patience it must take to work with trees. I had a friend once who was going through a difficult time with a physical problem that was quite undecided. She planted half a dozen trees on their property during the period when she was stewing over the outcome of tests. I thought it was an act of supreme faith. The trees are very lovely now."

"And your friend?"

"She succumbed after five or six years but she nourished the trees to the end. She said they were her legacy. A butternut for the squirrels; a red twig dogwood for beauty in winter and for the birds; a noble fir for protection of wild things when the weather was brutal; a sugar maple. . . . Each one was chosen for a particular purpose. It was, I think, a great act of love, to leave this legacy."

For a time they were both silent as they gazed at the lake that was such an unnatural, sapphire blue. The wind played on the surface in random patterns. It riffled a section that smoothed out again, then another, and another.

Suddenly Lois sat on the ground and hugged her knees tightly. Constance sat down near her. They both kept watching the unending patterns rise and fade on the surface of the blue water.

When Lois spoke again, Constance was taken aback by the harshness of her voice. "It isn't patience," she said, "it's desperation. So few people understand the situation we're in, how fast it could become critical. Tom Hopewell, Clarence, a few others. Earl knew at one time. You build a generating plant back in the Midwest, Gary, Indiana, or Chicago, somewhere, and the vapors rise and years later come down as poison, rains so acidic that lakes die, trees die, plants twist and writhe in their own brand of agony. Fish, frogs, aquatic plants, algae, all gone. And the lake looks like a reflection of heaven. Isn't that ironic, that it should be so beautiful and so deadly?"

"But can't it be countered?"

Lois continued to stare at the lake stirring in the soft breeze. In her mind's eye she saw the ghost trees, saw the figure rising from the waters, David's blind eyes wide open. . . . She shuddered. "A seedling puts down a deep tap root," she said, almost as if lecturing. "A zone of undifferentiated cells forms where the rootlet and soil merge, and then the acid releases the aluminum in the soil and that means the tree is doomed. The tree no longer absorbs the potassium it needs, the calcium, magnesium, manganese, whatever nutrients it relied on before; aluminum replaces them or seals the cells that would take them in. Desperately the tree puts out surface roots and they take up the nitrates that also rain down from the heavens. In this form, in this amount, more poison. Or else drought comes along and the shallow roots wither. Our need for electricity, heat, light, our need for crops, fertilizers, they doom the forests. Can we undo it? No one knows. No one."

The breeze that had felt so welcome only moments ago now was chilling; the lake that had been so incredibly beautiful now seemed a mockery. Constance hugged her arms about her. "Why are you telling me this now?"

"You said patience. But that's not it," Lois said, following her own line of thoughts, paying little attention to Constance. "Patience is benign, maybe even saintly. Sebastian has patience. People with too much patience are dangerous. They're the ones the world listens to, wants to hear, wants to follow. Not us, the doomsayers. Do you have any idea what kind of hours we're putting in here at the farm? Clarence, Tom, I? We're not driven by patience!"

"Yet you were willing to drop your work and come chat with me," Constance said. "Why?"

Lois pressed her forehead hard against her knees. Her voice became muffled and thick. "You, your husband, you have to leave all this alone. It's over with. The sheriff's satisfied, everyone else is. I have to get back to my work. We all do, yet as long as you're still asking questions, saying it's still open, no one can."

"Why do you drive to the farm now? I thought you enjoyed the walk?"

Lois looked up then and said sharply, "It's late when I stop work, too late to walk home. I'm too tired."

"Or afraid to walk through the woods in the dark suddenly?"

"That's absurd."

"I think it's very sensible not to be alone in the dark around here," Constance murmured.

Lois took a deep breath, started to say something, and turned to look at the poisoned lake instead. Very quietly she said, "There's nothing in this for your husband. Warren paid him; he won't stop payment or anything. Just leave, let us all get on with the work we have to do."

"Your husband thinks he can delete Earl Malik from living memory?" Constance asked.

"Last night," Lois said, speaking to the wind, the water, the air, "Warren and I talked a long time. There's something he has to do, something very important to him that he must do. He had a heart attack a few years ago, before we were married. Coming that close made him reexamine his life, everything he's ever done, and he realized that the most important thing is . . . what he has to do now. Anyway, we have to get all this . . . this trouble behind us so we can both get on with these other things. We simply have to." Her words rushed out suddenly, and she was almost whispering. "He knows how to manage things, make things work out. He always has known how to do that. For him there's no mystery to politics, how to make people do what he wants them to do. It will be weeks before Jill can touch Stanley's money, but he will lend her some so that she can go back to Paris where she wants to live. She has friends there. That poor girl never was here long enough to make any real friends, always back and forth, back and forth. He told me last night that she never quite finished high school. She went to a private school in France, and another one in Switzerland, another one in England, but altogether she never actually graduated, never went on to college. That explains her outburst about me, her jealousy of my work. She never had a chance."

"And Charlie's warning last night, that an identification will be made eventually? What about that?"

"You don't understand!" Lois said, her voice rising. "Warren can manage all that. He can manage Charlie, too,

194

if he has to. I believe him. He's always been able to manage things. Except for Shelley. How shrewd she must have been to get that agreement signed early. She understood him thoroughly. She used to taunt him about inheriting the land here, about selling it piecemeal, plowing up the lawn to put in tract houses or something. She was a devil! She taunted him about Jill, how the line had run out, how there'd be no heirs to keep the property in the family. She made him believe Jill could never bear a child, that the land would go to strangers and be destroyed. I knew how important it was to him, to leave the property to his own blood. I even stopped taking birth-control pills last year, thinking that maybe I would be the one to provide the heir." She laughed bitterly. "I was so convinced of the rightness of providing him with a child that I actually lost the pills, misplaced them beyond finding again. Is that a Freudian slip or something?" She put her forehead on her arms again. Her words became nearly inaudible. "I know the order of things now. I guess I always did but I let myself pretend to be stupid. His daughter, his grandchild, his land, and then me. That's the order of things. And it's all right. Jill is young enough. She'll marry again and present him with grandchildren. I have my work. He has his memoirs to complete. And we have to get on with it. We have to!" When she raised her face, it was tear-streaked. She ignored the tears that were still flowing. "We'll do it Warren's way. He'll take care of everything. Father knows best and all of that."

Constance regarded her for several seconds, then turned to look at the lake again. "When did *your* father die?" she asked. "You loved him very much, didn't you?"

Lois scrambled to her feet. "What do you mean?"

"Oh, you married your mentor years ago, and you let him take you into dangerous if not illegal waters. Although he finally betrayed you, when he turned up again, you paid him handsomely, out of pity, out of remorse, out of fear. Only you know why. And now you are willing to let an-

195

other father figure plan your future for you, take you into dangerous waters, perhaps betray you. And this time, through enough love, enough patience, enough forgiveness perhaps you can atone. Children feel such guilt, such betrayal when parents die prematurely that occasionally they spend a lifetime trying to rewrite that particular past. It never works, you know. Actually, it's one of the most egotistical fantasies of childhood, that you as a child could bring about the death of your parent through wishing. The more sinned against you feel, the more forgiveness you must offer."

Constance had been gazing at the blue lake, but now glanced at Lois, who stood rigidly before her as if paralyzed. "You and I both know that Clarence Bosch is well aware of your past. As director of this project he would have been informed. That's how the system works, and we know it. He values your work and your honesty or you wouldn't be here, and you know that, too. He'll keep you until the grant runs out, unless you are arrested. He has nothing to lose by it—not at his age, with retirement coming. And he has much to gain through your work." She shrugged slightly, stood up, and began to brush traces of leaf mold from her slacks. "No, you're not going along with this just for yourself and your work. But why? To protect your husband? I wonder why you think he needs your protection. A deep-seated psychological need of your own, or a concern of greater immediacy?"

Lois turned ashen and swayed. She held onto a tree for a moment, then pushed herself off and ran staggeringly. She bumped into another tree a second later, steadied herself, and continued to run toward the quonset hut. Constance watched.

When Lois was out of sight, Constance started up the path that led to the Zukal house. She was startled when Charlie stepped out from behind a tree and held out his hands to her. Wordlessly he drew her close and held her, stroking her back.

When she pulled away after several minutes, she studied his face. "You were watching?"

"For a while. I got here first and decided to walk around the farm a bit. I didn't want to interrupt you. Are you okay?"

"Fine," she said wryly. "Doctor's fine, patient is a mess." They started to walk together, his arm around her shoulders, and she told him what Lois had said, that Warren would arrange things. "Manage things, is how she put it," Constance said. "Including you. He could be a very difficult enemy, Charlie. He has a lot of power around here."

Charlie tightened his grasp of her shoulders and did not reply.

CHAPTER 15

When they were within sight of the mill, Charlie stopped and said, "Anything interesting in town?" He was watching men stack lumber torn down from the interior of the mill; the little rooms were all gone now to make way for the large work space Bobby would need. Next week, he thought distantly, Bobby and Flora and their two children were due to move out from the city.

"It's a fascinating little village," Constance said. "I think if a grasshopper sneezed in that town word would be out to everyone within ten minutes. And anything to do with the Wollanders or the farm is prime news, of course. And the people who work out here for the most part either live in town or have relatives who do. Every sneeze is reported."

"So tell me," he said in a growly sort of way.

"I am," she said in her equable sort of way. "First, Clarence Bosch didn't drive to his daughter's wedding the weekend that David died, after all. His wife drove over to Long Island on Monday of that week and he flew out of

Albany at noon on Saturday. They drove home together, arrived Sunday night late."

Charlie grunted. "What on earth made you go after that tidbit?"

"Curiosity. Usually the wedding is in the hometown of the bride. I just wondered why not this time. It's because the groom is in the navy and had a very short shore leave, and his parents live on Long Island and could swing the affair, and he had to report for duty again on Sunday at noon. They all decided that on the whole it could be managed better without extra traveling for the bride and groom. And Clarence Bosch didn't have to leave home until after ten-thirty on Saturday to make his flight."

"Check. Next."

She told him about Ellen from the trailer court, and about someone's cleaning out Earl Malik's possessions. This time he cursed softly.

"That's Warren Wollander's doing. He's managing things, the bastard. Go on."

"Warren's secretary's sister is a teller in the bank where Lois banks." She said this rather flatly, not liking the implications. "Everyone in town could have known that she was withdrawing large sums of money. On the other hand, Jill has charge accounts everywhere and Stanley wrote the checks. He was very generous, they say. She lost a rather expensive gold bracelet a few weeks ago and he just bought her a new one. And you never know where you're going to see her flashing past in that little *foreign* car of hers."

He chuckled as her voice took on the tones of disapproval she had registered when listening to the townspeople. She was a good mimic.

"And the mill was a regular den for years and years, but recently it's been quiet, for the last ten years anyway. It's because those kids don't have to sneak around to do things now the way they used to. They just live together openly and don't care who knows it." Again she was mimicking

199

one of the people she had talked to that morning. It didn't matter which one, Charlie knew; if he ever talked to that person, he would recognize that voice instantly.

Constance gave him a complete summary of her talk with Lois and they were both silent after this for several moments.

"You know," he said at last, "the case I made for her being It could even work. She certainly had reason to kill Malik."

"And David?"

"He could have tumbled to the fact that her ex was hanging out, that she was seeing him."

"And Sadie? And the campaign against the Zukals? I believe Clarence Bosch, that this little parcel of ground would be meaningless for the work she does."

"Yeah," he said. "I know. But maybe Malik knew more than she told us about the setup here, the bees and all. Maybe he actually did it the way Greg thinks he did, and then she had to kill him, to keep him from striking again."

"Good heavens!" she cried. "What for? Malik, I mean?"

"David because he caught on to his being here. Sadie because he hated dogs. The bees because he wanted to worry Warren to death so Lois would inherit the plantation and he could step in and run it."

Gravely Constance nodded. "And then Lois told him about her prenuptial agreement, that she won't inherit, after all, and he hit himself in the head, turned on the gas, lay down and died out of remorse. I'd buy that."

Charlie scowled. "What else did you hear?"

She told him a few more things she had heard in town, mostly confirming what they both had already known. Wollander had this county in his pocket; it was hinted that he owned the sheriff, that he was the one who had made Greg Dolman stop operating a speed trap years ago, but that he had allowed it to go on until Greg had made a killing first.

"Your turn," Constance said finally.

"Not as much as you turned up," he said. "An anonymous phone call to the zoning commission started the whole investigation from that department. Everything's in apple-pie order. No one knows if it was a male or female who called. Period. And no one even looked at this place for the past four years until the Zukals showed up. There was a little interest earlier, but nothing serious."

"That reminds me," Constance said. "Apparently Sebastian has at least half a dozen rather wealthy patrons showing him real estate all over the county."

Charlie grimaced. "And one of them will buy a place for him, want to bet?"

"No way. You know very well that I never bet."

He laughed outright and took her hand. "Let's pay our respects to the Zukals and be on our way."

"You're not going to Wollander's house?"

"Nope. If what Lois said is right, there's no point. Let him stew about it. Next time we talk, let him come to me."

Sylvie had one of her green kerchiefs tied on her red hair. She had on baggy pants and an orange-and-blue plaid shirt with the shirttails out. She was standing with her fists on her hips, glaring at Al on the porch, when Charlie and Constance reached the house.

"Charlie, tell him what they do when you shoot a deer out of season. Just tell Mr. Thick Skull, will you?"

"Dear God," Constance breathed. "Did you buy a gun, Al?"

"What's this, a third degree, all of a sudden? I ain't got a right to have a gun?"

"Did the deer keep you up all night?" Constance asked him.

Al gave her a suspicious look. "Yeah. Lights go on, lights go off, on, off, all night. And you look out and it's like they're getting ready for Christmas or something, getting ready for the long ride." He looked at Sylvie with a scowl. "I told you, I ain't going to shoot *at* them, just shoot and make a noise, scare the bejaysus out of them so they'll

201

go have a meeting somewheres else. What's the crime? A man can't shoot a gun?"

"All night," Sylvie said. "You wouldn't believe it. All night. The lights go on and you look out and it's this monster with horns like this." She spread her arms wide. "Just looking back at you. Red eyes. Like the devil in the movies, you know what I mean? Real red eyes. And just standing looking back. Like they own the world or something." She frowned in puzzlement. "I thought deers was supposed to be scared of people."

While Constance talked to Sylvie about deer and the hypnotizing effects of light, Charlie went with Al to inspect the gun, which turned out to be a twelve-gauge shotgun. He gave Al the name and address of an expert who would teach him to load it and how to shoot it, and extracted a promise that Al would not even try until he had instruction.

"Well," Constance said in the car, driving home again. "If he does try to shoot that thing, it will buck and he'll think he's broken his shoulder. A shotgun!" She glanced over at Charlie who was scowling at nothing in particular. "Don't you have any ideas? This is giving me the willies."

His scowl deepened and he didn't even bother to answer.

In his dream Charlie was hiding bitter pills in bleu cheese and feeding them to Brutus, who gulped them down as fast as Charlie could prepare them. He woke up enough to hear rain and reluctantly got up to take care of the windows. He closed the bedroom door without a sound and dodged all three cats as he made his way through the house, checking windows. The cats always became manic if anyone got up at night or if anything unusual took place before breakfast. Ashcan wove in and out between his feet, and Brutus sniffed his ankles, his knees, and swatted Candy, and made a nuisance of himself. Then Candy and Ashcan raced after each other, and Brutus ambushed them both at the door to the dining room, and all of them wanted to go outside. If he was up, they forgot about their own swinging door that he had installed to end the doorman's job he had inherited somewhere along the line. Doorman to a bunch of dumb cats, was how he had put it then, and he repeated the phrase now as he stood with the door open, and they sniffed the air suspiciously, and then cursed him for making it rain.

He poured himself a bit of bourbon, added water, and went to the refrigerator for a piece of cheese, and Brutus was back inside at his feet magically, watching for a dropped crumb. He could move faster than thought if cheese fell, and he could hear the refrigerator door from anywhere in the yard, especially in the middle of the night. He could hear the can opener from the next county, Charlie thought sourly, dancing around the cat. Cues, Constance had said. He had learned all those cues and they were indelible in his brain, new synapses had been formed, and probably never would be erased again. At least, not without extensive countertraining.

Charlie sat at the table and found that he was no longer thinking of the insatiable cat, but of Sadie, who also had learned cues. The trainer had transferred the cue to Sylvie, he was thinking. A word, maybe, or something in the introduction that let the dog know it was all right to take food from her new mistress. And in turn Sylvie could transfer a cue to Al. He remembered what she had said, they both had to handle the dish and food for a few days, and then Al could do it alone. Scent, Charlie decided. That cue was scent. Sylvie's scent had to be on the dish while the dog was learning to accept Al, too.

He nodded to himself. The rain stopped and the sky was lightening, not in a proper dawn because there was still too much overcast; he realized he did not really want the bourbon. He got up to make coffee instead. A moment later he caught a flash of movement as Brutus jumped on his chair and snapped up the pieces of cheese Charlie had left on the table. The cat streaked away as Charlie watched in resignation.

A little after seven Constance stood in the doorway as Charlie moved about the kitchen muttering. Muttering in their house could mean either that the person speaking needed reminding that what was being said was unintelligible, and at those times it was okay to interrupt, to join in, to ask questions. The other muttering was different: it was not to be interrupted. Muttering at seven in the morning, alone in the kitchen, was definitely the other kind. He was making pancakes, his voice a soft rumble; the aroma of coffee was rich and irresistible. She entered the kitchen without a sound, and he looked at her with an almost blank expression and said, "But why?"

"I give. Why? What why?"

"I think I know how someone got rid of Sadie, but Jesus, why? What was the point?" He glanced at the clock on the stove. At seven-thirty he would call Brenda Ryan, and it was taking hours for the time to creep to that number. Several hours had passed since the last time he looked at the clock, two minutes ago.

Constance blinked, and he grinned at her. "I'll bring coffee, you sit." He poured a cup for her and brought it to the table where she was yawning. "I'll pretend you're awake. Ready?"

"In a second." She drank some of the coffee first, then nodded.

At nine-thirty they drove up to the Ryan Kennels. The sun had broken through the clouds and the morning was brilliant and pleasantly cool, fresh-smelling, sparkling with water droplets everywhere. The trembling drops looked as pure, sweet and life-giving as they were meant to be.

Brenda Ryan was waiting for them. This morning she was wearing a bright-pink-and-white print dress, and pink earrings that looked like bracelets. Three hundred eighty pounds, Charlie thought, shaking her hand, no matter what she had told Sylvie. She had a very firm grip. A large black Labrador retriever was at her side. Brenda's fingers brushed the dog's head, and it began to wag its tail languidly, as if out of duty rather than interest.

"This is Duchess," Brenda said. "And if you can get her to eat, I better go into another line of work."

"You held back part of her food this morning, so she'll have an appetite?" Charlie asked, suddenly not quite as certain as he had been only moments ago. He was carrying a shopping bag.

"Sure did, but it wouldn't make any difference. I mean, most dogs will eat whenever food's available, hungry or not, unless they're really overfed. And I don't overfeed my dogs."

For a moment she looked as if she dared him to comment on that, but he pretended no automatic comment had come to mind, and he and Constance moved into the office, which instantly became very crowded.

Brenda watched as he began to rummage in the bag. First he pulled out a plastic-wrapped package of latex gloves. He pulled on the thin rubber gloves without a word and felt inside the bag again. This time he took out a package that held a scarf. He handed it to her unopened.

"Would you mind taking out the scarf and tying it on your head a couple of minutes?"

She hesitated, watching him through narrowed eyes, then shrugged, sending her patterned dress into a flurry of motion. Her hair was bouffant, curled, sprayed, dyed, with smells Duchess would recognize instantly, Charlie thought, hoped. He watched her put the scarf over her hair and tie it loosely. Next he took out a can of dog food, and finally a can opener.

He held up the can for her inspection. "Gourmet dog food," he said, unnecessarily; she was already nodding at it. "Just tell me this," he said, opening the can. "Is there anything in particular that you do or say when you feed her?"

"Nope. She's trained to stand back and wait, and then

eat. Don't have to do anything more than put it down for her."

"Good. I was afraid there might be something else." The top came off, stuck to the magnetized opener. He put it on the desk. "If it's going to work, that's probably time enough for the scarf," he said. "Let's finish. I'll take it now."

His uncertainty was increasing by the second. Duchess had not shown so much as a flicker of interest at the sound of the can opener, or the malodorous contents of the can. Brutus would be climbing his head by now, Charlie thought gloomily. Brenda handed him the scarf and he spread it out on the desk and began to spoon dog food onto it. He put a few spoonfuls down and cast a doubtful look at the beast who sat there looking as inscrutable as a damn Buddha. Sighing, he wrapped the food enough to move it, and lowered it to the floor, and stepped away from it.

"Now, I guess we just wait," he said. "You didn't give her a signal to sit still or anything, did you?"

Brenda was looking very interested now. She shook her head. "She's waiting to see if I'm going to give her a signal. See her look at me?"

Charlie didn't see the dog move a muscle.

"If this works," Brenda said soberly, "I'll have to change my methods, take it into account." She became silent now as Duchess began to shift.

The dog stood up, still apparently waiting for a sign, and when none was forthcoming, she ambled over to the food on the scarf and sniffed it with interest, then sniffed all around it, and back to the scarf again. Then she gulped it down in two bites. She licked her chops and sat down again.

"Goddamn it!" Brenda muttered. "I never thought of that. Of course, you'd have to have an in, get something that belonged to the owner, but even so, it's gotta be trained out. Goddamn it!"

Charlie looked at Constance who was smiling, more at

his relief than at his victory. "So now we know how," she said. "But why?"

She drove back. He talked.

"We made such a fundamental mistake," he said. "The dish was found at the mill and we assumed that food had been put in it over there. Let's rethink the whole thing. Someone doctored the dog food and put it at the edge of the property. Sadie wouldn't have barked unless someone actually stepped over the line, and that wasn't necessary, after all. Just reach in and lay down the scarf with the food on it, then stand back and wait. You saw how that mutt wolfed down the food. Two bites and done. Then the poisoner reached in and grabbed the scarf back and was finished. David found the scarf and returned it to Sylvie. I'd guess he didn't realize until later what it meant. There could have been traces of the food on it as well as grease, or he could have seen someone with it earlier. He saw something, that's for sure. So he was next."

He became silent, brooding about it. Finally Constance said, "Charlie, it doesn't make much sense, does it?"

"Why not?"

"Well, killing David because of the dog poisoning, and then killing Earl Malik because of the bees. It just doesn't make sense. Neither of those things, killing a dog, or moving bees to the station wagon was a capital offense; a reprimand, a fine, that's all either warranted. Murder to prevent discovery is just too much. In each case the response to being found out was too great. It keeps getting muddled in my head. I mean, it seems to be what happened, but it's so senseless."

She was a good driver; when she needed to pay close attention she focused on the road and other traffic, then her thoughts were tightly contained. After the road was clear again, the other thoughts took precedence. It was an automatic process that she didn't question. Now traffic

207

thickened a little and she passed a Grand Union truck, and a Honda, and a few minutes later she glanced at Charlie and started to speak. He was slouched in the passenger seat, his chin tucked in, a scowl on his face.

She held the words and looked straight ahead again. Beside her, Charlie stirred, and the words were in his head just as if they had been uttered. He grunted again, considering. They had made a second, more serious fundamental mistake.

Warren Wollander was going over the several days' stack of accumulated mail with his secretary, Carla Mercer. Pleas for money; would he put in an appearance at a dinner for Representative Lorenzo; two committee meetings were coming up, an agenda was needed . . . a policy meeting in Washington. . . . Tiredly he rubbed his eyes when the phone rang. He motioned for her to take it, and he leaned back in his chair with his eyes closed.

"I'll ask," she said. "It's Richard at the gate. He says Sebastian is out there and is asking permission to come in."

With a jerk Warren sat upright. "Let him come in. And you can get started on that stuff. We'll continue this afternoon with the rest of it."

She spoke softly into the phone and hung up. She gathered up papers, checked around the desk, and left for her own office down the wide corridor, toward the rear of the house. Warren went to the window to watch for Sebastian.

Sebastian's car, a powder-blue Cadillac, came into sight at the exact spot where someone had vanished the night Jill had announced her pregnancy. He rubbed his eyes again, harder this time, as if to erase the memory that was filled with pain, and he walked through the study, through the hallway to the main house entrance, and admitted Sebastian before he had a chance to ring the bell.

"I would like to see Mrs. Ferris," Sebastian said.

"Come in. This way." Warren pushed the door shut and

started back to the study. When Sebastian hesitated, he motioned with his hand. "Come along."

At the study, he waited until Sebastian was inside, and then closed that door and stood at it. "Sit down, if you'd like. This won't take long, but you may as well be comfortable."

"Mr. Wollander, I have no wish to take up your time. I really would like to see Jill." He remained standing in the middle of the room.

"I know. I'll call her in a minute." He studied Sebastian for another moment, then started walking slowly toward his desk. When he spoke again, his voice was machinelike, completely expressionless, as if he were reading from cue cards. "Sebastian Pitkin. Boy evangelist. Petty thief. Trick knee that keeps you out of the army but permits you to sit in lotus. Married twice, divorced twice. One son, sixteen years old now. Expensive tastes and the ability to indulge them without any taxable income. Out of the country for seven years, never accounted for."

Not a flicker of expression crossed Sebastian's face. He listened almost gravely, as if checking off the items against a list in his mind. When Warren stopped, Sebastian said, "I would like to see Jill, if you please."

"Of course." Warren had come to a stop at his desk. He moved around it and reached for the phone and paused once more with his hand on it. "I have very little influence outside this state, but for various reasons a good deal inside it. Did you know that many IRS investigations arise from information gathered first at the state level?" He picked up the phone and touched a button. The wait was brief. "Jill, Sebastian is here, in my study. Will you come down, please?"

Sebastian's expression continued imperturbable. Warren sat down and leaned back in his chair and neither said anything more until Jill entered.

"I came to see how you are," Sebastian said, studying her face intently. "I was concerned about you."

"Well, as you see, I'm fine. In mourning, but okay."

"Are you doing your meditations? Are they helping?"

She shrugged. "Not really. That served its purpose, and I appreciate all you did for me, but I think I'm through with that now."

"Jill, you are the best student I've ever had. You have enormous promise. Don't let it slip away because of this tragedy. Let this experience strengthen you; find its meaning and grow from it."

"See it as opportunity?" she said bitterly. "Look, Sebastian, for a time I believed I could follow your path, but no longer. I'm sorry."

"I have the name of a camp, up in the hills about an hour's drive, they tell me. It's a private camp that has come on the market. Go there with me, Jill. A ride up into the hills, a walk under the trees. We won't even have to talk if you prefer silence during this healing period. Silence brings its own power to heal the soul if you let it. And, yes, see it as opportunity to learn, to grow, to contemplate the absolute in a way that has never been available to you before, because you were not prepared before to face it."

She was moving restlessly about the room. She looked irritable and impatient when she took a breath and said, "Leave me alone, Sebastian. I wish everyone would just leave me the hell alone."

"I know he had me investigated, and that he told you things that he learned, but, Jill, I already talked about those things in our group meetings. Think back. You know I already talked about those things. Each one, every mistake filled with pain and regret became an opportunity to grow. And we grow or we cease to exist. We all have things in our pasts that are better left behind. We talked about that, too, Jill. Remember?"

She whirled around to face him. "What are you saying?"

"Only the truth."

"Well, listen to me, Sebastian! I don't have anything in my past that can hurt me now. Nothing! And I have no intention of helping you finance a school, or a church, or a camp, or even a barbecue! Now leave me alone!" She ran from the room and slammed the door after her.

"You'd better go," Warren said in a flat voice.

Sebastian looked at him, then looked past him out the window. "There is an image in my mind," he said softly, "of a puppet master whose fingers drip venom that runs down the wires that control the puppets, and the puppets absorb the poison, more and more until they are sickened and die of it."

He turned and walked from the room. Warren swiveled in his chair to watch out the window until the blue Cadillac curved around the birch trees and disappeared. He felt chilled and there was a tightness in his chest that he hadn't felt since his heart attack five years ago. His hands were clenching the arms of his chair so hard that when he forced them away, they hurt.

Gradually the noises of the house and yard returned. The sound of a riding mower swelled and receded; he could hear the rustle of Mrs. Carlysle in the hall, and a door closing somewhere in the back of the house. Outside, birdsong that had been silenced by Sebastian's departure now resumed. Slowly he arose and walked out through the side hall, out into the yard where the overnight rain had refreshed everything. Two gardeners were at work in the flowerbeds where majestic delphiniums made a deep blue backdrop for golden irises, and masses of pink sweet williams and carnations were intermingled with clouds of baby's breath. The lawn glistened with raindrops in the shade where it had not yet evaporated. So much beauty, he thought. So much beauty. He found himself standing under the oak tree that he thought of as his tree and he touched the bark almost tenderly. He wanted to wrap his arms around it as far as they would reach, press his cheek into the trunk, and weep.

211

CHAPTER 16

When Constance came within sight of their house, she slowed down. A pale-blue Cadillac was in the drive and leaning against it was Sebastian.

"Well, well," Charlie murmured. "Well, well."

She pulled into the driveway and stopped a short distance from the Caddy; Sebastian straightened up. He looked grim and very angry. "Hi," she called pleasantly, getting out of the Volvo; she headed for the front door with her key in her hand.

"I want to talk to you," Sebastian said to Charlie.

"How'd you even find me?" Charlie asked, following Constance.

"Jill said you lived around here somewhere. I asked at a gas station down the road. I said I want to talk to you. Do you mind?"

"Well, of course not. Come on in." He looked at Sebastian with disbelief. "You don't mean out here, do you?"

"It will take just a second."

"In the house," Charlie said firmly and entered without glancing back again.

Constance had gone on through to the sliding door to the patio which she opened, and then continued to the kitchen, moving around cats without paying any attention at all to them. Candy was complaining in a loud voice and Brutus was looking his slitty-eyed meanest. As soon as they saw a stranger, Candy streaked away, back through the cat door to make her escape, and Ashcan pretended he was a rug.

"Well, sit down," Charlie said to Sebastian, motioning toward a chair at the dinette table. "Honey, you going to make coffee, or you want me to?"

"I'm doing it. Or would you rather have tea, Sebastian?"

"Neither one," he said. He did not sit down, but glared at Charlie, who did. "I have a message for you to deliver to your boss, Wollander. Just tell him that if he, or anyone else, harasses me in any way, I have enough information to make life uncomfortable for him, and I'll not keep it to myself."

"You mean about that woman? What's-her-name?" Constance asked from the kitchen end of the long room.

"That's what I mean. I'm sure he would prefer not to have everyone in the county looking at him with raised eyebrows the next time he presides at a committee meeting. Especially the one on ethics in government that he's so fond of."

"Gave you the bum's rush, did he?" Charlie asked with interest. "But Jill's still on your side, isn't she? I mean, she's of age and all."

Abruptly Sebastian pulled out a chair and sat down. He looked uncomfortable, and for a moment Charlie wondered if he should offer him a cushion for the floor instead.

"Jill's completely dominated by him," Sebastian said. "I didn't believe she would fall into that kind of trap again but he's controlling her; she's like a doll that he moves around here and there."

The fragrance of brewing coffee began to float around the room. Constance brought cups and saucers to the table, then cream and sugar. She talked as she moved about, al-

213

most as if absently, "Of course, we can tell him that, but I don't see what difference it would make, do you, Charlie?" Her back was turned when she paused, not really long enough for him to answer. She picked up the carafe and came back to the table with it. "I mean if everyone already knows . . ."

"Well, everyone doesn't know that he had a motive for killing David Levy," Sebastian said harshly. "I can rake that over a few times and see how he likes it."

"Oh, really," Constance murmured, and now she sat down and poured coffee for them all. "Do you take sugar? Cream?"

He looked down at the cup before him in surprise, then back to her. She was smiling easily.

"Why don't you tell us about it?" she said. She looked at Charlie with raised eyebrows and he nodded almost imperceptibly. "You see, Sebastian, we aren't working for Mr. Wollander anymore. He fired us, I'm afraid. But we are working for Mr. Levy; we are investigating the death of David Levy."

Sebastian set his mouth in a tight line. He pushed back his coffee cup and seemed ready to leave.

"The sheriff is convinced that David's death was accidental overdose," Charlie said evenly. "I'm convinced that it was murder. But the sheriff may have the last word. Again, I just don't see why Wollander would give a damn about what you think."

"The sheriff will say what the puppet master tells him to say. Wollander would go to any length necessary to prevent a word of scandal from touching his wife, and David had more than just a word. He had a whole history to talk about. That's motive enough." Now he stood up.

"Sit down," Charlie said sharply. "Are you really so naive that you think you can get away with blackmail, especially with someone as powerful as Wollander?" Sebastian didn't move. Charlie waved toward the chair, the coffee on the table. "You'd better sit down," he said tiredly, "and hear me out. You see, the natural response to your little blackmail threat is to say that you had even more motive. You wanted the property for yourself—"

"I didn't. I told you, Jill didn't have a cent. I wasn't expecting to get that property at any time."

"I know quite well what you told me. Now I tell you things. I said sit down, damn it! I'm getting a crick in my neck."

Sebastian's eyes were bulging more than ever, but he sat down, his face flushed, his hands clenched.

"Use your own method and relax," Charlie muttered. "My God, you'd think I had a gun to your head. Relax, damn it. See, this is how Wollander could play it. David sees you and Jill together, maybe he even hears her telling you there's nothing she won't give you if you can help her get pregnant. And that means the mill property. Then the Zukals arrive and they have to be driven out again. First the dog, then David." He paused, then looked at Sebastian with a hopeful expression. "By the way, you haven't come across a stray thermos, have you? David was missing one."

"No, I haven't. And you're stringing a line of BS and you know it."

"Oh well," Charlie said blandly, and continued. "Anyway, the Zukals dig in, get their backs up, and another dirty little trick is called for, this time the bees in the station wagon. And this time a transient sees what's happening, and he has to get it, too. But now Jill has inherited a mint, and, no doubt, the Zukals will clear out, and the mill will be up for grabs again, but suddenly Jill's giving you the cold shoulder, telling you to get lost, and you want to retaliate by spreading dirt on the old man. That's how he'll play it, Sebastian. Believe me, I've seen the type many times, and that scenario will hold up. Yes indeed, it would work just fine. If anyone has to leave a tidbit here, another there to clinch it, I'd guess tidbits will be strewn around." He sighed and drank his coffee. "And as you said, the sheriff will buy whatever he has to sell."

215

Sebastian's head began to shake from side to side, as if he had nothing to do with it, was not even aware of it. His lank hair swayed back and forth. His gaze remained fixed on Charlie, who had to turn away because it was too damn eerie, he decided.

"It wasn't like that," Sebastian said finally. "It wasn't. She never even mentioned pregnancy until after Stanley was dead. I had no idea. She never promised me anything for anything. I was in the role of guide to meditation, nothing more than that. And she was a good student. That day at the mill was the only time we were ever alone together for more than a counseling session a few times at the house, where there were always others about. I have witnesses. He can't stick me with anything like that. I have too many witnesses."

"She seems to have found plenty of time to blab to you about the family, about David. Not in front of all those witnesses, I'd bet."

"No. Of course not. We had private counseling sessions. She was very disturbed in the beginning, very. She seemed to derive comfort, serenity even, from our sessions—for a time, at least. She never had anyone to talk to before, not even her mother, certainly not her father or stepmother. She needed to talk to someone and I filled that role for her. She talked a lot about her father, how much she hated him, and the reasons. Good reasons, I can see now, but the emotion of hatred was harming her, truly harming her." He looked very earnest, very sincere. "That emotion, hatred that fierce, does far more damage to the hater than to the one who is hated. I was teaching her that lesson."

Constance got up and took away his coffee, which had become cold. She refilled the cup and brought it back and this time he lifted it and sipped.

"So Wollander found out that David knew something about Lois and might tell it out of turn," Charlie said. "Is that it then? Just that? Will you keep adding more details as needed?"

216

"What more?" Sebastian took a deep breath. "From what Jill has said about her father, that was more than enough, Mr. Meiklejohn."

"Just Charlie," he said, then added with a grin, "Doesn't have quite the same ring as when you say 'Just Sebastian,' but it's the best I can do. And, no, that isn't enough, not even for a man like Wollander. What's the rest of it?"

"Never mind," Sebastian said. "I'll tell him myself."

"I doubt it. You had a chance and blew it. Don't be an ass now. You wanted us to do your dirty work for you. Pass the word that you're talking to people, no matter about what, just talking. He would then go to Jill and ask what you could possibly know that gives you any clout, and she would stew and steam over it, and maybe even come up with an item or two, and then the high and mighty Mr. Wollander would treat you with respect. Or at least leave you alone. But, you see, Sebastian, you're playing in a new league here, a new game, new players, and you don't know the rules they play by. You don't even know the name of the game. It's *Put the Bugger in His Place.*" He stood up lazily and stretched. "I'm afraid, Sebastian, old buddy, that you've been used, and now you're being sent packing. Just the way it goes." He smiled kindly at him. "And you know very well that I won't help you in a blackmail or extortion scheme, now don't you?"

Sebastian glared at him and pushed himself up from the table. "Try this one, then," he said harshly. "Who was the man Lois Wollander was keeping on the side in the trailer court? Does the whole world know about that little affair?" He stalked from the room, with Charlie close behind. Constance began to clear the table.

"I wonder just how much about that he actually knows," she said when Charlie returned, grinning.

"Remember that question we asked about Sebastian back in the beginning?" he said. "I've got my answer. How about you?"

She tilted her head, considering, and then said, "I think

we probably agree. Poor man," she murmured. "He's trying so hard to keep his toe in the door. You really shook his
tree for him, and you offered no comfort at all to soften
it."

"Hah! That's my mission for today, shake trees, see
which nuts come tumbling out. And as for him, he tried to
put the bite on the wrong woman, that's his problem. And
Daddy came to the rescue. I'll give Pete Mitchum a call
now."

Three times Charlie had had to tell Pete, nothing yet,
still working on it. The boy's disappointment had been hard
to take each time. Mr. Levy's disappointment had been
much harder on the two occasions that Charlie had returned calls from him. Soon, he thought, soon.

"Nothing definite yet," Charlie said to Pete when he appeared a few minutes later. "I could use some help,
though."

Pete nodded with enthusiasm. "Whatever I can do, Mr.
Meiklejohn." Although he had been disappointed, his faith
was undiminished.

Constance brought a plate of cookies and a can of soda.
Now and then she made Scandinavian delicacies that her
grandmother had spoiled her and her sisters with, and she
always gave most of them to the Mitchum boys. Too much
butter, too much cholesterol for Charlie, who could stand
to lose a few pounds, she thought, but she didn't nag about
it. Instead, she made the special cookies that he loved and
let him have a few, and gave the rest away. And the reason, she knew, was the way the boy was looking at Charlie
at that moment. Charlie pretended not to notice that the
Mitchum boys had a serious case of hero worship, and he
harrumphed if she hinted at it, but there it was. Fortunately
he had never said anything like give me a hand, will you, or
one of them might well have run for a saw.

"What I want is four or five guys about your size,"
Charlie was saying, opening the map he had found in
Malik's trailer. Pete Mitchum stood five inches taller than

218

Charlie, and his brothers were just as tall and broad. He nodded with a serious expression now that they had got down to business.

"Here's Spender's Ferry, out the county road here to the farm," Charlie said, pointing. "And the mill property. Now, as soon as you cross this bridge, all the land on the left is state forest." He traced the curvy road, and then stopped. "And this is the Wollander driveway, in about ten feet from the fence here. State forest on the other side of the fence." He pulled out a felt-tip pen and drew a wavy line on the map, the boundary, and then drew in the Wollander driveway. "Along about here, I think, is a clump of birch trees that will be your guide. The driveway turns just past the trees and goes on to the house. I want you guys to start at the county road, on the state forest side, and search the woods from the fence on in for about three hundred feet, from the county road on past the birch trees another thirty feet. It's a lot of ground to cover."

"Naw, it's not that much," Pete said. "What are we hunting for, Mr. Meiklejohn?"

Charlie glanced at Constance. "I'm looking for a thermos," he said. "And you might not find anything at all, but I want a good show of a bunch of guys searching. Carry big bags, wear gloves, pick up anything and everything that doesn't belong in the woods, even beer cans. Now, someone will probably come over to see what you're up to, and just tell them you're working for me, and you're searching for a thermos. You might even find a thermos, but I don't want you to fix your mind on that. Chances are you won't find it. If you do find one, don't open it, just chuck it in the bag and keep on searching until you cover the area. Got it?"

"Yes sir!" He looked like a horse at the starting gate.

Charlie thought for a second. "It could be that the sheriff or a deputy will come along and order you to leave. Don't argue. Just tell them you're working for me, and that you're on state land and have a right to be there. Tell them

219

where I am, at the Zukal place, if they want to talk about it. If they insist that you leave, do it. Bring your loot over to the Zukal place. I'll be there."

"What if they try to take the bags away from us?"

"Well, don't let them," Charlie said mildly. "One of the things you'll have to have is a whistle. Use it if they want to steal your loot. I'll come running. But I doubt it will come to that."

Pete looked ecstatic. "They won't get it away from us, Mr. Meiklejohn. Don't worry about that."

"Okay, I won't. Now, about time. It will take you a while to gather your forces, round up the bags, the whistle, gloves. Do you think you can have it all together by four?"

"Yes sir!"

"Good. When you finish, come over to the Zukals' and leave the bags, and you're done."

Charlie watched Pete cross the yard at a run. When he reached the fence this time he didn't bother to climb it; he put one hand on top and vaulted over as easily as a deer.

"One more little chore, and then lunch, and then off to the wilderness to shake a few more trees." He grinned at Constance, who looked up from cutting dense wheat bread. She already had roast beef out, and lettuce, and other good things, he saw with approval.

He dialed the Wollander house. Carla Mercer, Wollander's secretary, answered on the second ring.

"Charlie Meiklejohn," he said. "I'd like to speak with Mrs. Carlysle, please."

There was a pause on the other end, and then she said, just a moment; he nodded in satisfaction when he heard a click on the line. He put his hand over the mouthpiece and silently formed the words: "They're taping it."

He waited almost two minutes before Mrs. Carlysle's tentative voice said hello.

"Mrs. Carlysle, this is Meiklejohn," he said in a brisk voice. "I need some information that I think you can help me with. Would it be convenient if I drop over at about one, or one-thirty?"

"Oh, no, I couldn't. I mean, I'm working. What is it?"

"Not over the phone, please. It won't take more than a minute or two, I assure you. And it has nothing to do with you personally." She made a throat-clearing kind of sound which he ignored. "I don't want to bother the family anymore and I believe you can tell me what I need to know. About one, then. I'll come around to the kitchen." He hung up, and looked over at Constance. "Is it lunch yet?"

At one-twenty-five he and Constance walked from the woods onto the Wollander lawn. Since he had planned to make them wait until almost one-thirty, he was satisfied with his timing. He was humming under his breath.

"I think we have a reception committee," Constance said softly.

"Pretend you don't notice."

Warren Wollander and Lois were on the patio watching them all the way. Warren moved stiffly to the edge of the flagstones as they drew near.

"I want to talk to you," he said.

It sounded to Charlie much more like an order than an invitation. "I have some business with your housekeeper, and then I'll be on my way," he said pleasantly.

"I don't think you have any business with anyone in this house. And I don't want to broadcast what I have to say. Will you come up here, please."

Still not a real invitation, Charlie thought with regret. He shrugged, and he and Constance changed course and headed for the patio. "All I really want to know is who hauls your trash away, and to where," he said, still on the lawn a few feet away. "I thought the housekeeper was the logical one to tell me."

Lois was staring at him in bewilderment. "Why?" She looked as if she had not slept enough for a month, and the

221

effects were ravaging. There were hollows under her eyes and she was very pale.

Warren gave her a sharp look and she sat down abruptly in a chaise. Charlie could imagine the scene that must have taken place a short time ago: Warren in his good, gruff, masculine voice saying, "I'll handle this. You just keep still."

"I'm still on the trail of that missing thermos," Charlie said with a shrug. "The way I figure it, David had to take the pills somehow, and it could be that he dissolved them in lemonade and did it that way. But then, where is the thermos? See? If it turns up in a landfill somewhere with traces of quaalude and barbiturates, then we'll know, won't we?"

"You're still harping on that?" Warren said in disbelief. "My God, everyone else is satisfied that it was an accidental overdose. What I want to tell you, Meiklejohn, is that I am convinced, as is the sheriff, that the culprit was that transient in the apartment. We're both satisfied that nothing more is to be done except get on with life now. I don't want you nosing around here any more. You are no longer in my employ, and if you enter this property again, you will be treated as a common trespasser. Is that clear?"

"Mrs. Wollander," Charlie said, looking past Wollander, "was that thermos you bought a regular, glass-lined one, or stainless steel?"

"Just a regular one, glass lining, I guess." Her voice rose. "Are you going to search the landfill? For a thermos?"

"If it comes to that. First the woods. I thought of the lake, but an empty thermos would float, you see, so I gave that up. I thought that if David took it with him when he swam that morning, he could have left it at the edge of the water, but someone would have spotted it, either there, or floating around." He was pointedly ignoring Warren Wollander, who was livid with fury now. Charlie gazed across the lake. "I'm hiring a few of the workers to put in some overtime, after-hours, to search the farm. Eventually I may have to tackle the landfill."

"There could be a dozen such thermos bottles in the landfill!" Warren Wollander said harshly. "You're wasting your time, and right now you're wasting mine. Get out, Meiklejohn."

"I know there could be others," Charlie said. "And we'll haul every damn one in for laboratory examination. You realize how hard it is to hide something if people make a determined effort to find it? Very hard, Mr. Wollander. Very hard."

Lois had risen, and was gazing at the lake also. Hesitantly she said, "It could be in there. At the bottom. If he didn't put the cap back on, it would fill with water and sink." She looked at her husband. "I think we should call in someone to make a search of the lake. If they find it in there, that will pretty much settle it. Then we'll know."

"I already have someone lined up," Charlie said. "But that's good reasoning. I don't think you leave the cap off myself, because you might lose it, but it's possible. If nothing turns up at the farm, or in the woods, bright and early tomorrow morning you'll see people in the lake. Even if it's in the water, filled with water, there probably will still be traces of the drugs. It doesn't take much to show up in a good lab with good technicians. I have them lined up, too."

"I won't tolerate this," Warren said. "I won't have people here in the lake."

"But the Zukals will," Charlie said easily. "I looked it up in the county records. They have as much right to the lake and what goes on with it as you do. And my people will enter through their property, not yours. Are you going to give me the name of your trash collector, or do I have to do that the hard way, too?"

"Get out of here!" Warren turned and stamped back inside the house. After a moment, Lois followed him.

"She looks dreadful," Constance said in a low voice as they retraced their steps across the lawn.

Charlie shrugged. His face was set in hard lines, his eyes were flinty, like chips of coal. "Let's go see Bosch," he said.

Constance felt chilled. This was how he had become just before they both retired: hard, merciless, finally showing as little sympathy for the victim as for the criminal. The fact that he had become like this was what had made her declare an ultimatum: He had to quit the force, or she would leave him. It came back over him from time to time, that unswerving, unpitying coldness that once had threatened their marriage, threatened everything in her life that she cared about. When he turned into this kind of iceman, the chill extended out from him to enwrap her.

In fact, Charlie was not thinking of Lois at that moment, nor of Constance, either. That order, "Get out of here!" reverberated in his head. All his years on the force, as a fireman, an arson investigator, a city detective, he had been subordinate to men with power just like that, power to decide when to prosecute, when to plea bargain, when to persist, when to call off everything. The power to order, "Get out of here!" and never have to look back to see that they were obeyed. You stay with it long enough, something rubbed off on you, he had come to understand finally. Something that couldn't be washed away. Not as simple as hatred, or contempt, not necessarily corruption. But something rubbed off that lingered, that made you see them all as pieces moving in an insane game—the politicians, prosecutors, judges, cops, those who lashed out and those who were lashed, victimizers, victims, all players in the same hellish game. Each and every one of them willing to do whatever it took to survive the game. Even him, Charlie knew, and the knowledge filled him with icy fury, because he wanted, needed, a world built on sanity and reason and law, and they, the ones who made the game rules, had destroyed it, and had forced him to participate in the destruction. By the time you were smart enough to realize that something had rubbed off, you were a bona fide member of the wrecking crew, and the stain, the something, had penetrated right down to the bone marrow.

With those few words, *Get out of here!* Wollander had established his place in the game, Charlie's place, Lois's, everyone's. Those few words had caused to surface a deeper bitterness than Charlie had experienced for a long time.

He felt Constance take his hand, and then squeeze it hard, and he looked at her with surprise.

"Nothing," she said. "Onward. Let's go shake Clarence Bosch's tree."

Charlie grinned at her, but it was superficial. It did not touch his eyes. His eyes looked like dull chips of stone.

"Look, Dr. Bosch," Charlie said a few minutes later, "I don't give a shit if you like it or not. I want to hire your people. If I can't, then I'll bring in outsiders. I'll get a court order if I have to, but I want the search made today."

They were standing outside the admin building. Bosch was grayer than ever, more troubled than ever. "Do you have any idea of what all this nonsense is doing to us? Do you? We're weeks behind schedule. Weeks! I told you my caretaker here found nothing. Nothing!"

From the corner of his eye Charlie could see Tom Hopewell approaching, not in a big rush, but covering the ground. "Did you get a look at that man in the apartment?"

Bosch shook his head. "No. I looked in the window, but he was just a man on the floor."

"How long have you known about Lois Wharton, who she is?"

Bosch looked startled. He glanced at Tom who was only a dozen yards away, and motioned him not to come closer. In a low voice he said, "I won't have you dragging any of that into this mess, Meiklejohn! That's uncalled for. It has nothing to do with anything here and now. Lois Wharton is a brilliant scientist, doing brilliant work, and that's all I intend to say on that matter."

"Why did you mention that you left town for your daughter's wedding late the morning that David died?"

"Oh, my God, what are you driving at? I didn't conceal it. It simply never came up."

"I bet." Charlie waved to Tom Hopewell to join them. Brusquely he said, "I'm hiring some of your workers here to search this end of the farm when they knock off for the day. Any objections?"

"What the hell for?" Tom Hopewell demanded.

Why didn't he buy some new jeans? Charlie thought irritably. He was tired of these worn-out clothes, worn like a badge of merit, a symbol of his dedication to work, his unawareness of the amenities.

"If David took pills dissolved in lemonade, he might have left his thermos at the edge of the lake, or he might have dropped it on his way back to his apartment. I want a thorough search made of the grass at the lakefront on this side, and through the undergrowth from the lake to the apartment units. Understood?"

Tom Hopewell blinked, and Clarence Bosch raised his eyes beseechingly toward the sky. Bosch said, "You know how much area you're talking about? The whole side of the lake?"

"Absolutely. Do you know precisely where he went in, where he came out? Do you know precisely where he might have sat down to take a drink? Or the exact path he followed back to his place? The whole damn side!" Grimly he added, "If we don't find it today, I'm sending in divers tomorrow to search the whole damn lake bottom!"

"Jesus God," Bosch whispered in despair. "Let's get them started and get it over with. For God's sake!" He looked at Tom Hopewell. "Tell Henry, let them do it now, for God's sake." He reentered the admin building.

Tom Hopewell looked at Charlie, then at Constance bitterly. "This is a damn fucking mess. Come on, meet Henry Tremont."

*　　*　　*

When they returned to the Zukals' house, Al and Sylvie were both yelling at a strange man, who was dressed in olive-drab shirt and trousers. A red slash insignia was on his shirt pocket. "I don't care! I don't want no deers looking me in the eyes all night. You can't fix them lights so no deers set them off, what good are they?" Sylvie was screaming. Al was saying, an octave lower, but more menacingly, "I think youse guys loused it up so we'd buy more of your fancy systems. Systems! Systems to get dough!"

"You're from Frederick's Security?" Charlie asked the man who was very red in the face.

"What's the matter with these people? They nuts or something?"

"Al, I've been thinking about your problem," Charlie said soothingly. "Let me talk to the man, okay? I'm Meiklejohn," he said. "You?"

"Bergman. Carl."

Charlie took his arm and steered him toward the mill.

Al hesitated, started to follow, hesitated again. "Leave them alone!" Sylvie said. "Let Charlie take care of it, like he said. You deaf or something?"

"Sylvie, could I have a drink of water?" Constance asked then.

"Water? Hell, we can do better than that for you," Al said in evident relief that he had an excuse for not following Charlie. "A beer? Vodka? Even coffee. I say a beer would go all right. Come on in."

A few minutes later, when Charlie joined them in the kitchen, Constance was pouring freshly brewed coffee over a tall glass of ice cubes. "And that's all there is to it," she was saying. "Once when I ordered iced coffee the waiter brought me a steaming cup of coffee with a single ice cube melting away in it."

They all looked at Charlie. "Al, Sylvie, I guarantee that no deer will keep you awake tonight," he said. "And, Al, if you have another beer, that sure would go down just right."

227

CHAPTER 17

A few minutes after four Greg Dolman arrived. Charlie watched him leave his sheriff's car and walk toward the Zukal house, stiff with anger. The trouble with Greg, Charlie thought, was that he looked like a bookkeeper, not a lawman. Or even a preacher, he decided; Greg would look at home at the pulpit. Not a fire-and-brimstone type, but the soft-spoken, even mournful type who suffered over the sins of his congregation, and frequently told them so.

Charlie leaned against the porch railing, his arms crossed, a slight smile on his face as he imagined Greg sadly exhorting the sinners to sin no more. "Afternoon," he said.

"What the hell are you up to?"

"Just leaning against a porch rail, taking life easy."

"You're messing with the wrong people, Meiklejohn. I told you—"

"Is that the sheriff?" Sylvie yelled from inside the house. She, Al, and Constance trailed out to the porch. "I want to know what's the good of having a sheriff who don't do no

228

sheriffing," Sylvie said. And Al said, "We think, Mr. Sheriff, you don't look too hard when it don't suit you. Charlie here, me, and Sylvie, we don't think that tramp carried no bees nowhere."

"I don't give a damn what Charlie thinks," Greg snapped.

Charlie lifted an eyebrow and glanced at Constance. "I think we should take a little walk, Greg. Constance, you want to come along?"

She nodded.

"This won't take too long," Charlie said to Al and Sylvie. "Greg? Let's wander down this way a bit."

They walked toward the mill. The sound of workmen had diminished, and the numbers were down now, but there were still several of them coming and going. Today, a Con Ed truck was parked near the mill between a van and a pickup.

"What the devil are they doing now?" Greg muttered.

"Looking it over to see if the waterwheel is in good shape, looking over the dam, the sluice gate, things like that," Charlie said. "This is going to be a working establishment very soon now, it seems."

When they were past the mill, on the edge of the property overlooking the lake—which appeared bluer than ever—Charlie stopped. Briefly he wondered if the acid content of the recent rain had already affected the lake. How blue could it get? He glanced at the sheriff and said, "Greg, there's a murderer running around doing murderous things, and I intend to get him. I take it the boys have shown up by now in the woods, and that Wollander sent you over to give me a warning. Right?"

"Charlie, do you have a shred of proof? Do you have anything better than the scenario I have? If you do, unload it, and then let's talk."

Charlie shook his head. "The problem as I see it," he said in a meditative way, "is that I'm not real sure who you're working for. I mean, is it the Zukals? Then why

229

didn't you find out who killed their dog, and who's been making life hell for them? Is it the public at large? Then why didn't you go after David Levy's killer? Is it Wollander? If it is, then anything I say will end up on his table, and that would put a crimp in my plans."

A vein throbbed in Greg Dolman's temple, and his face became redder. "If you have information, it's your duty to tell me," he grated. "And if you don't cooperate, I'll go after your license. And you know I can take it if you're playing games with me."

"And you haven't answered my question," Charlie murmured. "You see, what I thought I might do is contact Captain See at the state police detective bureau. I've known him for more than twenty years; we used to work together back in the city now and then. Good man, See."

"You're trying to blackmail me!" Greg Dolman cried in disbelief.

"Gentle persuasion," Charlie protested. "I've had a lot of role models around here these past few days. Wollander's washed up, Greg. Did you know that?"

The sheriff snorted and jammed his hands down into his pockets.

"Oh, he probably would deny it himself, but that's the way it is. He's bowing out voluntarily, he thinks, but actually I think his days are numbered by forces even bigger than he is. Writing his memoirs, I hear."

A new intentness stilled Greg. He glanced from Charlie to Constance.

She said, "You remember when Eisenhower retired, Greg? He gave this impassioned warning about the industrial-military complex. Rather like biting the hand, don't you think? And Admiral Rickover? He did about the same kind of thing when he retired, a dire warning about the dangers of nuclear submarines, nuclear weapons of all sorts. This seems so common, doesn't it? The insider who gets out so often has an overwhelming desire to tell all. Educators do it, preachers do it, politicians. Even actors."

She gazed thoughtfully at the quiet lake. "Funny, isn't it? When they start to tell about whatever it is they are leaving, they don't seem to stop. They go all the way."

"I don't believe you. He wouldn't bow out, no matter what. The game he's playing is the only game he knows."

"But he's tired of it," Charlie said quietly. "Too many upstarts. The New Age politicians probably turn him off. Managerial types with their clipboards, spin-control specialists, four-second sound bites. It's not his game any longer, and he knows it. And he knows a lot of other things, too. He's been around a long time."

Very softly Constance said, "Think about the little remarks you must have heard in the past few years, the never-confirmed rumors you must have heard. Probably you didn't want to have to think too much about them, but I suspect they're floating around. Aren't they?"

He looked at her sourly. "There are always rumors." He turned to Charlie. "For Christ's sake, what are you after? Give me something."

"A killer. I told Wollander the same thing. I simply want him to leave me alone to do my work. If I ask his wife a question I don't want his answer. Or the housekeeper, or the daughter. And I want to know that if I tell you anything, it stays with you. I don't want him second-guessing my every movement. And I sure as hell don't want you getting his permission every step along the way."

Greg Dolman looked meaner than ever, his eyes little more than slits. "Not enough, Charlie. He says you're after a thermos, guys searching the woods over there, people searching the farm on this side. Hell, it's all over town, that you're after a thermos. Why the thermos? Tell me something I don't know about the thermos."

"It's the key to the mystery," Charlie said, and if Greg Dolman heard the undercurrent of mockery in his voice, he gave no sign of it. "If we find it in the right place, it'll mean David Levy probably took the drugs himself. If it turns up in the wrong place, it'll prove murder. See what I mean? The key."

Greg Dolman's indecision was painful to watch. He glared at Charlie with an expression of near-hatred. Abruptly he faced away. "Beat it, both of you. I have to think."

"But not too long, Greg. It's going to be you or Danny See. I want an official lawman around if the thermos turns up. Wouldn't like to be accused of rigging the sails the wrong way. Know what I mean? We'll be up at the house." Charlie took Constance's hand, and they left Sheriff Greg Dolman standing near the swinging bridge staring out at nothing in particular.

"Charlie," Constance said as they walked back, "did you ever really work with Danny See?"

"We need definitions," he began.

"I thought not."

"Dolman doesn't know one way or the other and the very thought of bringing in the state police makes him ache in a place he can't reach with ointment. But Danny did come to town a couple of times, you know. He took some workshops in investigating arson. It just happens that I conducted a couple of them. So there."

She nodded. "I wonder if Greg fully realizes that he's between the rock and the hard place."

"He does now. Bet he'll be back in half an hour, and then he'll hang around like an attached shadow. Bet?"

"You know I won't. Besides, why do you suggest a bet only when you know you'll win?"

"Because I hate to lose," he said with complete honesty.

Constance looked through picture albums with Sylvie and made all the right comments about the pretty daughters and beautiful grandchildren. Her comments were true, it was a handsome family. And Al and Charlie played the "Did you know X?" game. It had turned out that Charlie was on a special investigative force during the period that the Bronx was burning most fiercely, the time that the butcher shop Al's father had started was burned out.

"Did you know Mort Wurstman? Over on Trinity?" Al asked.

"Yep, and the son Dooley."

"A bad one, Charlie. Real bad. Got sent up."

"I know. I was part of the crew that sent him."

"Really? Good job, but it shoulda been done years before. Did you know Sal Maldane?"

"The hock shop? Sure. He's okay."

"Yeah, for a hock-shop guy. He got burned out, too."

"Prettiest case of arson you could ever hope to see."

"Yeah? Thought you said he was okay."

"Doesn't mean he can't light a fire, now does it? He *is* okay."

Then the sheriff came back, still glowering, but his mind made up. "You hanging out here these days?" he asked Charlie meanly.

"Until the boys get through and bring the stuff over. And the people at the farm check in. Want some dinner after that?"

"Yeah. And talk. Especially talk."

Tom Hopewell arrived first with Henry Tremont, who looked a bit like a tree himself, brown and tough. No sign of a thermos on the farm grounds, he said truculently, and he'd swear to that.

Charlie thanked him nicely, and asked Tom, "Will people be around at the farm for a while?"

"Are you kidding?" Hopewell said fiercely. "Most of the night is more like it. I tell you, we are running a little bit behind, like three weeks behind by my figuring."

Henry Tremont seemed to plant his feet even more firmly, and cleared his throat. "Dr. Bosch," he said deliberately, "he don't like the idea of people coming and going all night, taking bees, getting in the apartments, and such. We're putting on a couple of extras at night for the next

233

week or so." He said this as if it implied a warning to Charlie, who nodded gravely.

Then several cars pulled into the driveway; Tom Hopewell and Henry Tremont stalked away, and Pete Mitchum and his friends spilled out of the cars and expanded like foam monsters released from too-small boxes. Pete shook his head in regret, no thermos, and Charlie said that was all right. He said hi to Pete's two brothers and was introduced to the three boys he did not know. He introduced them all around, and it was obvious that they didn't want to leave, but he thanked them nicely, too, and sent them away. They had deposited four plastic garbage bags on the lawn before the front porch.

"We had witnesses to it all," Pete said before he left. "Sheriff deputies stayed right with us the whole time."

Charlie grinned. "I thought they might."

Pete grinned even broader. "I thought that's what you thought," he said in triumph. He swung around and returned jauntily to his old Ford that he kept looking spiffy.

Charlie regarded the bags, and shrugged. "Might as well have a look," he said. "I bummed a tarp from the carpenters." He spread the clear plastic tarp on the ground. Al helped position it and weight it down with rocks, and then Charlie emptied the first bag. About what he had expected: mostly beer cans, a few soda-pop cans, a few bottles. A beret. A leather glove that had started to mildew. Sodden newspapers. He used a stick to push stuff to one side as he went through it all. Nothing of interest. Greg Dolman held the garbage bag open and Charlie and Al lifted the tarp and dumped the stuff back in and tied it. The next bag had a syringe with a rusty needle, partly dirt-filled, and a broken Swiss Army knife in addition to miscellany much like that in the first bag. There were many spent shells; hunters made use of that land in season. The third bag was more of the same. Two condoms, and a string of dime-store beads, and a little silver-colored pillbox were among the junk. Charlie pushed the pillbox to one side with the stick, and

234

Constance picked it up carefully by the edges, using a tissue. The fourth bag had nothing to interest Charlie.

"What's that?" Greg motioned toward the silver box that Constance had put on the porch rail.

Charlie was through and all the trash was again packaged up. He looked at the pillbox without touching it. "You have any gear in your car?" he asked. "Might as well check for prints. Probably aren't any, but let's give it a go."

Greg went to his car and returned with a fingerprint kit. There were only smudges, worthless. Charlie picked up the box then and turned it over thoughtfully. "Real silver," he said. "It's just beginning to tarnish."

"That's too small to hold dope," Greg said.

"I know." The box was only an inch and a half on the side, and about a quarter-inch deep. Charlie opened it, empty, and then slipped it into his pocket. "It's a pretty little thing." He stretched. "Let's leave these people in peace for now," he said. "Al, Sylvie, thanks for the use of your place. See you later."

Greg Dolman followed Charlie and Constance to the Volvo. "Now where are you going? Is that it for today?"

"Dinner," Charlie said firmly. "Remember? We take you to dinner? I suggest you follow in the police car, or do you want to ride with us?"

"I'll follow," he said. "Where?"

"I spotted a roadhouse about ten miles out of Spender's Ferry. Don't know a thing about it, but that's where we're headed."

"Now," Greg Dolman said in the roadhouse. They were seated in a booth with drinks before them.

"Now," Charlie agreed, studying Greg thoughtfully. He knew Constance didn't trust the sheriff any more than he did, but she had said sensibly, "What choice does he have but to go along with it?" Charlie wished he knew.

"First," he said finally, "I'll want you to stick closer than a tick the rest of the night. Deal?"

Greg flushed a deep red, but nodded.

"I don't want any alarms going off, or any of those private security people nosing around. You, as a representative of the law, can handle them if they do turn up. Okay?" Again the sullen nod. "Okay. I've been all over the place today baiting a trap, and I'm pretty sure that it will be sprung tonight. Late tonight. I'll want you, or someone, to be there."

"Tell me what you're up to, Charlie. No games; no puzzles, just what you're up to." Greg took a swallow of his bourbon, straight up, and added, "You know I cut loose today, damn you. Wollander suggested I talk to you and let him know what you were doing. Well, I haven't gone back since. So, I guess you could say I'm committed." He sounded very depressed.

"Right. All day I've been broadcasting my belief that David Levy was drugged by the contents of his thermos. And the thermos is missing. That you already know. Everyone in the damn county must know it by now. I made it plain that if the thermos doesn't turn up in the lake, or on the edge of it, or on his route back to his apartment, it will prove beyond a doubt that he was murdered, and the investigation will go forward. But if it does turn up, I'll have to accept that he probably did it to himself. I think everyone concerned with this mess wants it over with, wants me to accept that David killed himself accidentally."

Greg scowled. "Goddamn it, Charlie, what if the damn thermos is in the lake? Then what?"

"It isn't. Not yet anyway. I think someone will make an attempt tonight to put it there."

"Oh shit," Greg said in a low voice, disgusted and discouraged. "You're fishing. You don't have anything, do you? You've been around, Charlie. You know there's people you don't play mind games with."

He was not even questioning his own acceptance of the game rules, Charlie knew, and Charlie understood without a doubt the process Greg Dolman was going through; looking inward, searching for his own way out of this predicament, probably examining the words he would recite to Wollander. Brusquely Charlie said, "When I walked away from NYPD, I walked away from those people who like to tell you what to do and when. I'm calling the plays tonight, Greg, and, by God, you're in! Shut your face and stop the bellyaching!"

He couldn't stop Greg, if the sheriff decided to take a walk, Charlie knew, not short of pulling a gun anyway; and he didn't have a gun along. The moment hung there while Greg made up his mind. Finally he lifted his drink and finished it.

"He didn't take the thermos to the lake for a morning swim," Charlie said, exactly as if neither of them knew what had gone on during that brief interlude. "He had a routine. Up early, a swimming workout, back to the apartment for breakfast, and then to work. You don't take a thermos for a workout when you're a minute away from home. No, the killer took it. Maybe to plant it on someone else, maybe to lace lemonade with dope to make it look like that's how he took the stuff, maybe for some other reason altogether. But the accidental death was accepted so easily there wasn't any real need to do anything with it. It's been stashed away somewhere all this time. If it was tossed, then our killer probably has a new one in hand. I'm betting on it."

"You're planning to stake out a whole damn lake in the middle of the night?" Greg shook his head.

"Part of it, Greg. Just part of it." Charlie pulled out a notebook and began to sketch rapidly. "Here's the lake." It looked like a teardrop. "Over here, the farm, with extra guards patrolling, and lights on. Not a good way to approach. Next, the Zukal place. Security lights everywhere. Even worse. On around the state forest land, and to the Wollander property. Again, guards everywhere. On past, and there's the orchard. Dirt roads back among the trees. Short walk to the lake from there. So, just this end, near the Wollander beach. It's the best place, after all. Toss the thermos as far as possible. It lodges among the rocks on the bottom and looks like it rolled in when David swam that morning." He took a gadget out of his pocket and placed it on the table. It looked very much like an infrared television control. He pushed it across the table to Greg. "I had the Frederick's Security Company put in a light, a portable unit. This controls it. It'll light up most of the lake. We'll catch our killer in the act of getting rid of the thermos, and then the real work can begin, the nitty-gritty detail work that cinches things. First you have to have a direction, then you can run with it. You know that's how it goes. I know it, too."

"You've got someone in mind?" Greg asked, a new intentness making his face taut, his eyes narrowed.

"Oh yes. And a lot of little things to corroborate it, but we need something big now."

Their dinners were brought then and they were silent until the waiter had left again. They all had ordered steak because they didn't trust anything else in the menu. The steaks turned out to be very good.

"Start at the beginning," Greg said. "Give."

"You won't like it," Charlie said; he stopped chewing to speak. "You see, it starts with the dog Sadie." Greg made a low groaning sound and Charlie said, "Sorry about that, but that's the way it goes." He looked thoughtful then and said in a wondering sort of way, "I just remembered Captain Bertlesman. For God's sake, good old Cap Bertlesman. He used to come in to deliver lectures when I was a green-as-grass rookie, back when the dinosaurs roamed. He used to say, 'Get the who and the how, and let the shrinks take care of the why.'" Charlie looked apologetically at Constance who had made a noise that was not quite a snort. "Didn't say he was a nice man," Charlie murmured. "Anyway, that's what I have for you, Greg. But only the how for the time being. If there aren't any slip-ups, you'll get the who in a couple of hours. Why will take care of itself."

For a moment Greg Dolman simply looked puzzled, but then a dull flush spread across his face. "You son of a bitch!"

Charlie nodded. If there were any slip-ups, he knew he needed that card in the hole; he might have to persuade Greg to tag along another time. Greg looked as if he wanted to reach across the table and choke him, and that was all right, as long as he didn't move in that direction. Charlie waited.

"Go on," Greg finally muttered.

Charlie described how he and Constance had demonstrated how to get a trained dog to take food from a stranger. "So, no problem," he said. "The killer dosed dog food with insect spray and killed Sadie. But then David came across the head scarf. Maybe the killer saw him with it, or they even talked about it. Anyway, David had to be next."

Greg was attacking his steak ferociously, as if this might be his last meal. Indigestion in the making, Charlie thought sadly.

"So, everyone knew about David and his vitamins, and his morning swim." When Greg made a growly sound, Charlie explained about the cookout and the meticulous report David had written to his father. "So, as I said, everyone knew. Everyone involved in this mess, in any event. No one was questioning the death of the dog; and now if David's death could be made to look accidental, so much the better. And the vitamins showed up. Heaven sent," he added drily.

Greg shook his head. "How you going to prove that, Charlie? No way."

"Wrong, Greg. Two facts. One, the company David ordered his vitamins from shipped them on the fourteenth, from Rochester. They would have been delivered by the

239

sixteenth, but they aren't listed among his effects. Two, examine the autopsy report, the contents of the stomach. You see, a few of those vitamins were time-release doses, the vitamin C, for example. No vitamin C is listed, and it would have been there in granular form for many hours, only gradually dissolving, being absorbed. Our killer entered the apartment, swiped the new shipment of vitamins, doped some of the capsules, and substituted them for the ones on the counter. Then, when David was dying, or even after he was dead, the killer returned and took away the doped containers, replaced the untouched ones, and it was done. There was one too many of each one that was in capsule form, but who would notice? Who did notice?"

"And the thermos?"

Charlie shrugged. "An ace in the hole, probably, but one that wasn't needed, not until right now, anyway." He looked with regret at his plate; his steak was nearly gone and he had no real recollection of eating it.

"So," he said. "Two down. No hubbub. No real investigation. On to the next item, moving the bees. And the tramp. You know, Greg, if you had found a bottle, that would have been much harder; much, much harder. But either the guy was so drunk that he turned on the gas and forgot about it and then fell down and bashed his head in, or he was sober enough to walk through the woods carrying a hive of bees. But not both. Let's say he was sleeping off a drunk under a tree and he hears someone messing around with the hive, and he follows out of curiosity, or even calls out. Our killer has to act fast now. A witness is the last thing on earth needed at this moment. Probably he said something like, 'Let's duck inside one of the apartments and talk. The watchman will spot us out here.' Something like that. And he picks up a rock. Inside the apartment, a quick bash on the head, turn on the gas, close up the place, and get back to the work at hand. There must have been a wallet, and he lifts that, just to muddy the waters. You could see the outline in the hip pocket," he added. A distant, thoughtful look crossed his face. "It might even turn up," he said. "And the rock, of course, gets tossed into the lake, one among five million others."

"And not an iota of proof," Greg Dolman muttered. "Not a single print anywhere."

"But that's proof," Charlie said. "Why would the tramp wipe his prints from the gas stove? Now that wouldn't have made any sense at all."

The waiter cleared the table and they sat in silence until he returned with coffee, and then left again.

"I don't like it," Greg said. "We need more people. Three's not enough. Too much territory to cover."

"Too many people and you start tripping over each other."

"How you plan to go in? Your car's a dead giveaway and so's mine."

"We'll park in the Zukals' driveway, about a third of the way to the house, where it curves, out of sight of the road and the house."

"And those damn lights they installed blast you. You said yourself, that's out."

"Um. The lights won't come on after ten tonight. I fixed that with the security guy today. He's the only one who knows," he added. "Not even the Zukals are in on it."

Greg thought some more, and they ordered more coffee. "Have you considered that the damn thermos might have been ditched someplace not accessible now?" Greg asked finally.

Charlie looked at him in surprise. Constance had asked the same question. "Sure. But I think a thermos will end up in the lake tonight, if it gets that far. One's pretty much like another, and who would pipe up and say it's not the same one? And I'd put up money that it will have measurable amounts of methaqualone and a barbiturate," he added grimly.

Greg was not happy about any of it, Charlie knew, and he also knew there wasn't a thing he could do about that. It was chancy; the killer might not have the thermos, or any thermos. He might be throwing a party that no one would show up for. Maybe the damn thermos was already in the lake. Maybe David had lost it himself days before his death. He understood that Greg was going along with it for now, this one night, and if it didn't work out, he'd be back in Wollander's pocket tomorrow. Case closed, again.

What if he was wrong? He didn't believe it, but it was a possibility he began to consider. What if they had read all the signs wrong? What if. . . ? He felt Constance's hand on his thigh under the table and looked at her. She knew, he realized, and she was saying, it's okay. He felt some of the tension seep from him, and he covered her hand with his.

Constance now said to Greg, "We both have dark raincoats in the car. Do you have something to put on? That shirt will be like a beacon."

It was going on nine-thirty. Right or wrong, Charlie thought, it was time.

CHAPTER 18

Charlie had positioned both Greg and Constance, and he no longer could see either of them. Greg had complained. "Hey, it's been a long time since I pulled an all-nighter."

"So go to sleep. You'll wake up when the lights come on."

"If."

"When. But, Greg, if you start snoring, I'll come over and kick you in the butt."

Constance was invisible, merging with a clump of bushes until not even a nighthawk would have been alerted to her presence. Charlie admired, and even envied, her ability to go into a meditative state—alpha state, she called it—effortlessly. She would be wide awake and alert and totally relaxed for as long as it took. That had been part of her aikido training and she had mastered the skill, but he had not been willing to learn it himself and he could not say why. She had explained it, rather too airily, he thought. "You aren't willing to give up any control, even to yourself." Maybe that was it, maybe not, and now, he was wishing he did not have a cramp in one leg, wishing that time would pass faster, wishing this was over.

Greg was against the bluff at the edge of the beach, his back against the rise, no doubt. And no doubt he was asleep. Now and then Charlie had heard his rustlings, but not for some time. Charlie was farther down where the bluff was not so high and he could see over the edge if he tried. Some large round rocks were on the top here, and he hoped his head appeared to be just another such rock when he stood up to look.

At first, he was thinking now, you didn't hear anything. Or only those noises that were expected, insects, cicadas, crickets, distant traffic sounds, a whippoorwill and a faraway echo of an answer. Then other sounds became noticeable—a bird flapping its wings, a bat's high screech, a small animal moving in the grass. No fish jumping, he thought with regret; no frogs yelling *here I am*. Two does and a buck had come down to drink and had stood outlined against the sky briefly, but they were not fooled by human immobility; they had left fast, the sounds of their feet loud, and with a snorting sound almost horselike.

No new stars had appeared in a long time. At first, he had been able to pick out a section of sky and study it, count the stars in it, close his eyes for a count of ten, and when he looked again the number of stars in the sector had doubled, tripled, quadrupled. But the slow swing of the heavens was impossible to see without a reference point; he tried to align certain stars with a tree branch, only to lose them when he closed his eyes again. Too many of them now.

He cupped his hand over his watch face; it was twelve-forty. He had not expected any action until after twelve, after one even, but time was being contrary; it had slowed to an unbelievable crawl. He stood up to scan the area again, and now that his eyes had adapted so well to the night, he could make out individual trees, individual bushes. He hoped Constance was stretching from time to time, and he knew that Greg had done that earlier, but not for too long a time. He inched away from his position and eased himself to where Greg was propped up, sound asleep.

He shook him lightly, and put his fingers over Greg's lips. "Get up and move back and forth a couple of minutes," he said softly. "I'll keep an eye out."

Greg made a mumbling noise and pulled himself upright jerkily. He had become stiff already. He bent and stretched a few times and then walked down the beach and back, then again.

"Okay," he whispered. "Thanks."

"Yeah. It's nearly one. Thought you'd want to know."

Charlie carefully made his way back to his position and studied the landscape again. Nothing. He wanted to go check on Constance but he couldn't do that. He would be silhouetted if anyone happened to be watching. But, he told himself, he had put her where he did because he knew he could trust her not to fall asleep and not to stiffen up, and he had put Greg where he did because he knew Greg would do both.

The doubts that had troubled him earlier kept swimming back into his mind. What if nothing happened? What if he was overestimating the lure of the bait he had spread around altogether too thick all day? He personally would suspect a trap, he told himself, and then told himself to shut up. If it didn't work, well, he'd think of something else. But the other part of his mind, the part that resisted the idea of achieving a meditative state, and that now was arguing with him over the futility of this night watch, that part would not shut up. Instead, it was saying, if it doesn't work there probably won't be another day for you, asshole. He would lose Greg's cooperation, and did he really think he had enough evidence to stir up any interest with the state cops? Dummy.

He shifted his weight. Now he was keeping a close watch over the top of the rise, but even this, that other voice was

245

saying derisively, how long could he keep this up? He was damned uncomfortable. His was the worst possible position he could have claimed; nowhere to rest his weight, no way to lean against a tree for relief, just stand upright and watch, or sink back down on this side and be blind. He was cursing himself silently when a figure appeared.

His hand closed over the infrared control in his pocket and drew it out. The person had vanished again, blended into the shadows of trees and shrubs. He didn't move, barely breathed, and presently he heard a sound that was new, then another. Footsteps on grass, hardly audible but there, coming closer, apparently hurrying.

Charlie caught an eclipse of a cluster of stars as the figure started down the slope to the lake, and now he counted silently, *one, two, three, four.* He pressed the button on the infrared control, and was blinded momentarily by the brilliance even though he had been expecting it.

He already had started to run the dozen steps to the woman in the black raincoat, when she lifted her face and screamed. Constance had materialized at her side, one hand on the thermos held in the air ready to be thrown, the other on the woman's wrist.

"Hello, Jill," Charlie said and took her other arm. Greg was right behind him.

Charlie had to admit that Greg behaved admirably during those first few seconds. He blinked a lot, but that could have been from the blinding lights. He looked at Charlie with large questions in his eyes, and when Charlie nodded firmly, he managed a nod also.

Two security men were racing toward the beach, one with a gun drawn, both with flashlights that were no longer needed. The portable spotlight array had turned the entire end of the beach into noontime glare.

"Mrs. Ferris," Greg said soberly, "I'll have to ask you a few questions. Let's go inside." He swallowed hard, and then recited her rights in a swift monotone.

Charlie gave Constance a quick look; she nodded, very

somber, tired. She carried the thermos; it was filled, the top on loosely, ready to slide off any second. Charlie kept a grasp of Jill's arm; the sheriff waved the private security men out of the way, and they all walked toward the Wollander house where lights were coming on upstairs and down.

By the time they reached the patio Warren was hurrying toward them, tying his robe belt. "What the devil is going on?"

"I couldn't sleep," Jill said shrilly. "I was taking a walk by the lake and found the thermos in the water and then they all jumped me."

"Take your hands off her!"

"Inside," Charlie said. "Come on, inside."

Wollander grabbed at the thermos, and Constance easily fended off his hand and kept moving with Charlie and Jill. Warren looked past them and yelled at his security men, "Get these people out of here! Right now!"

"Mr. Wollander," Charlie said patiently, "it's over. Now, let's just go inside and talk. The sheriff will have to use your phone to call his deputies, and while we're waiting, we can talk things over."

"You heard what my daughter said. She found that damn thermos."

"Filled with tap water. I heard. Greg, do you want to just go straight in with her? Constance can bring a car around if that's the only way to handle this."

At the door to the house Lois said, "Come in." She held the door open as they all passed her, and then pulled it closed again. She was in a long gray robe and slippers, her hair disheveled.

Warren glared at Greg. "Do you know what you're doing?"

"Yes, sir. I'm afraid so."

Lois led the way to the study and when they were inside closed that door also. "What happened?" she asked then.

Charlie released Jill's arm. "You'd better sit down," he

247

said, not too unkindly. She sank down into one of the leather chairs and drew up her feet into it. She looked childish, like a sick little girl. He felt in his pocket for the silver pill box and handed it to Lois. "Do you recognize this?"

She turned it over and over, then looked at him sharply. "Where did you find it? That's mine. Or just like mine."

"I think it's yours."

Warren walked stiffly to his desk and sat down. He picked up the phone and began to punch numbers. "I'm calling my attorney."

Charlie shrugged and spoke to Jill. "When they arrest you," he said, "the first thing they do is search you thoroughly, and there will be a medical examination. By a gynecologist." He heard the phone clatter back to the receiver but did not turn to look at Warren. "I'm not a doctor," he went on, "but I have it on good authority that there are certain physical symptoms that are present in the event of pregnancy; even if a pregnancy has recently terminated in any way, the signs are still there. Will they find the right symptons, Jill? The right hormones, the right physiological changes?"

She was staring at him speechlessly, the color gone from her face, her lips.

"When they send the thermos to the lab, will they find tap water? And maybe methaqualone and phenobarbital? You know the sheriff will have to search your rooms here. You must have had access to those drugs recently if you put them in the thermos. Are they still up in your room? Will they find them?"

"There's medicine," she said, keeping her gaze on him as if hypnotized. "My medicine. Stanley's. Maybe what you're talking about—"

"Jill, for God's sake! Just shut up! You don't have to answer his questions. Just shut up until an attorney is here to advise you." Warren's hand was on the phone but he did not lift it again.

She turned her wide, staring gaze to him, and began to shake her head. "Just shut up. Be still. Be good. Do what Daddy tells you. If I'm not good, you'll send me to Mother, and if she gets tired of me, she'll send me back to you. Back and forth. Back and forth. I saw the letter she wrote to you. She showed it to me, laughing and laughing. We both laughed. See another doctor. Get more opinions, and more, and more. Remember? It can't be true. I don't believe it. See this man, he's good. Remember? She dragged me to one doctor after another in their prissy white coats, with their prissy fat fingers, and they kept telling her the same thing, didn't they? All of them. Over and over. Then a new letter from you would come: Try this one, that one, this treatment, that treatment. And she wrote to you again and again, and still, try this, try that."

When she became quiet, Charlie said in a low voice, "You're barren, aren't you?"

"Yes," she whispered.

"And he's known that for many years, hasn't he?"

She nodded. "Yes."

"Did you take your stepmother's birth-control pills and use them?"

She nodded again.

"To make it appear that you had had a miscarriage?"

"Yes! Why are you asking me all this? You already know the answers! Yes! Yes! Yes! To everything."

"And the only victim you ever really had in mind was your husband, Stanley."

"Yes. Of course. Yes!"

Behind him Charlie heard Warren Wollander make a choking, sobbing sound. He did not look at him. He was gazing instead at Lois, who was pasty, and looked as if she might faint. The fury in his low intense voice was startling when he said to Lois, "He's known from the start about the fake miscarriage, about the fake pregnancy, about the killings. He was going to throw you to the wolves if necessary to save her skin."

Behind him he could hear Warren Wollander using the phone. His voice was toneless. "Get over here," Warren said. "We have desperate trouble. Come now."

Greg called his deputies then, and asked Warren if he would need a search warrent. Warren said yes, but Jill said no. Greg spoke into the phone again, ordered a search warrant drawn up, and began to say what it should include when Charlie interrupted him again. "Tell the judge you're also looking for a solid gold bracelet carved with flowers." Greg looked mystified, but included the bracelet.

"We'll have to wait," he said uncomfortably when he was done.

"I'll make coffee," Lois said. She left without a glance at Warren.

Charlie looked at Constance, almost expecting her to go after Lois, but she moved her head fractionally and did not get up from her chair.

In a very low voice Warren said, "Greg, you don't have to do this. We go back a long ways."

Greg Dolman looked more uncomfortable but Charlie noticed that Constance tightened her grasp on the thermos. Son of a bitch, he thought, she still didn't trust Greg Dolman worth a damn.

"Jill," Charlie said softly, "one question. Why did you take the thermos?"

"You mean there's something you don't already know?" she asked bitterly. "When I went to the apartment to switch the vitamins, I found that I had left the cod-liver oil here, and I couldn't replace it. I panicked. I was afraid someone might connect it to the dope, and I thought that I could mix the drugs in the thermos if anyone questioned anything."

The deputies finally arrived and they all watched as the thermos was decanted into a sterile jar that was sealed and labeled, and then the thermos was put into a bag and sealed and labeled. The attorney Warren had called turned

250

up, looking mean and sleepy. Charlie and Constance began to edge toward the door. Greg followed them.

"I'll want more," he said tiredly. "Tomorrow, sometime. What's that about a bracelet?"

"Tomorrow," Charlie said, just as tired as Greg. "I told Sylvie and Al we'd drop in around one. And before that, our phone will be off the hook and the doors sealed tight."

Greg didn't argue. He nodded, called one of the deputies to drive them over to collect their car, and turned back to the routine that awaited him inside.

Charlie looked past him for just a moment; the lawyer was in a chair drawn up close to Jill's. His face was inches from hers and she was still huddled with her feet under her, still looked like a sick little girl. He took Constance's arm and they left.

When they were once again in their own car, heading for their own house, Charlie said with a groan, "I am wiped out from here to Thursday and I ache from top to bottom."

"When we get home, soak first and then I'll give you a Swedish massage."

He squeezed her thigh. "You're good."

"And after I do you, you can give me one," she added. He squeezed her thigh again and she covered his hand with hers.

CHAPTER 19

Charlie woke up grinning, and was still grinning broadly when he entered the kitchen to find Constance making waffles. Fresh strawberries were marinating on the counter. She eyed him suspiciously.

"So you ate the canary, after all?"

He laughed out loud. "Dreaming. I was dreaming that I was married to Sylvie and I kept trying to dump her in the lake so I could run away with you. See, even in my dreams, I'm chasing you like a fourteen-year-old with two bucks running after the only whore in town."

She raised her eyebrows and looked like a schoolteacher with a recalcitrant eight-year-old. "You're just after my body. I always suspected that."

"Damn right," he said, nuzzling her neck. "And I would dump Sylvie in the lake, or run Sophia off a cliff, or ditch Elizabeth in a second to get at you."

She reached behind her and gave him an indecent tweak that was just short of vicious. He howled and danced away, tripped over Brutus and Candy, and ended up at the table, laughing and cursing.

"Are you ready for breakfast, by any chance?" she asked demurely.

"If they only knew," he said as soon as he could speak. "Oh, if only they knew, all those people who are ready to canonize you. Saint Constance. Hah!"

She brought him a steaming waffle covered with strawberries, and a pitcher of cream on the side. "You realize that this is your ration of high-caloric food for the day," she said severely. "Steamed fish for dinner. Fruit and carrot sticks for lunch."

He caught her wrist and kissed the palm of her hand. She leaned over and kissed the top of his head.

Al Zukal met them in his driveway. He had a look of total disbelief on his face. "Charlie! Lois said Jill's the one! That skinny girl? What for?"

"Is Lois here?"

"Yeah. Sylvie said you said she should call Lois and get her over here. She's been crying real bad, Charlie."

They turned to see the sheriff's car coming in the driveway.

"I didn't know we was going to have a party," Al muttered.

"Sorry," Charlie said. "I thought this would be the best way to wrap things up. You and Sylvie will want to hear where you stand now. And Lois needs to know a few things. Okay?"

"And if it ain't? Yeah, yeah. Come on in."

They sat at the kitchen table where Sylvie had coffee ready, and two kuchens, one apple, one cinnamon. Constance shook her head firmly at Charlie. Greg Dolman, he noticed, aggrieved, had a very large piece of both coffee cakes.

Lois was in jeans and a T-shirt and sneakers. Her working clothes. Her eyes were red-rimmed and swollen. She did not speak when they came in, but ducked her head and moved her cup around and around in the saucer.

253

"This won't take very long," Charlie said briskly. "Constance and I came to the same conclusion at the same moment, I think. We had been misdirected royally, and as soon as we admitted that, the rest began falling into place. Actually, Constance is the one who said it must be Jill."

"Everything pointed to her," Constance said, "but we were all so busy looking the other way we couldn't see her as a suspect."

Lois looked at her in bewilderment. "Nothing seemed to point to her. I thought she was pregnant and I lived in the same house with her."

"I know. But when I went to her room there wasn't a single book about pregnancy, no books on babies, no books on how to achieve pregnancy. None of the things you'd expect an anxious mother-to-be to have around. The drugstore in town has a nice selection, so it wasn't that they aren't available locally. She simply wasn't interested. And I kept wondering why she was here. It's obvious that she is not fond of her father, and she has no friends here, so why was she here?"

"They were redecorating their condo in the city," Lois said. "The place was completely torn up."

Constance shook her head. "She could have gone on a trip, or to an apartment, or to a hotel, or to visit friends, a number of things. But she came here, and stayed. Anyway, once we decided we had made a fundamental mistake, we backtracked, and it kept coming around to Jill when we asked: What if Stanley had been the intended victim from the start? After that it was obvious." She lifted her coffee then and Charlie knew the rest would be up to him.

"We backtracked all the way back to the day you and Sylvie came here," Charlie said, nodding to Al. "And that made us realize that Jill already had a plan in mind by then. I'll just take it step by step. She has no money of her own and is jealous of Lois because she is independent. She saw her mother as a kept woman all her life, and resented it, and she saw herself repeating the pattern with her husband.

Out here he could be with her only on the weekends and it gave her time to think and make her plans. It's really very hard to arrange an accidental death in the city, without drawing suspicion, you know. But out here? She learned about the bees, no doubt, when they arrived." Lois looked up, startled, and nodded slightly. Charlie went on. "Stanley was allergic to bees. It could be made to look accidental if he got multiple stings, and no suspicion would be attached to her, especially if she was a grieving widow who also had lost her child. But how to get him to where the bees would attack? That must have presented itself as a massive problem, until she found Sebastian. I think she brought Sebastian out only to verify that she had gone into the mill, into some of the little rooms with him. She had no hope of buying any property, or anything else. Stanley gave her gifts, and paid her charge accounts, but you can't buy a piece of property like this on your Visa card. So, why take Sebastian into the mill, unless she had a different purpose altogether? She claimed to have lost a heavy gold bracelet, remember?" He glanced at Greg who nodded.

"We found it in her room."

"I thought you might. Anyway, she said it was lost, and Stanley filed an insurance claim, and got her a new one. But if she could get the bees into one of those little rooms, and close the door on them, and then tell Stanley that she remembered that she had worn it the day she showed the mill to Sebastian, she could get him to open the door to go look for it. The rooms would have heated up just fine by midmorning; the bees would have been swarming around in a rage, just as they were later. It would have worked. The mill used to have a reputation as a hangout; kids could have moved the bees as a prank, and poor Stanley. She would have turned her big eyes on you and said she had no idea why he went in there, just as she did later about the station wagon."

He turned to Sylvie, "But you showed up. And then a

255

dog arrived. And carpenters began taking the mill apart. Everything she had planned was going to hell all at once."

"She killed Sadie?" Sylvie cried. "But how? Sadie didn't even like her. And why?"

Charlie detailed how Sadie could have been poisoned. Then he asked, "Sylvie, when David found one of your scarves and returned it, was there anything funny about it?"

"Filthy. It was filthy and I threw it away. I didn't even want to wash it."

"Mud? Grass stains? Filthy how?"

"All that and greasy." Her eyes widened.

"Greasy," Charlie said. "David found it and later on he must have made the connection. How he connected it to Jill I don't know, but he did, and she had to get rid of him, too." He shrugged. "As for why she killed Sadie, that's pretty obvious now. She still needed to be able to cross the bridge to collect the bees, and she needed a place to put the bees so she could send Stanley to them. Not on the Wollander property, too suspicious. If not the mill, then this house, or the station wagon, but not if a watchdog was barking its head off at her. It must have come to her, there was the perfect smokescreen; she could arrange things so that it looked like an attempt to get the newcomers out of the neighborhood; kids could take the blame."

His face tightened. "But David saw something and found the scarf. Maybe he saw her toss it. Maybe he even asked her about it, accused her of killing the dog."

"I don't understand what the fuss was over the thermos," Lois said. "What were you doing?"

"Well, it was missing. So the killer must have taken it. I was sure she had tampered with the vitamins, but why take the thermos? And I thought, if she had taken it, she would see this as a chance to sew things up good and tight. Let someone find it in the lake and be done with it.

"So now everything is in place for Stanley's death. She has announced her pregnancy, everyone is jubilant, even though Warren Wollander actually knew she was barren. He kidded himself at first about believing her, I imagine. She had taken the birth-control pills in order to plan exactly when she would start bleeding, and, to a certain extent, how much."

Al looked uncomfortable and shifted in his chair, and Sylvie's mouth pursed; Charlie was talking about things men didn't talk about, their attitudes clearly said.

He went on. "That night Warren saw her walk on the driveway to the place where it comes very close to the state forest. Why the midnight walk? Why the raincoat? Not to meet Sebastian. The raincoat was to hide under. A shadow moving out among shadows. Lights were still on, people still awake and she didn't want to be seen. And the reason could have been to throw something away. Not in the house trash because she already had said she had lost a bracelet and people might be sifting through trash more carefully. She had enough pills for her purposes, the rest could be flushed down the john, but there was the silver pillbox, and she had to get rid of it. She could have returned it to your bathroom, but if you knew it was missing before, that would raise questions, and she didn't want any questions about birth control or pregnancy to come up."

"You were looking for that?" Lois exclaimed.

"Not really. For something. I didn't know what she had tossed, or even if she had tossed anything, and it could have been the thermos, although I didn't think so. But that's what they found.

"So everything was ready, at last. Stanley came up for the weekend. He had a medicine cabinet full of medications, including some heavy-duty sleeping pills. If he didn't take one himself, she could see that he got it. And in the night she went over to move the bees to the station wagon. Then a witness showed up, a transient. He was drunk, but he saw what she was doing, and must have started to make a ruckus. She got him to enter the apartment and hit him

257

on the head, turned on the gas, and left to complete her real mission of murdering her husband."

Al made a grunting sound and Sylvie shifted in her chair, but no one spoke. Lois didn't move at all.

"Saturday morning Stanley has an appointment with Al, here, and she has her regular class, service, whatever it is, with Sebastian. What's more natural than that she would drive? Stanley doesn't like wandering in the woods; allergies, you know. She pulls up in the driveway to turn around, where she can see in the wagon, make sure the bees are still there. She says, 'Oh, I think I lost my bracelet in the station wagon. Seeing it has just reminded me. Be a darling and get it for me, will you? It's in the back. Do it before you start talking to Al, or you'll forget.'"

Lois made a deep throaty sound and closed her eyes.

"Right. So now it's done. I suspect that she stopped in the driveway, out of sight, long enough to hear the yelling, and then went on to Sebastian's meeting. Daddy shows up and rushes her home, she gags herself in the bathroom, takes out the tampon, and becomes an ashen-faced widow who has just lost a baby. But she won't let a doctor near her. There's only one more thing she has to do and that's get Sebastian over and tell him she was pregnant. She said he knew, that he was already advising her, and she has to make sure that he actually knows, just in case someone mentions it. She makes a big scene about seeing her spiritual advisor, and finally she can relax, wait for her inheritance to work through the legalities, and take off for France."

There was a long silence, broken finally by Lois. "And last night, it was all planned? All just a trap for her?" she whispered.

"Sure. There was no proof yet. I was pretty sure that if a scene started with her father present, taking over, giving orders, she would confess." *Get out of here!* She had killed three men to escape those orders. Charlie had not simply been pretty sure; he had known beyond doubt that when

258

she saw that trap closing yet again, she would escape in the only way remaining. He said no more now, but watched Lois, and wondered if she saw escape as a possibility.

Lois sat unmoving for several seconds, then she shook her head hard. "He must have known, but he was so desperate to believe," she said, nearly inaudibly. "And he was as happy as a child. She lied about her pregnancy exactly the same way that her mother lied, to hurt him, to make him know he had to choose." She closed her eyes very tightly for a moment. "No man should be forced into that lifeboat with his wife and child," she whispered. Abruptly she turned to Greg Dolman. "Sheriff, I'd like a word with you alone."

Constance stood up. "We should be on our way, too. Dr. Wharton, is Jill under a doctor's care now?"

"Yes. They took her to jail and did the usual, I suppose, but then the lawyer got a psychiatrist in to talk to her. He will attend her. Why?"

"I just thought that if that is the case, we may never hear any more details, when she did this or that, or how, or who that man was in the apartment." Her gaze was very steady as she regarded Lois. "Between a doctor and a lawyer, she may never have a chance to make another statement. This is what she feared and dreaded most, isn't it? Never to be free, to be independent. She really is to be pitied, and so is her father. And you, of course. But you have your work. You may be the most fortunate of the three."

Lois moistened her lips and slowly she nodded.

"We can step outside, if that's all right with you," Greg Dolman said then, rising, pushing back his chair.

"It's nothing," Lois said, her voice low, but decisive. "I should be getting back." She held out her hand to Charlie and then to Constance. "Thank you both." She walked away, back toward the mill, toward the swinging bridge.

Greg Dolman shrugged. "We'll be tying up loose ends for the next few months, more than likely. We found the bracelet and the drugs, and the water in the thermos is tap water with something in it. They're analyzing it now. We'll have the doctor's report on Mrs. Ferris in a few days. I'll be in touch." He also held out his hand. Lois's hand had been like ice, his was sweaty.

"And I have to pick up that portable light unit and return it," Charlie said. "And youse guys don't have to worry none about being drove outta here, get it?"

"It don't work, Charlie," Al said. "The words are okay, maybe, but the tune's wrong, know what I mean?" And Sylvie said, "Watcha acting like that for, Mr. Wiseguy? Aincha got no manners? He don't mean nothing by it, Charlie."

In a few minutes Charlie and Constance were walking hand in hand toward the farm lakefront where the portable spotlights had been set up.

"One more little thing to see to," Charlie said, and gave her hand a squeeze.

She tried to think of what they had omitted; nothing came to mind. When they emerged from the tree sections, Charlie turned toward the row crops and began to peer up the paths. He waved when Tom Hopewell showed up between two rows.

"I'd like a word," Charlie called.

Tom came to them, his hands covered with moist dirt. "I heard," he said. "Everyone's heard. It's really over?"

"Yep. I suspect Lois Wharton will be back at work in a few days and gradually things will return to normal. There are a few missing pieces, but nothing we can't live with."

"Well," Tom said doubtfully, and eyed the corn row he had just left.

Charlie helped him look down the row. "You know, if I had gone into that apartment first, I would have been overcome with curiosity about the identity of the dead man. Especially since I rather like Lois Wharton and wouldn't want to see her injured in any way. But then, if I snitched a man's wallet, I might not know what to do with it, might even be tempted to keep it around, and I would resist that

temptation the way Adam should have resisted the apple."
Tom Hopewell's face turned crimson. Charlie patted him
on the arm. "Since I didn't find any such thing I'm not
going to worry about it. Just wanted to say so long. And
pick up those lights. See you around."

After they retrieved the lights and were in their car
again, Constance said, "I can't believe you told him to get
rid of that wallet."

"You've got a nerve! After you told Lois to clam up?
And right in front of the sheriff, too."

"Well, that's different."

Charlie began to chuckle and after a moment he was
laughing out loud. His laughter died when he turned south
to start the drive to New Jersey. In the back of the Volvo
was the box containing David Levy's few possessions. They
had to be delivered in person; this report had to be made in
person. Constance rested her hand on his thigh as he
drove.

Just before Christmas that year Lois paid them a visit. At
first she was awkward. "I really just wanted to tell you,"
she said, "Warren is very ill, did you know? Last week he
had his lawyer in and destroyed our agreement and
changed his will. He set up a trust fund to care for Jill as
long as she lives. But she may never be able to leave the
institution. Anyway, he also transferred the property, the
whole parcel of ground over to me, to use as an experimental farm."

Constance took her arm and led her to the kitchen and
saw her seated, then began to make coffee. Lois looked
almost dazed.

"There will be enough money to run it. I intend to hire
Clarence when he retires, as a consultant. And Tom, if he
ever stops chasing corn in Peru." She looked up at Constance and said in a tone of wonder, "I told Warren the
story about your friend who planted trees as an act of faith.
Last summer when I was planning to leave him, I told him

261

that, and he asked me to stay and help him through this crisis. He needed someone." She shook her head. "No. He needed me. I am grateful that he's lived long enough to know I forgive him. We are at peace. I wanted to tell you." Before Constance could say anything, she went on, "We're already working very hard to get things ready. Al Zukal put in his limestone beach and it looks exactly like snow. Maybe it isn't too late."

She didn't stay long. At the door, ready to leave, she hugged Constance hard, and kissed her cheek. "Thank you," she whispered and was gone.

They watched her back out of the drive and then looked at each other. "He'll stop chasing corn in Peru when Warren kicks," Charlie said. He glanced at the sky; it had started to snow. He closed the door.

And won't she be surprised at what he'll have to say!

Charlie didn't know if she had said the words, or if he had, or if either of them had uttered a sound. He cast a suspicious glance at Constance and then sighed. She was smiling that certain smile she sometimes had, and it didn't matter.